The Eternal Gateway:

Guardian

By SB Jones

This is a work of fiction. All the characters and events portrayed in this book are either the products of the author's imagination or are used fictitiously.

The Eternal Gateway: Guardian

Cover by: JR Fleming, www.jrfleming.com
Fonts by: KC Fonts, www.kcfonts.com, kcfonts@gmail.com
Edited by: Carolyn Johnson

ISBN: 978-0-9836818-3-0
www.TheEternalGateway.com
Want to find out about new releases? Join the mailing club at sbjonespublishing@gmail.com

Table of Contents

"I pictured this moment differently."
-Kail Falconcrest-

"You always have a choice."
-Angela Atagi-

"I will make sure you suffer."
-Camden Arland-

"I am going to let you in on a secret. She dies and there is
nothing you can do to save her."
-Xavier Ross-

"I want them to pay." "We will make them all pay."
-Bastiana & Vincent-

Five years later.

Chapter 1

Angela Atagi stood peering out of the window in the darkened room. The city of Stalbridge sprawled before her. Lights from the street level and from the windows of other buildings were bright enough to block out the night stars. She sighed and wondered how the world had become so terrified of the dark. She also did not like to be kept waiting. "This was a foolish plan from the beginning," she cursed under her breath, pacing the room. Several times she had to resist the urge to draw one of her Keratin war blades. She settled on returning to the window.

The airships that floated in the night sky were a common sight these days. Therion's forces had been slowly crushing any opposition one city at a time. A few of the new Juggernaut class airships were absolute monstrosities. They could hold over a thousand troops and even had smaller airships that could be deployed. *A city in the sky*, she thought.

Angela heard the door open and quickly close. It did not show on her face, but she felt a wave of relief pass through her. Kail Falconcrest had returned and judging by his movements, the mission had not gone well. She watched in silence as he went to the window to glance out of it.

"We need to leave," he said.

"Did they have the ring?"

Kail shook his head no. "It was a trap."

"I told you this was fool-," her scolding was brought up short by his lips on hers.

"I know, and you can yell at me later, but we need to leave now," he insisted, pulling her towards the door.

She followed Kail's lead and abandoned the safety of the room. Before they had rounded the first corner in the hallway, the people pursuing Kail had caught up to them. Kail swung around behind her before she heard the gunfire. The bullets bounced harmlessly off of the magical shield Kail brought up between them. The barrier filled the hallway as he traced a holding rune on the floor next to it.

"That should hold them for a while," Kail said.

The rune would hold the magic in place long enough for them to escape. She saw three men retreating back to find a way past the barrier as they continued to flee towards the rooftop.

Angela kicked open the door to the roof. The hot night air was magnified by the heat still radiating off of the rooftop from earlier in the day. Kail was right behind her. "There, this way," she said, pointing as they ran to the edge of the high-rise apartment complex. The next building was attached but stood two stories higher. Angela, using the natural ability of her extinct race to fly, took to the air and flew towards the top of the adjacent building. She watched as Kail used his magic to assist him. His speed increased and a soft blue glow of magical power left a trace where his feet touched the rooftop. Jumping off of the side of a maintenance room that housed environmental units, he soared upwards to catch the top lip of the next building. He almost beat her to the top, but she was there first to lend a helping hand. "You could have just teleported."

"Yeah, but it produces a lot of light, and I didn't want to make our position any more obvious than it is already," he explained. "Looks like our company has arrived." Kail pointed to the three armed men that burst onto the rooftop below.

"We are running late, and they will not wait forever," Angela urged. She did not like that the men chasing them had guns. It was one thing to fight hand to hand or sword to sword, but these new weapons could make anyone deadly in the few moments it took to teach them how to load the cartridge and point it in her direction. Both Camden and Kail had tried to get her to use them, but she refused in the end. *I will study the weapon, but I will not use it. My bow is silent, more accurate and just as deadly*, she recalled the conversation.

"Don't worry, they will be there. This isn't the first time we have been tied up," he said with a smile. "Ouch! What was that for?" he protested after she thumped him on his head.

"Do not let your power make you arrogant," she scolded as she continued to the rendezvous point.

Kail rubbed his head where Angela had hit him while watching the men on the roof below him. *One step forward for every two backwards,* he thought with a sigh. Leaving the edge of the building, he turned to catch up with Angela.

Treylane Armstrong, the lead soldier that had been chasing the two outlaws watched Kail step away from the rooftop above him. *Everything was going according to plan. There would be no escape for them this time,* he thought, signaling to his men.

Kail didn't use his magic to help him catch up to Angela. She had been mad at him for a while about this operation, and he was not looking forward to her scolding. *I need to make it up to her,* he thought. *Only problem is that even after five years I still seem to disappoint her more often than not.* Everyone he knew had long ago run out of advice for him regarding a relationship with someone whose race died a thousand years ago. Even his best friend, Camden Arland, was at a loss, but there were parts that he would give anything, even his life, to protect. One of those things was the red head in front of him.

"Angela stop," he pleaded. He watched her spin to face him.

"What Kail?"

"I need you. I can't have you mad at me. It's too dangerous now for us to just stumble through this like we did five years ago."

"Then lead Kail. We all know that you did not ask for this destiny, but it is yours. Saddle your power and fame and save the world. Survive that first."

"I love you, you know that," he replied.

"Yes, and I you," she said, touching his face. "We are bound in this forever, but the Mastersons will not wait that long."

"Let's not keep them waiting then," Kail said, now that the air between them was a little less fuzzy.

Chapter 2

"I don't like this," Kail said, surveying the edge of the city in front of him. It had been half an hour since they fled the safe room with the enemy in pursuit.

"It has the same feeling as an ambush," Angela agreed.

The pair kept to the roof tops as they made their way across the city. The buildings had become shorter and spaced further apart. Angela could always just fly to where the *Odyssey* waited if needed, but Kail had the choice of either continuing at street level, or start teleporting himself across the city.

"Stay in the sky to cover me," he ordered. Her reply was a muffled sound as she took flight. Kail took in a deep breath and made his way from the rooftops to the poorly lit street level. It was clear that the lamps in this part of the city had not been filled with oil in a while. He focused his power around him in a shield. *Better safe than sorry*, he thought, stepping into the dark street.

Angela drifted in the sky above Kail keeping watch as he walked block after block. Her bow was in her hands as was an arrow nocked and ready, just in case. Her life had changed so much in the last five years, but it somehow had managed to remain the same. She had to admit that the

Time Walker, Mr. Eleazar, knew what he was doing when he brought her here from her home, a thousand years in the past. She was a Keratin, a warrior born and raised to fight, and there had been nonstop fighting. The longer it went, the less likely it seemed they would prevail. Five years in this new time was still just more war in a life filled with war.

The prophecy seemed to be playing itself out as well. The power given up shall be returned and the last to rule, shall lord over all. The Guardian will fall and the door will open for revenge yet taken. The childless one will decide the fate of all. It seemed to be Kail with his magical heritage returned to him, the fall of The Guardian at The Eternal Gateway, and Therion well on his way to lording over all. Revenge and the childless one were still open for debate between them, but it had been a long time since it had been a priority.   Now it was about staying alive and avoiding Therion's forces.

Her eyes quickly scanned the city streets below, before she realized that she had lost sight of Kail. Cursing herself for letting her mind wander, she flew from one city block to the next looking for him.

Kail kept his head low and his steps quick as he made his way closer to the rendezvous with the *Odyssey* and the ship's owners, the Mastersons. The longer he went without some attacker emerging from the darkness, the more agitated he became. The whole thing with his mother's ring had been a trap from the start. It had been simple enough in the beginning to get away. But the fact that they had chased him all the way to the safe house told him that this had been planned out for a while. *Why would they just give up the chase now*, he wondered.

Kail stopped in his tracks when it became clear to him. *They haven't given up, they are following us to the Odyssey*. He mentally cursed himself for not seeing it sooner. Focusing his mind he let the divining magic flow. He could sense them now. More than twenty soldiers were in his immediate area with at least three of them looking at him right now. Changing his focus he found there were just as many keeping track of Angela in the sky above him.

Angela's search became more frantic the longer it took to find Kail. A red glow of light from behind caught her attention. Turning, she watched as a ball of red energy slowly drifted skyward back from inside the city near the safe house. "Why is he back there?" She continued to watch as the light blinked three times and then went out. *It does not matter that was the abort signal, and everyone is on their own.* Not knowing where the danger was that caused Kail to abort, she rose higher into the sky for general safety as she warred with her next action.

In the distance she could see the *Odyssey* lift from its hiding spot outside of the city. It was not the only airship that recognized the signal. She could see a second ship as well come into view and head in the *Odyssey's* direction. She understood now. *Foolish, foolish plan*, she thought. *Kail was right to abort.* Angela shot skyward into the cloud level until she was sure that there was no one on the ground that could see her.

Treylane Armstrong stepped out from the shadows on the rooftop. He watched the fugitive Keratin fly from his sight into the night sky. Neither he nor his men had been spotted by the outlaws, yet they had been clearly sniffed out. He signaled to his lieutenants that the mission was over as their prey escaped. *Perhaps they had been too loose with the escape*, he thought. *Next time they would give chase instead of just watch and follow.*

"Shall we place bets on who's at fault for this mess?" Rhonin Masterson asked the deck crew of the *Odyssey* as the airship left the ground having seen the signal.

"I know who will get in trouble if they find out we are placing odds on them," his wife Rayne replied with a smirk.

"Incoming airship," a voice squawked over the speaker on the bridge.

Rayne glanced at her husband, and he gave her the go ahead as he pressed a button, making yellow caution lights light up throughout ship. "Ready weapons and secure the ship," she spoke into the intercom that conveyed her order.

"Helm, proceed to rendezvous point Atagi," Rhonin ordered as he stood from the captain's chair and made his way to the front viewing ports of the *Odyssey*. He watched the city pass below him and kept a watchful eye on the second airship that now hovered over the area where Kail's abort signal had been spotted.

"They are not going to pursue us," his wife stated, joining him.

"No, whoever it was that lured us here knows they have been made," Rhonin agreed. "They know it, and we know it. It holds no reason for them to press an attack after failing the ambush. It's not Therion though. This enemy is thinking about the costs involved. Sponsored bounty hunters if I had to guess."

The mighty drive fans of the *Odyssey* roared as the airship lifted its passengers into the sky and out of the city. The ship banked away from where it had waited and ran its engines at full speed to where Angela should meet them in the sky.

Kail let the magic fade once he knew that Angela and the Mastersons had seen his signal. *They're going to be mad at me. I won't hear the end of this one for a while*, he thought. A small part of the sidewalk in front of him shattered from the impact of a bullet. Half a moment later the distinctive crack of a gunshot above him rang out into the night. Scanning the edges of the rooftops above him, he quickly found the soldier that had fired.

His magic from earlier was still wrapped around him as his mind cycled through a dozen attacks that he could put to use. *Perhaps manipulating time in such a way that it would take an hour for the man to fall from the rooftop while still hitting the ground with the full impact.*

"Do not let your power make you arrogant," Angela's words from earlier in the night filled his head as the second shot missed him as well.

Maybe this is why my father gave up his magic, he decided after becoming disgusted with himself.

Kail tore the air in front of him apart with his magic. The opening was dark on the other side, but he knew where it would take him. It was another trick he had discovered allowing him move very long distances. It drained more magical energy than a simple teleport or making himself invisible, but a part of him still had the desire to flaunt his powers and crush the attacker. He knew that when he arrived at the secondary rally point the drain of this much magic would remove the urge. Memories of rogue mages being stripped of their powers and placed under the watch of the Mage Council filled his thoughts with warning, as he stepped into the blackness and vanished.

Angela stepped onto the bridge of the *Odyssey*. She quickly made her way through the crew to where the Mastersons were standing at the front view ports. Rhonin did not need to ask the question out loud for her to answer. "No, we did not get the ring," she said.

"And the reason for the abort?" Rhonin asked.

"I do not know. They were already after us when Kail arrived at the safe house. It was all a trap of course. He must have found something more," Angela reasoned. "There was another ship that responded to his signal."

"We saw that too," Rayne said.

"I am going to get out of this armor. It may be a while before Kail arrives," Angela said.

"We should arrive at Silverton by tomorrow night. Camden and the *Snow Break* should be there as well," Rayne offered as Angela began to step away.

Angela paused, thinking about Rayne's words before responding. "It will be a good thing. Being away like this... It is hard." Angela made her way to the lower decks of the *Odyssey* to the single room she shared with Kail. When the two of them were not on board, it was used by other crew members. At first it had made her uncomfortable that they displaced other people when they were here. She recalled a conversation she had with the Masterson's and Kail about it.

"It's only one room Angela, it's not like we're taking over half the ship and making them sleep outside," Kail said.

"Besides, who is going to say no to a mage like Kail and the woman who can fly," Rhonin joked.

"This is my point exactly," she recalled her sharp reply. It was not until later that she understood that the crew had seen it as a great honor and respect to them when they came aboard the *Odyssey*. She found it odd that so many looked to them as great people, leaders, even heroes, and that they would never be as great as them. She pointed out that Rhonin and Rayne had no magical abilities, yet they were considered equals. None of them seemed to understand her side of the argument.

Angela let her mind drift over the past five years as she began to strip off the Imaera hide body armor. She remembered fondly the hunting trip they had taken to Canyamar. It had been six months after Kail and Camden had come to rescue her in Courduff. The giant jungle cats were deadly predators and took considerable skill to hunt. The Imaera's hide was prized for its ability to resist magic and, if damaged, to slowly repair itself. Also the fact that Kail's magic was useless against them and Camden's fared no better but her gifts were left intact, brought a smile to her face. By the end of the hunt, every Imaera they had were her kills. As she folded the leather armor leggings, she placed them next to its matching vest. A small chuckle escaped her lips, recalling that Suki for weeks never let the men forget that they came up empty handed. It was also during that trip that the playful wisp that had come to live in the *Snow*

Break's engine core disappeared. Something else had also happened as a result of that trip, something she was looking forward to when they arrived home.

Grabbing a small bag of items and a towel she headed to the showers. The shower area on the *Odyssey* had impressed her. Hot steam from the engine after it powered the main turbines was routed throughout the ship. It served several functions; the primary was that it provided heat for the ship when they cruised at higher altitudes. There had been more than one cold night aboard the *Snow Break* on which she and Kail normally resided. The steam pipes also could be tapped with tiny valves and nozzles to provide a warm shower. As the steam sprayed from overhead, it cooled back into water. Once it drained it was run through a filter to be returned to the system. Stepping into the hot mist of the shower Angela relaxed, clearing her thoughts of the failed mission to recover the ring.

Kail watched from his vantage point as the *Odyssey* approached. Closing his eyes he let the divining magic flow into his surroundings. He didn't want to make the mistake of teleporting on board only to have someone see. Unable to find any watchful eyes he was satisfied that the ship had made a clean get away from Stalbridge. Focusing, Kail transformed into magical energy, and teleported to the *Odyssey* as it passed overhead.

Snapping back into existence on the outer deck of the *Odyssey*, he made his way to the bridge. Rhonin was there in the command chair. Rayne it appeared was off duty and below. He did not see Angela either. "Did the pickup with Angela go ok?"

Rhonin nodded his head. "She came aboard several hours ago as planned."

Kail nodded at the news while glancing around the bridge. Hesitating for a moment he simply turned to go below deck.

"Do you want to talk about it?" Rhonin called before he left.

"No, I think once will be enough when we get to Silverton and meet up with the *Snow Break*," Kail replied before disappearing below deck.

Chapter 3

It had been a long night and following day for Kail Falconcrest. The *Odyssey* still had an hour of flight time before they arrived in Silverton. As the coming night crept over them, the *Odyssey* had descended in altitude in preparation for landing. Taking this opportunity, he watched from the outer deck of the airship as the lights of the city came into view on the horizon. His thoughts were interrupted as slender hands wrapped around him from behind.

"This is the worst and the best part," Angela sighed, resting her head on his shoulder as she took in the view.

"Do you remember that day? So many years ago when we were first at Silverton," he asked.

"It is a day that is hard to forget Kail. The first time you repaid me the favor of saving your life."

"I still dream about it. It doesn't always turn out like it did. Sometimes in my dream, I panic and do nothing. I am frozen in the moment as we flew by and you were left behind. Other times I teleport to save you and miss, so I fall to my death," he recalled, remembering the day when the *Colossus* had caught up with them over the skies of Silverton.

"But you did not hesitate, and you did not miss," she replied, giving him a small hug.

"I know. Things are different now. I have to think about what I do. If I mess up, even if only I suffer the direct consequences, a lot of people will get hurt."

"I will tell you again, the same as I have before. Do what you think is right Kail. That is all anyone can ask of you," Angela reminded him.

"I think this ship is spoiling us," Kail answered, changing the subject. Angela gave him a questioning look. "No more cold nights drifting in the air currents," he added with a smirk.

Angela rolled her eyes at the implication.

"I kind of miss having to keep each other warm," he continued.

"The matriarch of House Atagi is going to replace your usefulness as a bed warmer with an Imaera unless you choose your next words carefully," she said with all seriousness.

"You weren't cold last night." Kail leaned in to caress the soft lips of the unique woman next to him as his answer.

"What was that for?" Rhonin asked as his wife smacked the smile off of his face as he watched the younger couple on the deck of his airship.

"It's not polite to stare with a grin like that," Rayne answered him.

"Why not?" he asked puzzled.

"You are such a cave man sometimes you know. It has been sixteen days since we left Silverton. How would you feel if you hadn't seen them in that time?"

"But I didn't see them either," he countered with logic.

"Go land this ship!" Rayne ordered her husband. She watched as her husband turned with a confused look on his face to tend to the landing of the airship. Turning back to the front viewport of the *Odyssey* she eyed Kail and Angela one last time, smiling as she remembered years ago when it was Rhonin and her out there.

Suki looked at herself in the mirror of her cabin aboard the *Snow Break*. Her mind was lost to thought as she ran her fingers over the scar on her chest. Her tiny reminder of how life is fragile and also a warning about trusting someone too much. Five years ago, Xavier Ross had been part of the *Snow Break's* crew. That was until he killed everyone. Only her small ability to heal had saved her before Camden found her. She had considered using that magic a thousand times to smooth out the scar, but never went through with it.

Motion from the port hole caught her eye as she buttoned the blouse hiding the scar. The *Odyssey* had returned. Taking one last look in the mirror to check her appearance, she headed to the galley where the news of the ship was eagerly awaited.

Camden Arland sat on one side of the metal galley table that had been bolted to the floor of the *Snow Break*. He squinted with assessing eyes at his two opponents in front of him. The cards in his hand contained four spears and the general. A full flank. *There is no way to loose with this hand*, he thought. "All in," he declared, sliding his entire pile to the center of the table.

The pair across from him looked at each other with matching eyes. Twins, one with dark red hair, the other with dark brown. "Call," they both said in unison, laying down their cards.

Three spears, a diplomat and the king for one. The other had two spears, a diplomat, the assassin and the queen. He couldn't believe it. The diplomats let them combine hands against him and the assassin removes his general. That left his four spears against their five and the royal pair. "Cheats!" he accused as they scooped up their winnings between giggles. He tried to figure out how they were doing it and gave them a scowl when a large portion of the bet was eaten between them.

Suki stepped into the galley at that moment to save him. "I thought I told you two to let him win," she said, seeing the whole pile of snacks in front of them.

"This is a conspiracy," Camden concluded.

"Quit being such a sore loser," Suki scolded him, "besides it's time to go. The *Odyssey* is back," she informed them to the delight of the twin girls.

"If they play like this at four, think what they will be like when they are older. Nothing will be safe," he countered, waving his hands around.

"Amaya. Alyssa. Quit teasing him and let's go," Suki said, extending both her hands to the girls. The twins each took a hand and started to leave the galley. Alyssa at the last moment ran back to the table to swipe the last of the snacks as Camden was reaching for them.

"Hey!" he called after her as she made off with the snacks.

Ground crew at the Silverton airship field rushed to meet the *Odyssey* as its engines cycled down. The *Odyssey's* designated landing area was on the far side of the field away from the daily and weekly traffic of the trade and merchant dirigibles. It still had direct access to the train rails for easy resupplying of vessels classified as military.

The *Snow Break* was birthed on the same side of the field as the *Odyssey*. Suki along with the twins stood at the bottom of the lowered loading deck and watched as the ground crew handled the ship. She could tell by the twins fidgeting that they were anxious.

"It could be hours still before we can go over there," Camden's voice said as he came down the deck. Three sets of female eyes turned in unison to glare at him. "I'm just saying. No need to get in a hurry."

"Quit being mean," Suki scolded him again. They all watched for ten minutes or more before the hull of the *Odyssey* opened and the crew boarding ramp was lowered to the ground. "Wait!" she shouted as both Amaya and Alyssa started to run towards the *Odyssey*. Both girls halted in their approach as they saw who was leaving the ship. Gunners and part of the engine crew were the first to depart followed by the combined med and galley crew members. Suki watched as they failed to contain themselves as they began to inch towards the *Odyssey* again.

"We may as well go. There is no stopping them," Camden sighed.

Suki had only taken a handful of steps towards the twins as they suddenly darted towards the *Odyssey*. Stepping out of the airship was Rhonin and Rayne Masterson. The pair met with the Officer-in-Charge of the airship field who had been waiting for them since their arrival. Next was Kail followed by Angela easily identifiable by dark red hair that matched one of her daughters. Kail ignored the Officer-in-Charge who tried to get his attention as he ran forward to meet his twin girls who were about to reach him.

"It's ok. I won't tell anyone," she heard Camden whisper to her as she watched the Atagi twins reunited with their parents.

"Just walk slowly," she replied, giving herself time to dry her eyes. Kail had his arms out and grabbed them in a big hug. She could hear his faint laughter and teasing about how they seemed as light as birds. With them hanging from his arms he approached Angela who in turn took each one to formally greet and then again as their mother who had dearly missed them.

Chapter 4

Kail followed Angela down the hallway to the meeting room. He didn't particularly enjoy being the man in charge of what had been labeled as a group of outlaws, terrorists and rebels. Silverton was the only city that would have them. *Only because they blamed Therion for bombing the place five years ago with the Colossus*, he thought. It wasn't until much later that word had reached them that Bastiana and Vincent had returned to the city to take out their frustration when The Guardian had whisked them away. Camden's fortune helped as well. He had almost single handedly rebuilt the town. They had not known at the time, but the investment had returned itself a hundred fold in natural resources, talented people and most of all, a new place to call home.

Stepping inside the room after Angela, everyone present rose as he approached the table. The Mastersons were both there along with Brom Carter, the pilot of the *Odyssey*. Camden and Suki were present as well. With them were Harold Riggins, the first officer, and Lawrence Burke, the chief engineer of the *Snow Break*. Randal Wood, the Officer-in-Charge of the airship field, and Duncan Deline the commander of Silverton general, were on opposite sides of the table.

Kail started the meeting by going over the details of the failed mission to retrieve the ring from Stalbridge. Randal and Duncan grilled him for hours about every detail. Angela was not spared either. All of their statements, including the ones from the Mastersons, were documented. If the information they had regarding the artifact held true, it would be a powerful item to possess. Kail argued that if it were in the hands of Therion, defeating him at that point would become next to impossible. None involved with the planning of the mission had ever mentioned, or may not have known, that the intelligence about the ring also included that it had been created by his father, Duke Falconcrest. Nor did anyone bring up the fact that it may have been the wedding band he gave to his wife, Kail's mother. *They didn't have to because it was written on everyone's face that this was more personal than strategic*, he remembered.

The rest of the meeting passed as usual. Each bit of news that had come in was reported to the airship captains and to himself. Most of it was about supply chains, work orders, recruitment numbers and such. It wasn't until the spy reports were read that he started to pay attention.

"Aldervale has expanded their air field and is in the process of doubling the rail lines between it and Courduff," Duncan read. "Cahir, rumor has it, is not liking its arrangement with Therion and Courduff."

"Cahir?" Kail interrupted, "the city that Vincent and Bastiana controlled before joining up with Therion and Courduff?"

"That is what the report says sir." Duncan double checked.

Kail looked towards Angela at the news. She shook her head in response. The fights between them were ones that they almost never walked away from. "Continue," he prompted.

"The *Wind Runner* is still on assignment in Canyamar, but they have reported nothing new in the vicinity of The Eternal Gateway. Therion's outpost there is still being manned, and the supplies and personnel are still being delivered. No new reports on any changes or why Therion is still interested in the place five years after it was destroyed," Duncan finished.

Kail nodded after hearing the update about the *Wind Runner*. It was the first airship that they had built at Silverton. James Decisero had been captain of it since it was flight ready. His crew was just as diverse as the *Snow Break's* and *Odyssey*. Christi Strang, their chief medic was just as skilled as Suki, but lacked the magical ability was all. Malix on the other hand was a brute, but had the skill to pilot the ship like no other. Having the *Wind Runner* watch The Eternal Gateway was good experience for them. A part of him wished it was the *Snow Break* on duty there instead of being stuck with the administration of a city.

The meeting took a break for half an hour before resuming. Kail took the time to stand outside and watch the ground crews work on the *Snow Break* and *Odyssey*.

"Hard to believe where we are at now compared to where we started," Camden said, joining him.

"Mr. Eleazar didn't plan this out very well did he?"

"No. He didn't," Camden agreed.

"I don't know what we're doing anymore. Eventually Therion is going to send his forces and just crush us. Those new juggernaut airships of his are insane. We are out gunned and outnumbered. Honestly, I am surprised he hasn't done it already."

"Maybe he has bigger things to worry about like Cahir. I have no doubts that we're still on his bucket list and other resistance groups like ours are forming on their own in other cities," Camden suggested. "Something is coming to a head, we can all feel it. But you can't let anyone see you get down. You know how infectious it can be to morale when the people you look to for hope and inspiration, loose theirs. Maintain the illusion at least for now dirt farmer," Camden finished, causing Kail to smile at the nick name from his boyhood.

"You ever wonder what it would be like if Eleazar had never walked into our lives?"

"Yup, we would all be either dead or worse, and you would not have the love of strongest woman I have ever known or two daughters that are going to make your life miserable when they get older," Camden ribbed.

"I am so doomed," he admitted.

"Wait till they come home with boyfriends."

"Argh! I don't want to hear this," Kail shouted, holding his hands over his ears. "I am putting you in charge of boyfriend patrol."

"I'll get right on that!"

"Excuse me sirs, but it's time," Harold called to them from the outbuilding of the meeting hall.

Kail led the way back to the meeting room with Camden right behind him. The debriefing was over and the remainder of the time was spent for new issues. "I want to get more intel about Stalbridge. Find out who owns that other airship, and who it was that had men following us until we aborted the rendezvous. Also start screening some men for my daughters," Kail directed Duncan Deline.

Coughing, Camden spoke up, "I thought I was on that duty. But... I think it's a bit soon."

"What?" Kail stopped him before he realized what he had said. "No, no, no. I want to start looking at having body guards for them. Guardians in the background. I don't want these guys from Stalbridge showing up here and starting something."

"Oh, ok," Camden replied, looking rejected.

Kail looked to Angela. "What do you think?"

Angela could see that Kail's words had unintentionally implied that Camden and the *Snow Break* may not be up to the task of looking after their twins. She returned her gaze to Kail before answering. "I think that finding loyal men is a good idea. There is no safer place for them than the *Snow Break* when we are away, but they will not always be children. They will need guardians there for them when we cannot be," she finished, looking back to Camden.

Randal and Duncan presented request after request that had been funneled up to them from Silverton. Most of the items involving money he let Camden decide. Occasionally, if there were military variables to consider Kail decided instead. Again Kail's mind began to wander. He didn't know how long it had been before he noticed that no one was talking. Glancing around the room, everyone was frozen in place. Adrenalin made his heart race as he wrapped himself with his magic. Soon after, he marked the walls with runes to protect everyone in the room. *I didn't do this. Who is causing this? Only Therion or maybe Bastiana had the power to time stop*, he wondered. *Mr. Eleazar?* Kail made for the door to the meeting room but was brought up short. The door had changed. *That is the same door I saw five years ago at The Eternal Gateway.*

Reaching slowly for the door knob he recalled what he had seen years ago in the jungle of Canyamar. *Therion,*

The Guardian Eleazar and the Keratin. Gripping the knob he gave it a turn and opened the door. Instead of hallway, he saw the jungle of Canyamar lay before him in ruins just after The Gateway's destruction. He could even see in the far distance the *Snow Break* fighting against the *Colossus.* The impulse to stop the death of Camden's crew had him already stepping through the door when the sight blurred and time shifted.

"The door is shut," he heard the woman say.

It was the same girl from the past. *She doesn't know I reopened it.* Horror sank in as he understood now. *This isn't the past. It's the future.* The woman he was looking at had the same Keratin war blades as before, but she also had a side arm on each hip as well. *They have guns.*

Mr. Eleazar suddenly stepped in front of him on the other side of The Gateway. "I am more sorry than you can ever know Kail. But this is not your time or your fight." Mr. Eleazar slammed the door shut. Bright light began to seep around the edges of the doorway until it became blinding. Kail let out a scream before darkness overcame him.

Chapter 5

Kail slowly opened his eyes after the blinding light from The Gateway caused him to black out. He knew instantly that something was wrong. He wasn't in the meeting room anymore but instead on a bed. Sitting up and looking around the room, he saw that he was alone, but it was clear that there had been visitors. *The hospital in Silverton*, he recognized after looking out of the window.

"Finally," he heard Suki say as she entered the room.

"Something has happened. We need to get everyone," he insisted.

"We know Kail. Get back on the bed," Suki ordered him. "Go tell them that he is awake," she called out to someone in the hall.

"What do you mean you know? Everyone was frozen in time. I saw The Gateway and Mr. Eleazar."

"Slow down Kail. Everyone will be here soon. You have been unconscious for three days."

"Three days?" he repeated before remembering. "That's how long Mr. Eleazar was out after he saved us and our ship over Silverton five years ago," he said. *Maybe I did cause the time stop*, he wondered.

Randal Wood, the Officer-in-Charge of the Silverton Air Field, was the first to arrive. Camden and Angela arrived a few minutes later. Suki had managed to keep all of them from saying anything until she had gone over him with a fine tooth comb to check him out. Rhonin Masterson finally arrived and James Decisero followed.

"James?" Kail said stunned. "Why are you here?"

"The *Wind Runner* arrived twelve hours ago," Randal reported.

"Something has changed," James started.

"I know. The Eternal Gateway, it's back," Kail finished for him.

"That is our best guess. There was light and commotion from Therion's base when it happened. We stayed for half a day before we were forced to leave when reinforcements started to arrive." James stated.

Looking at Camden and Angela, "What happened at the meeting three days ago?" Kail asked.

Camden and Angela glanced at each other before answering. "We thought you might have fallen asleep," Angela started. "But we could not wake you."

"It got pretty scary there for a few minutes. It was like when you used to drift off before you could control your magic. When you used divination on accident," Camden said. "Then you seemed to panic, and the room was walled off with magic barriers and runes. A few moments later you screamed and went limp and the magic left with it."

"It was a time stop. Like the one Mr. Eleazar uses. I still don't think I caused it," Kail started to tell them what he saw. "The Eternal Gateway was there, closed like it was in the jungle."

"The Gateway was in the meeting room?" Angela asked.

"Yes, I saw the jungle destroyed on the other side," Kail answered. He looked at Camden and left out the part about seeing the *Snow Break* and *Colossus*. *He never has gotten completely over the death of his first crew.* "Things shifted just like before, and I saw the Keratin woman again and Mr. Eleazar was with her."

"The very same as before?" Angela questioned.

"No, I think this time I opened the door right after she shut it five years ago. Mr. Eleazar slammed it shut this time. He said that he was sorry before doing it though."

"What do you think it all means?" Camden asked.

"I don't know," Kail answered. "Randal."

"Sir?" the officer answered.

"Order the ships to be made ready. We're going to The Eternal Gateway," Kail ordered.

"Yes sir." Randal left the room with a salute and headed off as ordered.

"I don't think you should be going anywhere just yet," Suki objected.

Ignoring her protest Kail got off of the bed. "It wasn't the past that we saw five years ago. It was the future," he said. Kail explained the rest of what The Gateway showed him and about the guns the woman had. "We have to go to The Gateway."

Camden shook hands with James of the *Wind Runner* as they parted ways to board their airships. The Mastersons were already aboard the *Odyssey*, and the ground crews were already pulling back the last of the support equipment for the vessel. Once the ground crew was clear the *Odyssey* fired up her massive fan blades, and a few moments later she was airborne. Minutes later the smaller sleek *Wind Runner* lifted into the sky. A bright blue flash and the sound of the air cracking let him know that Kail had teleported to him.

"We're all ready," he heard Kail tell him.

"Just taking one last look is all. Can't be too careful," he answered.

"It will take us two days at top speed to get there."

"Two days," Camden paused. "This is it you know. Where everything starts to change," he replied.

"If The Gateway has indeed returned. Then yes, I would agree."

Camden and Kail watched as the *Odyssey* and *Wind Runner* rose higher and higher before circling Silverton as they waited for the *Snow Break*. The light on the tower changed from yellow to green, indicating that they were cleared for takeoff.

"Let's go," Kail said.

"You do know that some of us still have to walk," he joked, following Kail up the boarding ramp into the *Snow Break*.

Camden took his seat in the command chair. "Bring the turbines online," he ordered. The *Snow Break* had been out of commission for the last six months as the old drive fans had been removed and upgraded with a new metal turbine fan system. Also the old cabling system that ran through the ship had been replaced with an all hydraulic system as well. So far the ship had passed all of its test flights with the new turbines, but they had yet to really put her through the paces.

"Aye Captain," Harold Riggins answered from the helm.

As the hydrogen and oxygen fuel was fed into the engines from the core of the ship, the high pitched whine that was characteristic of the new turbines could be heard. Camden looked at the bridge crew as the *Snow Break* lifted off the ground. The new turbines were quieter than the original fan blades had been, but when they were brought up to full power make no mistake, they screamed.

"Status?" Camden asked.

"Engines are at ten percent. Twelve," Harold answered.

Kail raised his eyebrows in appreciation of the new turbines as Camden smiled with pride. The old fan blades needed sixty percent just to lift off or hover.

"Take the lead," Rhonin's voice crackled over the speaker. Radio was another new invention, a local one that a group from Silverton had produced. It didn't work very well, and it was hard to understand anyone on a good day. The not so good days, they were better off shouting at each other from the decks of the airships.

"*Snow Break* has the lead," Camden replied into the radio. "*Odyssey* and *Wind Runner* take up flanking positions."

The reply was garbled when both Rhonin and James tried to reply at the same time. *It needs a lot of work*, Camden thought. They were still working on the protocols when it came to radio conversations.

Suki and Angela were strapped in their chairs in the galley. Amaya and Alyssa were there as well. Suki had been happy that the twin girls were coming with them even though she knew that it went against all common sense to take them into harm's way. She knew that Angela had not been happy either, but there had not been enough time to find a secure location or the people to take care of them. The bounty hunters that Kail and Angela had run into at Stalbridge still had them on edge. Kail had told her that if it came to it, he would rip apart space and time to get them to safety. She harbored no doubts that he would.

During the last couple of years she had spent more time with the twins than their parents. Once they were old enough to be left alone without their parents worrying so much, Kail and Angela had slipped back into their old roles as leaders and fighters against Therion. It was never asked of her, but she had taken up the role of being their nanny and caregiver. Both girls had grins on their faces and had their heads huddled together whispering about how they were grown up now, and they were important people in this mission to The Gateway.

As soon as the light in the galley turned from yellow to green, the twins were out of their chairs making a fast escape from the room. She had not even seen Angela move, but their mother was already blocking them at the door.

"Settle down," their mother scolded them. "It is going to be very busy in the hallways and on the bridge. If you want to go there, you need act like you belong there."

"Yes mother," they replied in unison, following her into the hallway.

Amaya with her red hair let her sister follow their mother first. "Coming Suki?" she asked before following them into the hall.

"I will be right behind you," she said with a smile.

The hallways and corridors to the bridge were indeed busy. With a full crew to man every post allowing for rotations, the *Snow Break* was a cramped place compared to the old days when it had just been Camden, Kail, Angela and herself. She missed some of the privacy, but it was a fair trade when things got rough. Having all the cannons and guns manned properly made the *Snow Break* a very powerful ship. Several times in the past years they had gotten in over their heads but had come out alive because of the extra crew aboard.

The bridge was lightly manned. Camden was in his captain's chair, and Harold was at the helm. One other crew member was off to the side monitoring flow valves and pressures. Kail stood lower where the view was better. The twins quickly joined him but were not quite tall enough to see out of the glass. He had to lift them up so they could see. She could hear him pointing out the *Odyssey* and the *Wind Runner* to them on each side.

"What do you think we will find when we get there?" she asked Camden.

"A military base and a pile of rocks. Whether that pile of rocks forms an archway or door, I don't know."

"Do you want The Gateway to be back?"

"Yeah, I think I do. I like where we're at with Silverton, but if something doesn't happen soon, there won't be a Silverton for us all to live happily ever after in," he finished.

"Do you think this is the prophecy?" she asked.

"Prophecy? What are you talking about?" Camden questioned, standing up to face her.

Suki frowned. "The door shall open for revenge yet taken," she quoted the prophecy.

Camden sent a sharp look to Kail who wasn't paying attention to their conversation. Angela took notice when Camden stood and made her way over to them.

"The look on each of your faces says that you have knowledge of something important," Angela said in her accent from a different time.

"I was thinking about The Gateway and the prophecy. If The Eternal Gateway is back or open," Suki started before Angela interrupted.

"For the revenge yet taken," Angela finished, following her same line of thought.

"Yes."

"Kail," Angela called, causing him to join the conversation.

Suki explained again for Kail about the possibility of The Eternal Gateway's return and the connection to the prophecy.

"It's certainly possible. I think I will tell the other captains. We should at least be aware of that chance if The Gateway is there when we arrive," Kail said. They all agreed with the extra precaution as Kail kissed his daughters and told them to behave for him while he was gone. The twins nodded in unison, and Kail transformed into a ball of bluish light and teleported to the *Wind Runner*.

Chapter 6

Captain Wilhelm Bailon stood on the command bridge of the *Lotus*. Three days ago, Therion arrived in Aldervale aboard his airship, the *Inferno*, and ordered him personally to take command of the *Lotus*. Included with those orders, he was to provide escort for Therion's capital ship to Canyamar and the outpost at The Eternal Gateway. He had never seen Therion in person until that moment, and there had been many rumors and speculation about why he had suddenly been put in charge of one of the finest ships in Courduff's air fleet. His service in the Courduff military had been spotless, and his work in Aldervale had seen him quickly promoted up the ranks. His desire to command an airship was not unknown to his superiors, but for every airship there were fifty captains maneuvering for the opportunity to command one. Playing the political game wasn't something he was willing to do, and he highly doubted that anyone vouched for him. Taking advantage of an opportunity when it knocked on your door, however, was something only a fool let pass by.

The *Inferno*, following behind the *Lotus*, was one of the first juggernaut class airships. It was the prototype, after which the others were modeled. It was a bit smaller than the current ships being made by the massive metalwork and clockwork factories in Courduff and Cahir. It housed over seven hundred troops and enough firepower to destroy a medium sized city. Therion did not tell him anything about the mission to The Eternal Gateway, other than if there was anything that did not belong to Courduff, then it was to be destroyed.

"We should arrive in less than two hours," Cid Daltry reported.

"Thank you Lieutenant," he replied. Cid had followed his same career and was now reaping the benefits. Every time he had been promoted or assigned to a new duty, Cid had received a similar assignment. When Therion put him in charge of the *Lotus*, he had taken Cid with him. He also expected there to be some resistance with the existing crew of the *Lotus* when he took command, but there hadn't been any. He wished he had time to research the previous captain, but he barely had enough time to pack his things before they left Aldervale.

"They say that The Gateway looks different for each person who looks at it," Cid commented.

"I wouldn't know. I haven't seen it, and every report for the last five years says that it was destroyed," Bailon said.

"Why do you think Therion is moving the *Inferno* from Courduff to the outpost and taking the *Lotus* with him?"

"I don't second guess or try to speculate why we are ordered around. I only need to know the details they give me to complete my job," he answered. "The outpost is coming into view now. Ready the crew and ship lieutenant," he ordered.

"Aye sir," Cid clipped a salute as he returned to duty.

Therion stood alone in his private viewing deck on the *Inferno*. The *Lotus* held point in front of them as they neared The Eternal Gateway. Three days ago he felt the massive amount of time energy pass over the world. *Anyone with half a brain cell for magic couldn't have missed it,* he thought. The previous captain of the *Lotus* happened to be in the wrong place at the wrong time. *My patience for peons bickering for favor was already wearing thin.* When the time energy hit, he lashed out believing to be under attack. The *Lotus's* captain had simply ceased to exist after that. His name was already forgotten. *As it should be.*

He had no knowledge of her new captain. He happened to be the first person of rank in Aldervale who had simply saluted when he arrived instead of trying to lick his boots. *If he proves to be incompetent, he can be easily replaced,* he reasoned. A light knock from the door in the back of the room disturbed his thoughts. "Enter," he called.

He heard the sound of the door opening, but no one stepped inside. "The captain reports that the *Lotus* has signaled, and we are beginning our final approach to the outpost sir," a voice reported.

"And the captain needs my assistance with this task?" he questioned.

"No, sir. He wanted you to be informed is all," the voice reported with fear.

"You can tell the captain that if I want his information, I will get it from him."

"Yes sir," the voice quivered as the door shut.

The urge to simply teleport the rest of the way to The Gateway was increasing in its seduction. If he could unlock its secrets, he could control all of time and the destiny of the world as he saw fit. He closed his eyes and settled his emotions until the anticipation faded from his body. *Never become rushed, mistakes are made that way*, he thought, calming his mind.

Captain Bailon watched from the *Lotus* as the *Inferno* settled into the large clearing where the outpost built a landing strip. The *Inferno* was larger than it could handle and crushed several trees in the process. He made a mental note to have the air field in Aldervale expanded even more to make sure it could handle the *Inferno* or any of the juggernaut airships. *Maybe even three or four of them*. There wasn't enough room for the *Lotus* to land as well, but he was fine with that. They could remain airborne and at the ready if anyone was foolish enough to attack. The cities of the east were proving to be difficult to subdue, and it wasn't uncommon to hear of reports of them attacking isolated ships when they could.

"So that is The Eternal Gateway," Lieutenant Cid said. "Not exactly what I expected."

"What do you see?" Bailon asked.

"Looks like someone started to build part of a barracks or something and stopped," Cid explained what he saw.

"Interesting," Bailon said. "I see what I would guess to be the entrance to a grand church. Two towering spires of stone and massive wooden doors."

"The rumors appear to be true then. It's different for everyone who looks at it," Cid finished, turning to attend to his duties.

"I wonder what is behind those massive doors," Bailon said to no one.

Therion stood in front of The Eternal Gateway. Twisted black iron adorned the columns that supported the giant bronze door in front of him. It reminded him of a bank vault. *Fitting that it would present itself this way*, he mused. Both large and small cogs and springs clicked and ticked away as he studied The Gateway. As he continued to watch, some of the mechanisms were clearly of future origin and others seemed to fade and disappear while others took their place. He had tried to open The Gateway when he arrived in the simple chance that it was open to him. "I will unlock your secrets," he challenged.

Chapter 7

"One airship above The Gateway and a juggernaut on the ground," Rhonin's voice spoke over the radio.

"It is the *Lotus* and Therion's ship the *Inferno*," Kail added when his eyes came back into focus after using divination to discover who they were facing.

"And The Gateway?" Camden asked.

"It has returned as well," Kail confirmed.

"What about Therion?"

"I didn't stay long enough to find out or give us away," Kail said, walking to the front view port of the *Snow Break* to view the *Lotus* patrolling the sky around The Eternal Gateway and the outpost.

James Decisero's voice came over the radio next. "We won't get a better chance than now."

He's right, Kail thought. *This is a golden opportunity to strike while the Inferno is on the ground with only the Lotus to protect it.* Looking to Angela he waited. Staring at each other for a few moments he gave the order. "Do it," he said at the exact moment that Angela nodded.

Camden gave the signal and all of the status lights on the ship turned red. Crew ran to their posts and gunners strapped themselves into the cannons. Suki already had the medical bay locked down while making sure Amaya and

Alyssa were safe and secure. One by one as the crew checked in, the lights turned green.

"*Wind Runner*, draw off the *Lotus* while the *Snow Break* and *Odyssey* go for the *Inferno*. Get them to chase if you can, and we will pick them off from behind and then take your turn firing the *Inferno*," Kail ordered.

"Roger, *Snow Break*," James voice acknowledged.

Kail watched as the *Wind Runner* increased its speed and broke away from the *Snow Break* and *Odyssey's* formation. "*Odyssey*, *Snow Break* will take the lead. Follow us in."

"Copy, *Snow Break*," Rhonin answered.

Turning to face Camden, "I'll go out and block for us," Kail said as he made his way to the outer deck of the *Snow Break*.

"Incoming airships!" Bailon's crew reported.

"Report," he ordered.

"Three airships. Two are lined up and approaching from the west, and the third is circling around to the north."

"Keep an eye on the lone ship," he warned the bridge crew. "Bring us around, and stay between the other two and The Gateway. Therion is there, and the *Inferno* can take care of itself." He nodded to Lieutenant Cid.

"Ready battle stations," Cid called out as the *Lotus* maneuvered to guard over The Eternal Gateway.

"They are guarding The Gateway instead of the *Inferno*," James called out to Malix and the rest of the *Wind Runner's* crew. "Bring us in closer, and prepare to fire. Let's see if we can't get them to come after us."

Kail stood on the outer deck of the *Snow Break*. The wind sent chills down his spine as he watched the Wind Runner circle from the north. The whine of the *Snow Break's* turbines increased in pitch as they started their run on the grounded *Inferno*. The *Lotus* opened fire first. Several flashes of cannon fire lit along its side followed by explosions high in the sky. *She knows how to fight*, he thought. *Filling the air above them so they would have to fly through flak*. The *Inferno* still had made no attempt to try to become airborne.

"Alter the approach arc by ten degrees," James ordered. "We don't need to make it easy for her." The first outliers of the shrapnel began to bang against the hull of the Wind Runner.

"Malix agrees," the helmsman answered.

Kail returned his focus to the *Inferno* as the massive airship blinked to life. Dozens of cannons opened fire as they approached. The amount of firepower the *Inferno* possessed surprised him. *Reports are one thing, but seeing it is different,* he thought. The *Inferno* was going to fill the sky in front of them with debris. *I can block this, and if the Odyssey follows our path, she will be fine as well.* He let the magic come to him, pushing it forward and in front of the *Snow Break*. Almost instantly blue ripples appeared as pieces of the *Inferno's* cannon fire were deflected from their path.

Bailon approached the front viewport of the *Lotus*. The airship was coming fast. "Switch to direct cannon fire," he said. Eight of the *Lotus's* cannons went silent just long enough to swap out the ammunition.

"Airship identified," a bridge watchman called out behind binoculars, "It's the *Wind Runner*."

"We're dealing with the terrorists?" Cid commented confused, then added, "That would identify the other two ships as the *Snow Break* and *Odyssey*."

Bailon wasn't sure how he felt about combating Kail Falconcrest and his group. They had very little contact over the last five years since his half sister Suki had helped convince him to spearhead a rescue in Courduff. *I don't want to find out that I killed my sister, she won't be on the Wind Runner if her last letter to me is still true*, he thought. "Maintain position and focus on the *Wind Runner*. As I said the *Inferno* can defend itself and if the reports about their leader, Kail Falconcrest, are true Therion will have to deal with him personally if magic comes into play."

"It looks like it already has." Cid pointed out as the *Snow Break* made its run on the *Inferno*.

"Focus on the *Wind Runner*," he ordered loudly when Cid's comment turned half of the heads on the bridge. "I will not have us distracted from the danger in front of us. Is that understood?"

The "yes sirs," called out from every direction.

"The *Wind Runner* is opening fire," the watchman reported.

"Brace for impact."

The *Wind Runner* reached them, streaking past at full speed missing all of the *Lotus's* cannon fire. Deck crews on both sides were firing smaller repeater guns that lanced out at each ship. The *Lotus* also took no direct hits from the larger cannon fire. *Inexperienced or under-crewed*, Bailon assessed.

"That didn't go very well," James said bluntly. The *Wind Runner* had taken some damage on the approach from the flak cannons, and when they traded fire at the end of the attack run the sound of shells piercing the hull could be heard. One of the backup pressure pipes had been damaged on the starboard side, but no casualties had been reported.

"Malix thinks we try again," Malix said from behind the helm. His dark skin and piercings marked him as a native of the Canyamar jungles.

"Bring us around, and set us up for another pass. This time over the top of them," James ordered.

Therion watched the *Wind Runner* streak overhead after exchanging fire with the *Lotus*. *At least her captain is doing his job*, he thought as he returned to study The Gateway.

Camden gave the order to fire, and the *Snow Break* began to shudder every time a cannon was shot. The incoming fire from the *Inferno* was suicidal to fly into, but with Kail protecting them outside, reversed that. Still it was unnerving at best to charge into hell voluntarily.

Suki kept her eyes on the twins when the firing started. The excitement of being on the airship had suddenly worn off. The endless distant cracks and thuds from the ground fire had started several minutes ago, but when the deafening explosions of the *Snow Break's* guns joined, fear replaced excitement on their faces. "Everything is ok, your mother and father are out there."

"I don't want to be here anymore," Amaya trembled.

"I know honey, just cover your ears."

Alyssa didn't say anything, but there were tears forming in her eyes. *This is stupid, stupid, stupid,* Suki cursed. *When this is over, I am going to kill them all for bringing them along.*

Kail could no longer see the *Inferno* in front of them. The smoke and explosions firing from the airship filled the sky. It was also affecting his ability to concentrate and keep them shielded. He hoped that the *Snow Break's* gunners were faring better than he was.

Angela came to stand next to Camden on the bridge. "This is not good," she said surveying the situation.

Standing up from the captain's chair, "No, it isn't," Camden agreed. "Helm, increase speed and altitude to the maximum that the *Odyssey* can follow. We need to get into clearer air."

"Aye sir," Harold barked, pulling back on the *Snow Break's* controls.

"This is our only attack," Angela said. "We cannot defeat this even with the advantage of them being on the ground."

Camden reached for the radio and was able to contact the *Odyssey*. The Mastersons agreed that a head on assault wasn't going to work. The firepower the two airships had was just not heavy enough to finish off the *Inferno*, and Kail couldn't protect them forever.

The *Lotus* jerked from the impact of the *Wind Runner's* second attack. Smoke began to fill the bridge. "Put out those fires and vent the air," Bailon ordered. "Report!"

"Helm control is undamaged," the pilot reported.

"The lights on three of the cannons have gone red. Intercom is dead to the engine room but functioning everywhere else," Cid reported.

"Get a repair crew on that now. Helm spin us around and keep the damaged side away from the *Wind Runner*," Bailon ordered.

"The *Wind Runner* sustained heavy damage as well," the watchman reported. "Heavy smoke is trailing her from multiple spots on the hull.

Therion's focus was interrupted as stray gunfire from the battle above him kicked up the ground and bounced off of The Gateway. Frowning he watched as the *Wind Runner* passed over the top of the *Lotus*. Looking at his own ship on the ground he saw the telltale blue ripples of an abjuration shield protecting her attackers. "Falconcrest. Now that's cheating."

"That's it," yelled James, using a fire extinguisher to put out a fire in the hallway just outside the bridge. "Malix!"

"*Wind Runner* can run, but her teeth are gone," the dark man yelled through the smoke.

"Get us to the others. I am going below to help with the damage."

"Malix agrees."

James descended further into his ship putting out multiple fires along the way. Two of the gunners were dead at their cannons, and he helped a third to the infirmary. Christi, the ship's medic, helped him carry the man to a bed when he entered.

"We're done, Malix is getting us out of here. We have dead, Christi."

"Dead are a part of war, James," she said, tending to the injured man.

The air began to clear as the *Snow Break* and *Odyssey* climbed higher. Kail could see the smoke coming from the *Wind Runner* as it made its way in their direction. He signaled to the bridge to start breaking to port so they could fall in behind them. *We need to retreat*, he realized.

Camden gave the order to bring the ship around to arc away from the *Inferno* and out of her firing range to rendezvous with the *Wind Runner*.

Kail tried to puzzle out what started to happen at The Eternal Gateway. A blue light raced along the ground away from The Gateway. It jerked and cracked like a ground fissure as it raced in the direction of the *Wind Runner*. As it reached towards them, it began to cast light skyward along the path it drew. The horror that followed was seared into his mind.

Therion stood with The Gateway to his back. His hands were flexed like talons above his head as he channeled his magic into the ground in front of him. It raced along the path of least resistance towards the fleeing *Wind Runner*. More and more energy was poured into the spell he wove until it had reached ahead of the fleeing ship. Lifting his hands higher a massive tendril of electricity erupted from the ground in front of him. Earth and jungle were torn free as he pulled the attack out of the ground. The energy roped and rolled in the air as it began to reach into the sky. Excess magical discharge lanced out and set parts of the outpost and surrounding jungle on fire. The end of the energy finally tore free from the ground underneath the *Wind Runner* and whipped skyward. When the attack licked the hull of the doomed ship, Therion closed his fists and pulled downward, "Burn," he chanted through clenched teeth.

Kail saw the end of the energy attach to the back of the *Wind Runner*. When it made contact the entire tendril froze in its movements. Instantly the entire length of the energy snapped forward and slammed into the back of the *Wind Runner*. Color drained from the world and sound seemed to disappear when the energy exploded, consuming the *Wind Runner*. Everything turned into a bright washed out white color or pitch black shadow.

Camden held his arm over his eyes to protect them from the flash. He could see Angela's lips moving as she shouted something, but he couldn't hear anything she said.

The *Wind Runner* was gone. Exploded in its place was a cloud of liquid fire that rained onto the jungle below.

Kail didn't need to use divination to search for survivors because there were none. He poured everything he had into the shield in front of the *Snow Break* as the wash from the attack rolled over them.

Therion let the power surge one last time before releasing his hold on the magic. Flittering memories of the War of Antiquities danced in his head. It seemed a lifetime ago when the mage war unleashed devastation on such a level. *They need to learn who they are messing with*, he thought. *My own subordinates as well as the enemy.* "Magic still rules this world," he shouted. "Your toys in the sky are nothing!"

He stood watching as half of the jungle burned from the remains of the airship he had just destroyed. The explosion from his attack had started fires in the outpost itself as well as on the *Inferno*. Crew from the outpost were scrambling to combat the fires. He was too wound up to focus on The Eternal Gateway. Damage from the attack would have the *Inferno* in a state of chaos, and the noise from the outpost would be distracting as well. Focusing his power once more he teleported away.

Chapter 8

If this is death, then the living have it easy. . . .

Pain layered upon pain disjointed his thoughts. Darkness clouded his vision between each breath he managed to gasp through the burning pain. There were even new definitions of pain being created here. *I can see the bones in my hand*, he thought lying on his back. Ash drifted through the sky in a grey blizzard. The movement brought a wave of dizziness that threatened his consciousness.

Willpower alone isn't going to be enough this time. Fighting through the pain he blinked in rhythm with each forced breath pushing the pain further and further from his mind. It was easier than he expected. His brain had no objections to retreat from the suffering. He could feel the adrenalin start to fade from his system. *No, shock will kill me if I don't fight.* The pain was beginning to fade only to be replaced by the duller ebbing away of his life. Of all the desires and seductions he had faced in his life, none had been as sweet or as comforting as the thought of drifting to sleep, succumbing to the relief of the darkness.

It was the smell that brought him back from the abyss of death. *I will not sleep with the stench of burnt flesh. My flesh*, he chided himself. The pain returned, but this time he welcomed it, used it to fire his desire to live. He could feel the jungle floor beneath him in every detail. Every nerve ending screamed to let him know that death was not an option. Sound returned as well, and the storm of ash highlighted the roar of nearby jungle dying to fire. Again he looked at his left hand, burned, melted and useless as he pushed himself up onto his knees with the other.

Faint shouts were coming from all directions as he took in his surroundings. *I know this place*, he thought as recognition began to creep into the back of his mind, *I know... this time.*

"Over here!" someone shouted.

Through the smoke and ash a soldier ran over to where he had managed to kneel.

"Another survivor?" a second voice called out through the haze.

Courduff's uniform. The Gateway. He recognized the insignia on the soldier's uniform.

"Try not to move, sir. Stay still, you are badly burned. Are you a commander from the *Inferno*?" the soldier asked after seeing the remains of his formal clothing.

He couldn't speak, so he waved the soldier closer signaling he could whisper. As the soldier leaned in closer, he wrapped his good arm around the back of the soldier's neck, cupped his chin and with a hard jerk, spun the man's head until it faced the wrong direction. He needed to hurry, more soldiers were coming. Peeling off his clothing, he nearly fainted again from the pain. Cloth was melted into where his skin caught fire in the battle at The Gateway. His left hand was useless as he traded his clothing for the dead soldier's uniform. The last bit was to loop the man's identification tags around his neck.

He needed to get away from the dead body. Shock set in and the loss of blood took its toll as he crawled away. He could see a medic head his way against the silhouette of the flaming jungle. Darkness slid over him, and his final thought was, *revenge.*

Chapter 9

Captain Bailon stormed down the hallway with Cid following him as best he could. "I have our new orders," he said.

He heard Cid hurry, pulling out a clipboard.

"We're to return to Aldervale with the wounded. Once they have been offloaded, Therion wants us to oversee Courduff and Aldervale's security. He apparently can see to the defense of the outpost himself. What is the current report on the wounded?"

"We have fourteen on the *Lotus*. *Inferno* reports over seventy so far with another dozen in critical need of medical services that we cannot provide here at the outpost," Cid said, flipping through the clipboard as they continued to walk.

Bailon was angry at himself as well as the situation caused by Kail and Therion exchanging magical attacks. Everyone suffered, and there were no winners. Each side lost men and gained nothing. He was angrier at Therion. It had taken more than a day for Therion to return so Bailon could plead for the wounded to be evacuated. His reasoning told him that the ones that died while waiting would have died in route anyway, but any more deaths would be Therion's fault. Reason did nothing to calm him. "Inform the *Inferno* and oversee the transfer of their wounded to the *Lotus*."

"Yes sir," Cid responded, turning to his task.

"Cid."

"Yes sir?"

"And the number dead?"

Cid didn't have to check the clipboard to answer. "Fifty two, sir."

Therion ran his hand over his scalp. He had not had a chance since arriving at The Gateway to shave the growth away. The itch of new hair would pass in another day. For some unknown reason a part of him felt like this was a turning point, and a change in appearance would also accentuate the importance of that fact.

He had been staring at The Gateway long enough for the outpost crew to become used to his presence. Some had become brave enough to start telling stories using insufferable loud voices about their heroics in the battle a few days ago. *Pathetic*, he thought. *Perhaps I should promote one of the corpses. That should give them the hint that I prefer silence.*

The Eternal Gateway stood as a sentinel in front of him. The immense vault style door mocking his desire to open it, learn its secrets and control the destiny of time. *I control The Gateway now*, he thought. *It will only be a matter of time before I unlock its secrets. Time won't matter anymore.* A series of cogs turned and clicked, the distinct sound of a tumbler falling into place drew his attention. Therion squinted his eyes at The Gateway. *It's unlocking.*

The *Lotus* was making good time back to Aldervale. She was a fast ship, and the trip would take less than half the time with the engines pushed to their maximum. Also they didn't have to worry about playing escort for a slower ship. Captain Bailon was pleased with how quickly the transfer of the wounded had gone. Having Cid with him made all the difference.

"We should reach Aldervale in forty five minutes at the current speed," Cid reported.

"Make sure the casualty signal is turned on before we arrive. I want the hospital to have as much time to prepare as possible," Bailon said.

Ari Ebonmore stepped into her office at the hospital and switched on the light. On her desk were stacks of papers that seemed to grow every time she looked away. Ever since she returned to Aldervale after studying in Courduff, her life had been nothing more than a string of long days and shorter nights. Her father was very proud of her and a little more than relieved when she returned. He hadn't said anything, but she could tell that he was hurting on the inside. Her sister Sarah had left home after a fight with their father. It wasn't her fault, but there was some guilt that haunted her for not doing anything to keep her from leaving.

All those years ago when she had listened to that strange man and had become involved that night with pulling

Kail Kelly out of the lake. *No, not Kelly, Falconcrest apparently*, remembering the news briefs labeling him an outlaw. Then his aunt and uncle showed up with a wounded girl that could heal herself. All of this inspired her to become a healer. She quickly took advantage of the military that had been stationed in her father's inn and secured a spot at the medical school in Courduff. Jealousy had fueled her sister's anger. Sarah had spent a lot of time flirting and socializing with the officers and when her shy sister suddenly shot past her in life, it was more than she could handle.

She took a letter from her pocket and placed it into the top drawer of her desk. *One more to add to the pile just like it.* All were from her sister to their father. Each one was from a different place in the world. They never knew when or where the next one would come from, but as long as they continued to arrive they were satisfied that Sarah was ok.

There was a loud knock on her door and before she had a chance to call out for whoever it was to enter, the door jerked open. Felicia Carlson burst into her office yelling, "The *Lotus* is back!"

"Calm down Felicia," she said calmly. Felicia was young and often excitable, but her heart and mind were in the right place.

"No, they are back and they have wounded, lots of them!"

Ari's widening eyes were the only thing that betrayed the hammering of her heart. "They were not gone very long," her voice said calmly. She was already across the room and leaving the office before she realized it. "How long do we have before they transfer?"

"They just landed a short while ago. I don't know who took the call, but the airstrip had been trying to reach us for the last thirty minutes."

"I'll find out who was supposed to be on duty. Right now gather as much staff as you can, and get them ready to receive the wounded," she ordered. *Please, please no, not him,* echoed through the back of her mind.

"Yes ma'am," Felicia spun and ran down a side hall.

Captain Bailon stood outside of the hospital, watching as the wounded were funneled through the doors. Some were able to enter the hospital under their own power, but for every one that could walk there were three that needed to be assisted by gurney or wheelchair. He had broken protocol by seeing to the wounded first instead of reporting to his superiors at the airstrip and garrison. He knew Cid would hold them off until he made sure that there was nothing left he could do for the men under his command.

After the last of the wounded had made their way into the hospital he finally stepped inside. The front lobby was over crowded with staff tending the wounded, but he smiled. *She's brilliant,* he thought. The soldiers with the more serious wounds were nowhere to be seen. Only the injured who simply needed to be checked over or have bandages replaced remained.

Ari's hair started to creep into her face as she directed and oversaw the wounded. Finally the flow of soldiers into her hospital stopped. The worry from earlier had been forgotten once she started delegating responsibilities to her staff. However, they came back in a rush when she saw him standing in the lobby. She almost ran, but a giggle from Felicia brought her up short, and she smoothed out her nurses uniform before continuing.

Wilhelm Bailon reached up and tucked his officer cap under his arm when Ari approached. "Ma'am, I apologize for burdening your hospital with our need."

"It's quite alright officer. It is our duty to serve and help those in need. It is blessing that you were unharmed," she replied to his formal apology.

Bailon smiled in return. "Walk with me for a moment, and I will bring you up to speed before I have to report for debriefing." He extended his arm.

She placed her hand on his arm as they started to walk. *So formal*, she blushed. On the way back through the hospital he gave her a brief synopsis of what happened in the jungle of Canyamar at The Eternal Gateway outpost. She didn't ask, but she knew how much this weighed upon him.

"When time allows, may I call upon you Miss Ebonmore?" Bailon asked.

Ari smiled imitating his formality. "I would like that very much Officer Bailon."

"With your permission, I take my leave ma'am," Bailon said, putting his cap back on his head.

Ari nodded. "Good day officer," she said, watching him leave the hospital while unable to suppress her smile.

Therion had cleared everyone away from The Gateway. The last thing he wanted was some bystander to suddenly find himself as its new guardian. Stranger things have happened in his lifetime. The War of Antiquities, Bastiana's protective staff and the Duke's son were prime examples of being caught unprepared. Twice more the distinctive click of the locks on The Gateway sounded. Visually The Gateway was also changing as fewer and fewer of the gears spun or changed before his eyes.

Felicia found Ari by checking room to room. "Ari, here is the consolidated report of the wounded from the *Lotus*." She passed off a group of papers to her.

Ari thumbed through them quickly. "At least no one has died," she mumbled, keeping her eyes on the papers.

"There is one man. A burn victim, Doctor Porter has given up on him."

"I'm sure Doctor Porter's assessment of the man's condition is accurate. He wouldn't stop if there was anymore that could be done," Ari said. Looking at Felicia's begging eyes she sighed. "Alright, I will take a second look at him."

"You are the best burn specialist we have ma'am," Felicia said encouragingly.

"Lead the way."

The pair entered the room a moment later. Ari winced at the sight of the man on the table. Skull and facial muscles could be seen were the skin on his face had been burned completely away. Sinew and tendons were visible from his hand and a greater portion of his chest and legs were either a dark crimson, or charred black. "This man should be dead," Ari said. "No one should be able to live through this, especially after the days it took for them to get here."

"Doctor Porter says he refuses to die," Felicia said.

Ari assessed the man's condition the same as Doctor Porter, a lost cause, but there was something she wanted to try. "Isolate the man into his own room, and Felicia."

"Yes ma'am?"

"I'll need a butcher, a live pig, and a meat cuber."

Felicia's eyes widened as if she had grown a second head.

"Now Felicia!" Snapping the nurse from her confusion.

The Eternal Gateway gave off another chime. Therion watched patiently as half of The Gateway now stood still.

It had taken a lot of argument for Ari to convince the butcher to help her. Felicia hadn't helped by siding with the man's objections. "*You want me to make pig skin bandages?*" she remembered him saying. She had lost track of the hours, and the butcher had long since left for home after running thin strips of pig skin through the cube machine. There were several trays with the pig skin bandages suspended in ruddy salt water. She meticulously removed each inch of burned skin, muscle and even parts of bone from her patient. The pig skin was then placed exactly like she would have used a normal bandage. Each one was either sewn to existing skin or in many cases, back on itself. The cuber had cut hundreds of tiny slits into the replacement skin that allowed it to stretch and breath. He was going to be ugly, but the man could complain about that later if he survived.

"I brought you something to eat," Felicia said, setting a tray of food next to the one just like it from the night before. "You worked through the night Ari. It's daylight again."

"I'll stop when I'm finished," she said without looking up. She could hear the nurse circle around her.

"Do we even know his name?" Felicia asked.

Ari paused in her work furrowing her brow. "I don't recall."

"If this works in any fashion you could write a paper about it. Or they could lock you up for being crazy," she finished. Going through the man's belongings she found what she was looking for stuck to a piece of his uniform that they had cut off of him the night before. Peeling it apart she handed the identification to Ari.

Rubbing away the soot she read, "His name is Ross, Xavier Ross."

Chapter 10

"She still won't talk to you?" Camden asked.

"No, well, that's not entirely true, she says plenty. Yells is more accurate," Kail said.

"I can say something to Suki if you want. You know how attached she can get."

"Nah, she will come around eventually, besides she's right you know. It was absolutely foolish to rush. Nothing is worth risking my daughters like that," Kail said, slumping into a galley chair on the *Snow Break*. "We've done some crazy things, but this was reckless. And the cost..."

Camden looked through the papers on the table. "How long have you been working on this?" he asked solemnly, reading the top page. *Sir, I regret to inform you that your son, James Decisero, is dead.* The line was crossed out. *Sir, I am afraid this letter brings...* It too was crossed out. Three more pages of crossed out openings filled the spaces.

"In my head or just on paper," Kail sighed, rubbing his eyes.

Angela stepped into the galley and nodded to Camden.

"You know, you don't have to do this at all. Everyone understands the risks involved when they sign up,"

Camden suggested, standing from the table. "Angela," he nodded, greeting her on his way out.

Angela walked around the table to stand behind Kail and placed her hands on his shoulders to give them a gentle squeeze.

"That feels nice," he said.

Bringing her head down next to his she whispered, "Do not make yourself sick by doing this."

Kail squeezed her hand in acknowledgement. "Do you think we will one day look back upon all this and know if it was worth it or not?"

"Every day I have been here has been a gift," she said, remembering the Time Walker saving her life in a forgotten time a thousand years ago. "I see ourselves in the faces of our children, and I know already that it has been worth it."

Kail pulled away from Angela's hands and sighed. "You know what we have to do."

Angela moved to sit across the table and stare at him. "Knowing and doing are two separate things."

Kail had to look at the papers on the table to continue. Right now he didn't have the courage to meet her stare. "It won't be forever. Just until this is over or things change and it's safe."

"Rationalizing excuses will not help. I agreed. As much as I detest it, it is the right thing to do," she said harsher than intended when Kail flinched. "They will be excellent guardians, and we could not have asked for anyone better."

"I can't help but wonder if my father and mother sat somewhere having this same conversation."

Angela paused and recalled the stories about Kail being dropped off at the Kelly's doorstep by strangers. It turned out they were not even part of his real family. "I am sure the decision they made was just as difficult as ours. Whatever happens, we will be back. Promise me this Kail."

"I promise."

Angela smiled shaking her head. "Aldervale. I do not know if the idea is madness or genius. The rinun snake hides in plain sight. Hiding Amaya and Alyssa in Therion's backyard as Camden put it."

Kail shook his head. "Silverton is too dangerous now. We've been lucky that Therion hasn't come here yet, but there is no doubt that he will send forces here after what happened at The Eternal Gateway."

"We are not the only ones sending their families away. All of Silverton is preparing for the attack that will come."

"When that happens, Therion better lead the attack because if he doesn't, I will burn them all," he said fiercely.

"We will protect Silverton when the time comes, but do not lose your soul in the process Kail," Angela said as she stood. "Will you join me for bed?" she asked, holding out her hand.

"I need to finish this," he said, returning to the papers on the table.

Angela nodded and exited the galley.

Kail took a bottle of dark liquor from the cabinet and filled the bottom of a glass. Downing the drink in one swallow, he filled the glass again before putting the bottle back and returning to the task at hand.

Kail reviewed the words on the paper and took a sip from his drink as he tried to clear his thoughts from the previous conversation. He did not want to think about sending his children away while he wrote to James's father.

Sir.

It is my sad duty to tell you of the death of James Decisero.

James was given the task of watching The Eternal Gateway Outpost in the jungle of Canyamar. Recently The Eternal Gateway's return recalled James from that duty to report its arrival as well as the increased activity of Therion's forces. The decision to return to Canyamar was made quickly to take advantage of the sensitivity of the information. The *Wind Runner* along with the *Odyssey* and *Snow Break* encountered Therion's forces at the outpost. Tactical advantage was ours, and James was given the order to attack. He performed his task with courage and honor. Shortly afterward an attack from Therion, of unknown origin, destroyed the *Wind Runner*.

In the time James had served with me, I found his skill as an airship captain to be of superior quality. His actions and charisma quickly won the hearts of us all and his crew. His ability to complete his missions has saved hundreds of lives including my own.

I cannot begin to understand the loss you must feel. I believe that a life that was lived for a worthy cause continues to serve that cause even after death.

James saved the lives of many people. Those people are alive today to carry on that cause. The amount of good James brought to the world ripples forward for all time. We may not see the good James left behind, but not seeing it, does not mean it isn't there. These actions represent everything we fight for and I am grateful.

With respect,
    Kail Falconcrest.

Kail brought the glass to his lips to find it was long empty. He looked at the letter one more time to be sure it had everything he intended to say. Folding the letter he left the galley. The early shift had already started as he was saluted by a few of the *Snow Break's* crew. *So much for getting any sleep*, he thought as he made his way to his quarters for a change of clothing that would be more appropriate for the delivery of several letters he intended to make today.

Chapter 11

"Where are we going?" Amaya asked for the hundredth time.

"Aldervale, dear. The town where I grew up," Kail answered with endless patience as he stood on the bridge of the *Snow Break*. The airship had been in flight since yesterday after being resupplied and receiving new intelligence reports. Flying blindly into Aldervale, when they were arguably the most wanted people in the planet right now, was an awful idea at best. Even so they would have to land a half days ride by horseback or risk being spotted or reported. He had only been able to visit the Kelly farm twice in the last five years since the confrontation with Therion when he and Camden had brazenly walked through the front door of the Mage Council tower to rescue Angela.

"I don't want to go there," Alyssa whined, her eyes rubbed sore from crying.

"It won't be forever, my little bird. You will have a lot of fun. We have horses there and if you're lucky, there may even be a newborn colt," Kail said, trying his best to avoid another round of tears. "Also there is the market place. Did you know that I used to spend a day every week selling old roots? There was even this one old lady who would come buy just to kick the cart!"

That wasn't the most soothing thing to say as Alyssa's lips were quivering and a moment away from a new outburst. Amaya was whimpering about being sent to live with angry old ladies. Kail felt like he had just stabbed himself in the stomach with every passing moment that flew them closer and closer to Aldervale. He was ready to abandon the whole idea.

"When you are at the Kelly's," Angela came to the rescue, "you will be our ambassadors. The Kelly farm is very important and an influential part of Aldervale. You must be very careful though, there are many who do not like the people of Silverton. You must do your best to listen and learn from the Kelly's." Angela's words seemed to halt the sniffs coming from the twins as they continued to listen to their mother's words.

"She has a way doesn't she," Camden whispered to him.

"I won't argue you that," he replied.

"They are Keratin. War is a way of life for us," Angela said, stepping into the conversation with Camden and Kail. "All they needed was to be given a direction on which to focus." They glanced at the twins who now had their heads together talking about the role they would play helping their parents. "Give them a knife and a tree and when you look again, they would have a hundred spears, a thousand arrows and a fort built."

Camden glanced at Kail raising his eyebrows. "I know what to get them for their next birthday then," he said in mock seriousness.

"You're not getting them knives," Kail said, gesturing no with his hands.

"I was going to get them a forest," Camden said as he smiled.

"You are a year late for knives," Angela stated, looking back at the twins.

Camden looked at Kail and mouthed the words, "*Is she serious?*"

"*Not my department,*" Kail mouthed back, shaking his head.

Harold Riggings interrupted. "Sir, we are approaching the landing area. We need to lower altitude for the next twenty minutes before we arrive."

"Thank you," Camden replied.

The *Snow Break* rested in a clearing about a mile and a half from a small road leading out of Aldervale and into the southern territories. Few people used the road other than locals. Kail used his magic to scout the area and found no unwelcome guests waiting for them. The arrangement for horses had come through, and there were seven horses and one small traveling wagon waiting for them.

"One moment I am piloting an airship and the next I am piloting a horse drawn cart," Harold mocked sarcastically.

"If you do a good job, I could promote you to wagon captain full time if you like," Camden replied.

"No, no ambition here to climb the ranks. I wouldn't want the responsibilities," Harold replied as he helped load the wagon with the twin's belongings.

"This is going to be odd," Angela said, facing Kail.

"I haven't tried this on someone else before," he said as Camden and the twins stood watching.

Kail opened himself up to the magic once more. Illusion was one of the ten forms of magic Mr. Eleazar had taught him. Kail closed his eyes and ran his hands across his wife's face and hair. He could see in his mind's eye her angular features and striking eyes. He knew them by heart. He had never seen red flame hair like hers before, except again with the birth of their daughter who had inherited the same color. He could sense that the spell was complete, and all he needed to do was tie off the magic with a rune for it to remain. Stepping back he opened his eyes to look at his wife.

"Well, how do I look," Angela asked.

"Wow," was all Camden could say.

Kail looked at the unknown woman who faced him but sounded like his wife.

"You did not make me look like some recruitment poster fantasy did you?" she quipped.

"You're, unremarkable," Kail said.

"Hand me a mirror and let me see," Angela demanded. Grabbing a hand held mirror from one of the twin's bag she looked at the work of Kail's spell. The reflection looking back at her had dull brown hair and hazel eyes to match. She moved her head from side to side and squinted to see deep lines appear from the corner of her eyes. "Excellent, a face no one will look at twice or remember in passing."

Kail assumed that was a complement, but he wasn't sure. Amaya and Alyssa were looking at their mother's new face with disapproval and disgust. Suki finally joined them from the *Snow Break* and looked at Angela's disguise. She gave Kail a cold look and went to stand with Camden.

"Ok," Kail said, moving past the moment. *Suki was going to be mad at us forever it seems*, he thought. "Who wants to go first?" he asked his daughters. Amaya and Alyssa looked at each other for a moment before each pointed at the other. Kail smiled and ran his hands across his daughters' faces and hair. In a moment he was finished and like their mother now, two identical girls with brown hair stood before him. Gone was the stoic dark haired girl Alyssa and the more emotional red headed Amaya.

"How long do we have to look like this?" Amaya asked.

"Just until we get to the Kelly farm. Once there I will change you back. It's only a precaution as we travel." Kail let his magic flow over himself next and the man standing in his place had short brown hair, dull eyes, and a thick mustache.

Camden couldn't keep from laughing. "That's a nice mustache you have there."

"What's wrong with a mustache? Mustaches are cool," Kail finished as he added a grey felt bowler hat.

"Stop him, stop him now," Camden demanded when Kail added the hat to his disguise. "I would rather turn my whole body to stone and jump in a lake than look like that."

"Wait until I add the goggles," Kail teased.

"Oh, and what are the goggles supposed to do?" Camden wanted to know.

Kail smiled, "Nothing." He moved towards Camden only changing his hair color from the recognizable blond to a dark brown. "Suki?"

Suki shot him a glance when she heard her name spoken. "He looks fine, I don't need any changes."

Kail looked back to Camden who gave a weak shrug. "Ok, if everything is in order, we can head out. We're still half a day away from the farm."

Harold climbed up onto the wagon to start making his way through the forest in the direction of the road. Amaya and Alyssa shared a horse lead by Kail that followed after the wagon. Angela followed next with Camden and Suki bringing up the rear.

Camden let his horse lag behind and subtly forced Suki to match his stride until they could talk without easily being overheard. "I know you hate this plan, but you are being unfairly hard on them. Kail and Angela put on a good face, but this is killing them and once we leave without Amaya and Alyssa it's going to be worse. They are going need our support and not be reminded of the daughters they left behind."

Suki took a deep breath and sighed. "This isn't something that I can just forget about Cam. Every part of me says this is an awful idea, and I understand why they are doing it, and I can't fault them for it."

"Cam? Where did that come from?" he asked with a smug grin.

"I didn't mean it," she tried to take it back.

"No, I kind of like it. Of course, all my other girlfriends might get jealous," he teased.

Suki rolled her eyes and shook her head. "Keep it up you big lug."

"Does this mean I can call you Sue when no one is around?" Camden wasn't ready for her left jab. His horse jerked at the sudden motion causing him to roll off the back of the horse to land on the hard road.

"It's ok," she called to the others when they stopped to check out the commotion. "Brown hair made him a smart ass is all."

Camden dusted himself off and settled his horse before remounting. "That's going to leave a mark, and I'm going to feel it tomorrow. Good thing I know a good healer with magic fingers," he teased again.

Suki's mouth hung open with the fact that his tumble hadn't changed his attitude at all. "Not a chance," she said but couldn't keep herself from smiling.

"There she is," he said, seeing her smile for the first time in weeks. "Camden Arland, pleasure to meet you," he offered.

Looking at him slyly she took his hand apologetically and shook it. "Suki, Suki Leigh," she replied with a smile.

Daylight had less than an hour left when the Kelly farm came into view. "This place has changed, changed a lot," Kail said as they reached the outer edge of the farm.

"Looks like the Kelly's are doing well," Camden assessed.

"Those three barns were not there before, neither were those other outlying buildings," Kail pointed out.

"Are you sure your aunt and uncle still reside here?" Angela asked.

"The correspondence between us hasn't indicated that they moved or anything like that," Kail said. "They're either here, or they are not, either way we will find out when we get there." Kail took the lead as the party continued down the road to the start of the lane to the Kelly farm.

Jessica Kelly was finishing the last bit of kitchen work before settling down for the rest of the evening when she saw the group arrive. Sighing she called out to her husband, "Royce, looks like a group of travelers headed this way."

Royce Kelly came to stand by his wife to look out of the window. "They probably want a place to stay the night. Next thing they will want to try and peddle something to us or beg to work for food or a place to live. I'll go see if I can run them off."

"Just be careful Royce," Jessica told him when he buckled his pistol around his waist before going out of the front door.

Kail slowed his horse when he saw his uncle exit the front of the house. Noticing the gun he waved to everyone behind him to stop before climbing off of his horse. Taking his horse by the reigns, Kail approached where his uncle stood.

"Evening traveler," his uncle greeted.

"Evening sir," Kail replied.

"If you're looking for a place to stay, you can continue down the road to Aldervale. It's about an hour out. If you hurry, you can make it before dark. Tell the Ebonmore Inn the Kelly's sent you and they will cut you a nice deal for the night," Royce stated, resting his hand on the hilt of his pistol.

Kail eyed his uncle's posture. "I would like to show you something."

"Whatever it is you're selling, we don't need any," his uncle cut him off.

"I'm not selling anything. I just don't want to get shot."

"You have ten seconds."

Kail had not expected this from his uncle. Clearly times were different and obviously more dangerous. He filled himself with his magic to dispel the illusion hiding his features. He reached up and removed the bowler hat he had been wearing. "There are women and children watching uncle."

Royce's eyes widened at what he saw in front of him before quickly recovering. "You best put back on your hat. Come on in, and we will discuss what you're offering. Your friends can stable their horses around back," Royce finished and turned to enter the house.

Kail put the illusion back on as he settled his hat on his head before returning to the group. "He knows it's us, but there seems to be some problems. Take the horses and wagon around back Harold, and keep things ready just in case we need to leave quickly." Harold nodded and moved the wagon behind the Kelly farm house before returning to take care of the horses.

"You don't think he will betray us do you?" Camden asked.

"No, I think there are people working here for my aunt and uncle that are not friendly to us, or there might be a military presence. Remember they supply a lot of food to the garrison in Aldervale," Kail pointed out.

"If that is the case, then we should leave now," insisted Suki, glancing at the twins behind Angela.

"We are going to go inside, and if there is reason to change the plan, Angela and I will decide then," Kail finished the conversation with a hard look and headed to the front door of the house.

"What?" Suki asked Camden when he gave her a sharp look.

"You can remove your disguise, it's safe in here," Royce told Kail when he entered the house.

"It is you!" Jessica Kelly exclaimed when she saw for herself. "It's so good to see you. Oh my, look how much you have grown up. Such a man now," she said happily after hugging him.

"Almost five years now," he said, moving to hug his uncle.

Angela entered next, followed by Amaya and Alyssa.

"You remember Angela?" Kail introduced. His aunt and uncle's blank looks told him otherwise. "Oh." Kail waved his hand and Angela's striking red hair and sharp features returned. The same happened for Amaya and Alyssa as the illusion was removed.

"Oh my," Jessica stammered as she recalled the night Angela broke into the farm house with the innkeeper's daughter. Her eyes bounced between Kail, Angela and the twins. "Oh my!" as she made the connection. "The letters mentioned your twins, but here they are, and they are so big!"

Royce was the first to offer Angela his hand. "The side of my head remembers her fondly."

"Master Kelly," Angela greeted with a smile and slight nod, "Mrs. Kelly."

"And this is Amaya," Kail said, holding out his hand as the red headed twin took it. "And this is Alyssa." Her dark haired sister joined on the other side.

Shy looks were passed between the twins and the Kelly's before the girls said, "Hello," in unison.

"You know, I believe I have some cookies in the kitchen," Jessica offered. Both girls looked to their father and mother before being lead into the kitchen leaving the rest of the group in the living area.

The night had grown late with Jessica insisting on serving food and the inevitable catching up since the last time Kail had visited. Angela stood at the doorway to the room where Amaya and Alyssa were sleeping. She was etching her daughters' features into her mind so that when they were reunited she would notice every little change that time had brought. Kail and Camden were in the living room with Royce. Suki and Jessica were in the kitchen having a conversation over a sink of dinner dishes

"So," Royce asked, taking a sip from his drink. "Why do your girls have her last name and not yours?"

"Atagi," Kail started. "How many Keratins do you know?"

"None, well, one I guess."

"Well, turns out in her culture, the girls all keep the same last name as the mother. Boys do the same with their father's name. Males all come from this line, and females all come from the mother's line, or houses as she calls them. House Atagi," Kail explained.

"So if you had a son, his name would be Kelly or Falconcrest then?" Royce concluded.

"That's how it would work, yes."

"Why didn't you make her follow our custom instead?" his uncle wanted to know.

Kail gave Camden a tired look when the big man chuckled. "Angela isn't the type of person you could *make* do something unless she wanted," Kail started. "Besides, she said the boys were mine and the girls hers, so it was fair."

"We told them that their last name while in your care would be Kelly or Branson."

Royce took another drink. "That should work. It would be easy enough to convince people that they are Jessica's niece and her cousin. Especially after the *Lotus* returned awhile ago with large amount of wounded soldiers. War tears families apart left and right. Being here away from the hostile areas is a good enough reason for them to be staying here."

"We were at that battle," Kail said. "The one with the *Lotus*," he added in response to his uncle's confused face. "The twins were there as well," he continued softly. "Angela and I can't thank you enough for doing this for us."

"Well," his uncle sighed. "I wouldn't want my children anywhere near war if I could help it. You're not going to..." Royce wiggled his hands in front of him. "You know. Enchant us or something like when you arrived?" remembering the enchantment that had been placed on him and his wife, forcing them to believe Kail was their nephew.

"No, I mean, I can if you want."

"No, no. That won't be necessary," Royce quickly declined. The pause in the air emphasized the late hour. "So your party will be leaving in the morning correct?"

Camden nodded his head and Kail answered, "Yes."

"Well, before you do, we will have to have a look around the farm. There are some things I want to show you," Royce said as he stood. "I will see you gentlemen in the morning."

Kail and Camden stood and said their goodnights.

Royce Kelly opened the hangar style door to one of the three identical barns that Kail had pointed out as being new. Camden whistled in appreciation as the dawn sunlight fell onto the hulking machine housed there.

"It's impressive and expensive looking," Kail commented, taking in the steel behemoth.

"Hyperion's finest," Royce said with a smile. "I own six of them. It tills, picks rock, plows and plants all at the same time."

"Kerosene or exotic?" Camden asked about its fuel source.

"Both actually. Hyperion Industries provides both, and there is no way I would be able to get my hands on these babies without a military contract," Royce explained. "With just one, we can do a week's work in a single day."

"So why have six?" Kail asked. "One would have been excessive."

"We have expanded a bit," Royce shrugged.

"How much?" Kail asked taking the bait.

"One twenty."

"A hundred and twenty more acres?"

"Thousand," his uncle said with a smile.

"One hundred and twenty thousand new acres?" Kail said disbelievingly.

"Six might not be enough then," Camden added.

"Well, enough gloating. This is what I wanted you to see," Royce continued. "Here and here are the wheels for train transport. And if you look here, here, and here," he pointed out. "These are where different modules can be attached."

"Makes sense lets you customize the machine to your needs and given the size of these things, rail would be the only way to transport one." Camden said.

"Exactly, but those are mounts for military purpose. Hyperion is making smaller versions for people who do not have military contracts. My point is, these will be all over the place, not just here. When the military moves in on a new area, all they have to do is mount their weaponry and it becomes a machine of war."

"You're saying that Hyperion Industries and the military are selling these to the places they want to invade?" Kail asked.

"Yes, and the people are paying for them. Hyperion gets paid, and the military already has equipment deployed just waiting for them to arrive and confiscate it," Royce finished.

"We have Hyperion equipment in Silverton," Camden admitted. "It's top notch stuff."

"Well, they have to take it from us first, but now that we know the capabilities are there, it will be better," Kail said. "We will have our own people look into doing the same. If Therion attacks, we can convert Hyperion equipment over for our own use."

"Just be safe Kail," Royce finished as Harold brought the horses and wagon around. Angela and Suki were with him.

"Let us say our goodbyes Kail," Angela said.

"Alright," Kail said. "One day we won't have to sneak around like this uncle." Kail gave Royce a hug and returned to the farm house with Angela.

"That is something I don't think I would have the strength to do," Camden muttered while watching Kail and Angela walk away to say goodbye to their daughters.

Suki kept her back to the scene. "Let's not talk about it," she sniffled as Camden put his hand on her shoulder.

The trip back to the *Snow Break* was solemn and uneventful. Camden wondered if the cough Kail seemed to have picked up was contagious or just his way to cover up from breaking down. *Suki had run out of tears hours ago*, he thought, looking at her slumped on her horse. *Angela, stoic as ever*, he observed.

The events of the morning were quickly put aside when he noticed that Lawrence Burke was waiting for them a half mile from the airship. "We have a situation sir," Lawrence said when the group approached.

"What's going on Lawrence?" Camden asked, dismounting and looking around for an ambush or any immediate threats.

"He showed up yesterday, and we found him in the galley," Lawrence started. "We tried to get rid of him, but he insisted that he knew all of you."

"Who is on the ship?" Kail wanted to know.

"That's just it, he wouldn't tell us. But the weird thing is that he knows things. A lot of things and those eyes just creep us out."

"Is he dangerous?" Angela asked, removing her war blades from their sheaths.

"I don't think so. But I don't think we can get rid of him unless we use force, or you talk to him," Lawrence said, leading the way through the forest to where the *Snow Break* was landed.

"Harold, Lawrence, get her ready for takeoff. We will deal with our guest," Camden ordered.

Camden, Kail, Angela and Suki made their way to the galley. Kail lifted a hand that had a soft glow around it and nodded that he was ready. Angela held a war blade behind her back and nodded as well. Camden took a deep breath and walked in with Kail and Angela quickly flanking him.

"Well, it's about time," the man in the galley stated as he closed a pocket watch in his hand and stood from the table. Piercing blue eyes assessed them in turn. "I can see that I chose well."

The three of them were speechless as Mr. Eleazar walked around the table to greet them.

Chapter 12

Guards stood at their posts in front of The Eternal Gateway as the heat and humidity of the jungle pressed down on them. Therion had ordered them to keep anyone but a select few from approaching. Anyone disobeying the order would be charged with treason on pain of death. Scattered through the jungle, charred remains of trees stood as sentinels as they sent wisps of smoke drifting into the sky. A reminder to everyone of the power that Therion commanded.

Only one lock remained on The Eternal Gateway. Most of them had unlocked and settled on their own. Others Therion had puzzled out their riddles and workings. Lore on The Eternal Gateway was almost non-existent. Tales, legends, and stories passed around and forgotten. Validated accounts were even more scarce. There were a scattered number of people in history who could be directly tied to The Gateway. *The Guardian and the Keratin from a thousand years ago*, Therion listed. *The spy that Vincent used, Captain Arland and of course Falconcrest.* "Obvious with the direct interference of The Guardian," he spoke to himself. Vincent and Bastiana are tied as well to its history when they had destroyed it five years ago.

"Present ties," he concluded as he watched the final lock on The Gateway twitch. *Something is wrong with this one.* A simple clock face, polished brass numbers with black metal for the hour and minute hands. The shown hour was six o'clock. As the minute hand made its way to the twenty minute mark, it would blur and return to the top of the hour. "Six twenty," he riddled. "What is special about six twenty?"

He had tried to manually move the clock past the stuck time, but to no avail. Also if he wound the clock backwards it would hiccup at twelve fifteen, and five eight. "Three times... Three times when or where time seems to be broken," he reasoned.

The vibrations of the *Snow Break* in flight as it returned from Aldervale set the mood in the galley. Kail and Angela sat on each side of the metal table with Mr. Eleazar. Camden paced back and forth shaking his head each time Mr. Eleazar spoke. Suki stood in the corner listening to the argument.

"This is stupid. Stupid with a budget," Camden said, letting his feelings about Mr. Eleazar's request, no demand, be known.

"I agree with Camden," Kail said. "We don't have the equipment or manpower to assault The Eternal Gateway again. Therion is too powerful. You weren't there when he destroyed the *Wind Runner*. You haven't been here for five years. Why show up now? You have a lot of explaining to do. Look at you, you look half the age of what I remember."

"You do deserve some explanation. My life is not any different than anyone else's. Each day I get older the same as you. What is different is the order of my days. Just last week by my time, I approached Angela here. Of course she turned me down, but a few days later she had a change of heart," Mr. Eleazar said, eyeing Angela's reaction.

"That was over five years ago," Angela countered, not flinching from his words.

"For you yes, but not for me. My days are scattered through time, but none the less linear when you line them up."

"Why here, why now?" Kail wanted to know.

"As I was saying, I finished dropping Angela off, and I see everything went ok," Mr. Eleazar said, assessing her. "I decided to hop forward and see how things were working out. Something is wrong though. This is much later than I had intended to go, but while I am here there is no reason not to see how things are going. And the best place to do that is at The Gateway," he finished while adjusting his pocket watch with a puzzled look.

"He's lying," Camden stated bluntly.

"He is young and undisciplined," Angela corrected. "Exactly the same as when we first met. You can see why I declined his offer. Only when it was made clear there was no real choice did I say yes," she finished, recalling the moment when her warrior group had been ambushed and the Time Walker saved her from death.

"Don't defend him Angela," Camden continued. "He never told us anymore than what was necessary for him to get us to do what he wanted."

Mr. Eleazar pushed himself back from the table and threw up his hands. "My curse in life is to pay for things I haven't even done yet."

Camden watched Mr. Eleazar. "Go to another time to get your answers," he said.

Mr. Eleazar sighed and avoided everyone's eyes. "I can't. There is something wrong."

"Finally some truth!" Camden exclaimed, pointing at The Guardian.

"Camden," Kail said, shaking his head to stop.

"Time Walker, if you would excuse us for a moment please?" Angela asked.

Mr. Eleazar looked at everyone in the room before rising to his feet. "As you wish," he said, leaving the galley.

A few moments of silence passed before Angela spoke. "This is dangerous. He does not know what has happened."

"What do you mean?" Kail asked.

"He is the same as when I first met him, but also different. Remember five years ago when he saved us at Silverton. He said something about things had changed," she tried to get them to recall.

"Yeah, I remember, then we hiked through the Canyamar jungle, got attacked, betrayed by Xavier and he got himself killed when The Gateway exploded," Camden summed up for them.

"This could be where it starts, the changes and confusion," Angela presented. "Think about it, it is not a coincidence that Mr. Eleazar and The Eternal Gateway's return are connected."

"You're saying that he can only be where The Gateway exists." Kail said, following Angela's logic.

"When, not where." She corrected.

"Who cares?" Camden objected. "He left us high and dry that day. It wasn't him that saved you from that crazy Bastiana woman. That was all us. After that, nothing, all us again. Silverton, this war, everything. Us, that's it, just us."

"You have to help him," Suki finally spoke for the first time. Everyone's eyes turned to the sound of her voice. "And you're wrong, he did save you in Courduff. He brought the Masterson's remember."

Camden rolled his eyes but didn't object.

Suki continued. "We knew five years ago when he told us something was wrong. This may be the beginning, but this is where it might get fixed as well."

"Doesn't matter," Kail said. "It's already happened. This changes nothing."

"You don't know that," Suki pleaded. "We've become too caught up running a city, fighting a war, worrying about supply lines, hiding family" she scolded.

"Remember when this all started. It was just us, that's it. We fought, we escaped, and we won. We did more with just the handful of us than we have done ever since to try and stop this. And now the one man who brought us together asks for our help, and we sit here and bicker and tell him no. We owe him everything. Fortunes," she said looking at Camden. "Lives." Turning her eyes to Angela. "Love." Finishing with Kail.

Kail looked to Angela as Suki's words soaked in and saw the features of his children reflecting in her face. He looked to Camden next and saw that he knew her words were true but still hadn't convinced himself yet. "I'll decide when we return to Silverton," Kail said, ending the discussion.

Suki turned and stormed out of the galley. Camden glanced at Kail and Angela before leaving.

"Do what you think is right," Angela said from the far side of the table.

"That's the easy part," he said.

"Why do you hesitate then?"

"What if I'm wrong? How do I forgive myself or how could anyone forgive me, if I'm wrong?"

"You cannot be wrong," Angela said with confidence as she reached her hand across the table to his.

"I was wrong before at The Gateway. What I saw then, and wrong again with the *Wind Runner*."

"This is your destiny Kail."

"What if it's not my destiny?"

Angela closed her eyes and took a deep breath before continuing. "This is your destiny, my destiny, Camden's and Suki's. Cast this doubt from your mind and your heart. There has never been a moment like this in the history of the world. We were born a thousand years apart, yet here we are, together with two daughters. How can it not be destiny?"

"You're so beautiful, and I love you so much, you know that."

Angela smiled at his words. "And I love you, Kail Falconcrest."

Chapter 13

"Helm, take us up so we can get radio contact with Silverton," Camden ordered from the bridge of the *Snow Break*. "Comm, let us know when you reach them."

"Aye sir,"

Mr. Eleazar assessed what he saw as he walked the bridge. "Radio, that's early. Turbines as well from the sound of it. Changes indeed," he finished, turning when Kail and Angela stepped onto the bridge.

"Mr. Eleazar," Kail greeted. "Camden."

Mr. Eleazar turned with a nod. "Is Suki going to join us?" he asked when she did not follow.

"I don't think so," Camden said.

"Oh, I'm sure this isn't going to be something she wants to miss," Mr. Eleazar said with a glint in his eye.

"Bridge to infirmary. Suki, can you come to the bridge please," Camden said into the intercom.

"Be right there, sir," her voice came over the speaker. Camden winced at the word sir.

"Same old Mr. Eleazar. What do you know that you're keeping from us?" Camden asked.

"I'm not keeping anything from you. I just think she would like to be here is all," Mr. Eleazar said, feigning hurt feelings.

"Sir, we have contact with Silverton."

"Thank you comms," Camden said, looking to Kail.

"Get the Mastersons, Randal Wood, the Officer-in-Charge, and Duncan Deline of the Silverton infantry general," Kail told the comms officer.

"Yes sir."

Suki came onto the bridge. "Reporting as ordered, sir," she said stiffly.

"Now now dear," Mr. Eleazar started. "We're all friends here. We have been through so much together, or at least you have and I will later."

"Sir, they are on the line," the comms officer interrupted.

"Rhonin, Rayne, are you there?" Kail spoke into the microphone.

"We're here, so is Randal and Duncan," Rhonin's voice crackled back.

"The *Snow Break* is going to be delayed on its return to Silverton," Kail said.

"And the reason?" Rhonin asked.

Kail looked at Mr. Eleazar before answering. "Start on project Destiny."

"So it's time then?" Rhonin's voice said.

"Yes it is."

"We will start immediately. You all be careful, and we will be ready when you arrive. Silverton out," Rhonin finished and the radio chirped.

"Project Destiny?" Suki asked.

"It was Mr. Eleazar's idea really," Kail started still looking at The Guardian. "When we first went to The Eternal Gateway, he said, 'The Gateway has and will always be here. When the world was new and when the world was old. Everything changes, but The Gateway remains.'"

"That sounds like something I would say," Mr. Eleazar agreed.

Kail ignored the quip and continued. "When The Gateway was destroyed, I knew that it wasn't forever. So four years ago we put together a plan, no more like an idea."

"Who is we?" Suki wanted to know.

"Myself, Camden, and Rhonin," Kail answered. "It was just an idea, don't get all mad."

"And what is this idea?" Angela asked, wondering why she had not been included.

"That we go for it."

"Explain," Suki demanded.

Camden stepped in to help. "Basically the idea is that when the time came, or the opportunity, we would take it. Forget everything else and stab," he said, thrusting his hand forward.

"That's it? That's your big plan?" Suki said.

"Well..." Camden stumbled.

"Yes," Kail said firmly. "No more gathering and building armies. Just us, and we go. Like the way it was before all of this."

"You are bigger fools than I gave you credit," Suki continued to berate them.

"I agree with Suki," Angela started and held up her hand to stop any protest. "However a single strike force can accomplish what a marching army cannot. Therion would not expect us to attack again after such a defeat."

"Destiny," Kail said, nodding his head at Angela.

"Destiny," she agreed.

"And what do you think of all this nonsense?" Suki asked Mr. Eleazar.

"Simple in form and execution," he said. "No complicated plans to have fall apart, just a simple goal."

Suki looked at her companions faces before speaking. "Fine. We go for it and end it if we can."

"Now that that is settled," Mr. Eleazar said, clapping his hands together. "I am curious master Falconcrest. Care for a sparring match? I want to see how good of a job I do, or did that is."

"I think we can arrange that," Kail agreed.

"This brings back memories," Camden said, standing next to Suki and Angela on the outer deck of the *Snow Break*. The crew had crammed onto the bridge and stood looking through the viewports. Rumor spread quickly through the ship that the man of legend, The Guardian, had returned and was onboard. Camden had ordered the ship to hover in the sky and drift with the wind while Kail and Mr. Eleazar sparred.

Kail walked onto the deck of the *Snow Break* on the heels of Mr. Eleazar and heard the crew react when they arrived. Kail had changed into his combat gear. A black vest made of Imaera hide, left his arms and shoulders bare. Years of missions, skirmishes and keeping up with Angela had stripped away all fat from his body. Taut muscles defined his lithe frame unlike the hulking mass of Camden. The matching black Imaera hide pants extended down to ash grey soft soled boots.

Suki glanced away before she embarrassed herself in front of everyone by staring. However seeing Angela openly ogle her man she couldn't help but start coughing and muttered something about the heat in the air. Camden chuckled and rolled his eyes at the two women as he flexed his biceps as a distraction, kissed each one and winked. Angela failed to notice Camden's antics, and Suki made for the edge of the ship.

"Where you going?" Camden called.

"I'm going to stand here so when I throw up, it will be over the side."

"Alright, if you get in danger of being dissolved by your own stomach juice, let me know," he called to her.

Suki simply closed her eyes and shook her head.

"Just remember you two," Camden called. "This is my ship so don't destroy it by showing off."

Kail made his way to the far side of the ship's deck to square off with Mr. Eleazar. "Any rules?" he asked the time traveler.

Mr. Eleazar shook his head. "No, I don't think so. We can keep it civil," he added while straightening his jacket and set it aside. "A gentlemen's match."

Kail opened himself to his magic. Blue wisps of magical energy started to float off of his hands. Similar spots of magic were left on the deck floor of the *Snow Break* as he paced back and forth eyeing Mr. Eleazar.

Mr. Eleazar assessed Kail. *Alteration is where the boy is going to start*, he could see.

Kail could see that Mr. Eleazar was not going to make the first move. *Why should he, this was an assessment of what I can do*, Kail concluded. Kail extended his hand and used a blast of energy to push Mr. Eleazar back, then sprang forward with unnatural speed to close the distance while Mr. Eleazar was distracted.

Kail's attack came to an abrupt end when he closed within striking distance of The Guardian. The initial push had no effect, and Mr. Eleazar was more than ready for a brawl. Mr. Eleazar easily brought his arm up in time to block Kail's jab and pivoted underneath his outstretched arm. Startled, Kail was sent sailing and slammed onto the metal deck of the airship with a groan.

Angela's smirk turned into a frown, and Camden shook his head.

"I am sorry, should we start a bit slower?" Mr. Eleazar taunted.

Kail got to his feet and said, "No, I think this is good so far." Again Kail resumed a physical attack posture and approached Mr. Eleazar. This time Kail opened his mind to divination and the body of Mr. Eleazar began to blur. He could see the possibilities of where his opponent would shift and move depending on his choices. Mr. Eleazar with his ability to control time, and who knew what else, made seeing his moves difficult. Normal opponents had two or three choices at best. Ghostly apparitions of Mr. Eleazar started to appear in various places on the deck.

Mr. Eleazar grinned at Kail. "Like what you see? Divination while extremely powerful is not going to work like you want it to against me."

Time was all Kail needed. The longer he used divination, the clearer the paths would become. Kail's attack was to kick low and follow it up with one towards the head of Mr. Eleazar. Magic enhanced his speed and strength beyond that of even Camden and adding a small amount of abjuration to shield his body from the impact, Kail had discovered that he could kick and punch steel all day long and not get hurt while the metal was beaten and destroyed.

Mr. Eleazar blocked the two kicks, but the force of them pushed him back. *Those attacks had some power behind them*, he nodded approvingly. "That is an interesting use of shielding magic," he complimented.

"I don't know how much you're going to recognize. Five years is a long time to learn a few tricks." Kail advanced on Mr. Eleazar again.

Both men attacked and defended. Mr. Eleazar brought his arm down and caught Kail out of position. A second hard punch caught Kail in the chest and magical energy erupted against the Imaera hide armor. The blow lifted Kail off of the deck floor and sent him cart wheeling sideways. Mr. Eleazar was quick to press the advantage. Before Kail had even landed, Mr. Eleazar was there waiting. Mr. Eleazar swung his fists together over his head and brought them down on Kail slamming him even harder onto the *Snow Break's* deck. Kail's breath left him in an anguished gasp.

"You're holding back too much," Mr. Eleazar said, walking away from where Kail lay on the deck.

Kail was slower to get to his feet this time. Mr. Eleazar words rang true. "Define gentlemen for me."

A tingle of danger ran up Mr. Eleazar's spine, and he already was spinning around to counter it.

Kail's left hand was firing a solid bar of magic and his right was slinging smaller individual balls of energy that wove through the air on their path towards their target. Mr. Eleazar brought up his hand to brace himself for the impact by wrapping a barrier of magic around him. It did little good as the bar of energy slammed into him. The smaller attacks barreled into him and detonated with ear shaking explosions that knocked him off-balance. Mr. Eleazar teleported out of the attack to escape.

Kail was waiting and two of the images he had been keeping an eye on through divination came into focus. He wasn't sure which one would turn out to be the real Mr. Eleazar so he sent attacks at both.

Mr. Eleazar blinked back into reality escaping the multi-pronged attack from earlier only to have Kail's second attack slam him in the chest and drive him back into the safety railing that surrounded the deck of the airship. A cry of surprise escaped from his lips as the front of his shirt was dotted with tiny burn holes. "Good one, Kail," he said. "Very impressive."

"Gentle people, gentle," Camden yelled, trying to make himself be heard over the noise of the fighting mages and the whine of the turbines. Smoke rose from several spots on the outer deck of the *Snow Break* from magical attacks.

Light began to flash and spray from the two mages doing combat on the deck of the airship. Clashing magical energy from attacks, dodges and blocks echoed through the sky. Kail rolled towards the edge of deck, coming up on his side and extended his arm to deflect a series of magical attacks. Mr. Eleazar just as quickly found himself running as attack after attack exploded behind him, generating another shout of disapproval from Camden.

Kail failed to block the kinetic blow that caused his feet to leave the deck floor. He blocked the second attack in mid-air, but the concussive force sent him over the top of the safety rail. Vertigo washed over him for a second as the deck floor was replaced by a several thousand foot fall.

Mr. Eleazar grinned and snapped his fingers with a time stop. Kail hung out over the empty air in front of him. "Had enough yet?"

"Not even a setback," Kail taunted back frozen in the air.

Mr. Eleazar smiled and walked over to the safety rail in front of Kail and leaned casually against the top. "Yes, well, I am sure you could soften your landing." He turned his gaze at Angela. "Or I guess Angela could swoop down and catch you in her arms."

Kail smiled as he closed his eyes and gathered his power. He had avoided using chronomancy against The Guardian recalling what happened last time they sparred on the deck of the *Snow Break*. Mr. Eleazar had placed an attack behind him that he could not stop. This time however he would see how far he could push his powers.

Mr. Eleazar turned his head back to face Kail. "That—," his sentence stalled on his tongue. Kail was not hanging in the air in front of him anymore.

It took more than chronomancy to punch through a time stop of someone else's creation. The more Kail moved, the more the pressure built around him. He wrapped himself with his magic in a full shield that helped. Each moment he could feel his magic reserves drain even more. Mr. Eleazar stood in front of him with his back towards him. Moving quickly before the shock of his escape wore off. Kail wrapped his arms around Mr. Eleazar and held tight lifting the man off of his feet. "You had enough yet?" Kail grunted, mimicking Mr. Eleazar's earlier taunt.

"No!" yelled Mr. Eleazar. "You don't understand the physics of what you have done." The time stop ended. The void in the air where Kail had been was now a vacuum. The air around Kail where he moved had been compressed unnaturally by his violation of Mr. Eleazar's time stop. Nature took care of the rest. The deafening explosion of compressed air around the pair was nothing compared to the shockwave of air rushing to fill the void left by Kail.

All of the windows on the bridge of the *Snow Break* shattered in unison as the ship bucked fifteen feet to port. The entire crew was knocked to the ground as well as everyone out on the deck.

Kail's hearing was silent. Even the high pitched whine he normally encountered when noises were loud enough to hurt his ears was absent. His world was simply mute. His vision spun and everything seemed to be moving in slow motion. He could see Angela and Camden yelling something as they got to their feet and ran to the edge of the *Snow Break*. He pushed himself up onto his hands and knees and saw Mr. Eleazar lying unconscious on the far side of the deck. Stunned and blinking he saw Angela dive over the side of the safety rail and disappear out of sight.

Angela had only a few seconds to catch up to Suki and try to slow their fall enough that they survived hitting the ground. Whatever attacks Kail and Mr. Eleazar had been using on each other had gotten out of hand. When the *Snow Break* jerked, she saw Suki go over the rail. Her hearing rang and she could feel blood as it cooled on the side of her head from her ears as she flew her hardest to catch the healer as she fell from the sky.

Kail stumbled over to where Camden stood leaning over the side of the airship. He understood now what Angela was trying to do. Camden turned to face him still unable to hear, but he could see the big man's angry face yelling at him.

Angela quickly caught the falling Suki in her arms, but their rapid decent was a lot to overcome. Lifting another person into the sky was not something Angela was capable of doing. She poured all of her will into her ability to fly to try to slow them down enough, as the ground rushed up to embrace them.

This is my fault, Kail thought. Using magic to break a time stop left him on the edge of exhaustion, but the peril he was seeing unfold in front of him surged his magic back to him. Gripping the edge of the rail Kail screamed and made a wrenching motion with his hands that channeled all of his magic at a space below the falling pair. Blackness tore through the air below Angela and Suki. Just as quickly as the pair passed into the void, it snapped out of existence. Kail turned with red face and spittle to the open deck of the airship and tore another rift into reality. Visions of him saving Angela with teleportation all those years ago flashed into his mind when they crashed through the bridge because of the difference in momentum. This rift was inverted and Angela with arms wrapped around Suki shot out of the void skyward. Gravity would slow them and with the airship below them the fatal fall would be only a few dozen feet. *Angela should be able to take care of the rest.* Moments after the void snapped shut, Kail's eyes rolled backwards as he collapsed onto the metal deck of the *Snow Break*.

Kail woke in the infirmary. He could feel the small vibrations of the *Snow Break's* turbines through the hard bed, but he could not hear anything. His head and body ached from everything that had happened. Angela stood over him with a concerned look. "Hey beautiful," he said. It was strange, the vibrations in his throat felt funny when his ears registered nothing.

Angela smiled, grabbing a paper and pencil and quickly wrote something down for him to read. *"How are you feeling?"* was written on the paper.

"I feel like I got run over by an airship," he said. "I can't hear anything, it feels weird."

Her eyes returned to the paper as she wrote for a few moments. *"We know. No one could hear after the explosion between you and the Time Walker,"* was scrawled under the first message.

"You can hear me."

"Yes, Suki has been healing the crew," was written on the paper when Angela turned it back to him.

"Makes sense," he said, looking around the room. "Where is she? Why hasn't she healed me?"

An amused look crossed Angela's face as she began writing her response. *"Suki said that you are the last person she was going to heal."*

Kail sighed and looked up at the ceiling of the infirmary. "Yeah, I suppose I deserve that." He felt Angela nudge him to the edge of the bed as she crawled on next to him. She didn't need to use the paper for him to read the *thank you* from her lips. "You're welcome," he whispered back and held her in his arms.

Mr. Eleazar turned away from the entrance of the infirmary and made his way down the hallway. *Their relationship wasn't something I planned for*, he thought to himself. However he was concerned about Kail's power. It was far, far more advanced than someone even with his lineage, talent and time should be capable of producing. He could only conclude that in Kail's past, his future, that he had taught him too well. Nothing else could explain it. Escaping a time stop was thought to be impossible. Things were changed and wrong and needed fixing. Mr. Eleazar sighed. "Looks like I will have to go light when I teach him to use his powers," he muttered to himself.

Mr. Eleazar stopped and retraced several steps. In front of him was Kail and Angela's quarters. Curious he pulled on the door release and stepped inside. Calling the room spartan would have been generous. Mr. Eleazar frowned. *Life on the run did not allow one to have any roots.* He was about to leave when something caught his eye. Shoved behind a pipe that ran next to the bed was a photograph. Reaching over he pulled it from its hiding spot and processed what he saw. Two little girls with huge happy smiles filled the shot. *Sisters clearly*, he examined. *Twins maybe, but clearly not identical. Changes indeed.*

Camden cleared his throat from the hallway in front of Kail and Angela's quarters. "Well, did you learn everything you wanted to know?" he said stiffly.

"Yes... Yes, Kail has come a long way. I do apologize for what happened. I underestimated his determination," Mr. Eleazar said as he discarded the photo on the bed.

"That may be so, but you are hiding something again. I can see it in your eyes."

Mr. Eleazar glanced back at the photo on the bed one last time as he stepped past Camden. "I don't know yet. But I think I will have to find someone else," he finished and walked down the hall, brushing past Camden.

Camden stepped into the quarters and saw the photo of Amaya and Alyssa laying there. He picked up the photo and slipped it into his pocket. *Secrets upon secrets were going to be the downfall of them all*, he thought as he made his way to the infirmary to let his friends know that Mr. Eleazar knew about the twins.

Chapter 14

The front windows on the bridge of the *Snow Break* had been replaced with spares that were kept on board. The rest were covered by metal sheets normally used for patching hull damage in the field. "New rule. No more sparing with magic on the *Snow Break*. If you feel the urge to shoot fireballs at each other again, you can just exit to your left," Camden said, pointing. "Right there off the edge of my ship," talking specifically to Kail and Mr. Eleazar.

The crew enjoyed the show the two mages had put on, but no one enjoyed how it ended, least of all Suki. Being knocked off of the ship and then having to heal every person had not endeared her to Kail or Mr. Eleazar. The *Snow Break* cruised through the sky above the jungles of Canyamar. Angela and Suki stepped onto the bridge together, Angela made her way to Kail and Suki stopped next to Camden.

"We should arrive in a couple of hours," Mr. Eleazar started. He had given the first officer of the *Snow Break* the coordinates of a place far enough from The Gateway that they should avoid detection. "If we leave a little before dark, we should be at the outpost in the dead of night. Angela and Camden will support Kail and me while we make our way to The Eternal Gateway. Suki will hold back with two volunteers and only engage if we get into trouble. Anymore than that we will lose the element of being a small group."

"Agreed," Kail said to the plan. "How much time will you need once we get there?"

"I don't know, a few minutes, maybe more. Many more."

"Every moment we are there increases the risk," Angela said.

"I know, but there is something wrong with The Gateway. It is possible that I may not be able to fix what is wrong unless I am able to uncover the problem," Mr. Eleazar said.

"If its answers are what we need to stop the suffering of this war, then we will get you the time you need," Kail said. "If it gets too rough, the two of us should be able to teleport everyone away."

"And if Therion is there? There is a good chance he hasn't left the gateway outpost," Camden stated.

Kail looked at Mr. Eleazar before answering. "Then we deal with him and end this."

"Sounds good to me dirt farmer," Camden said, nodding as he turned to the first mate of the *Snow Break*. "Harold, you have the bridge. Let's get ready," he finished, leaving the bridge to prepare for the night assault on The Eternal Gateway.

Kail stood shirtless in his quarters. He had paused in changing into the Imaera hide body armor to look at the photo of Amaya and Alyssa that Mr. Eleazar had found. He remembered the day the photo was taken. Alyssa had discovered, "*A yucky worm*," as she put it and terrorized her sister with it. It didn't take Amaya long to find her own, and the two of them teamed up to chase Camden with them. *There are not enough days like that one*, Kail sighed to himself.

"Help me with the top," Angela said, interrupting his thoughts.

"Sure, hand it to me," he replied, catching her black tunic as she tossed it to him. "It's gotten a bit tight since we had it made."

"Yes, well, motherhood will do that. It was not something I put thought to then," she said. "You are responsible too."

"Yes, yes," he teased, helping pull the tunic over her head and chest.

"What are your thoughts about Camden finding Mr. Eleazar in our room?" Angela changed the subject as her head popped out of the top of her armor.

"Aside from what we already talked about, not much new. Mr. Eleazar is manipulative and talks in riddles."

"We need to be careful with our words around him. I do not think we should say too much about what happened the last time all of us were at The Gateway."

"What do you mean?" Kail asked as he adjusted her tunic.

"I believe it would be dangerous for us to tell him how the events unfolded. It could change things. How would you react if you were told that you died five years ago and that was what you now had to look forward to?"

Kail shook his head, "I don't know, I haven't died, but you did in a way, a thousand years ago. What if you knew that you had to go back? Would you do it, or try to change your fate?"

"Right now, no. I would not go back, but I might if I found out that if I did not meet my fate the rest of the world suffers," she finished.

"I still say it doesn't matter. What has happened has happened. The Mr. Eleazar then already experienced what we face today. Remember what he said about time being a river and changing its course, but in the end it still flows to the ocean regardless of what you do. No matter what we tell him or don't tell him, we still will end up in this same spot as we are now," he concluded.

"True, but the whole purpose is to change the river, not to stop it from the ocean," she countered.

Kail shrugged his shoulders and helped strap the Keratin war blades to her lower back. "As you're fond of saying, 'all we can do is our best and do what we think is right.' We don't know where the river flows or where he wants to make it flow."

"Everything I have done for the last five years is because of him. I am still unsettled with him regarding our children."

"Sit," Kail instructed and began to brush Angela's long red hair. Learning how to braid girl's hair had made him the butt of many of Camden's jokes. Two daughters had left him little choice but to learn. "Amaya and Alyssa are safe with the Kellys," he said, separating her hair into three parts. "I think Mr. Eleazar has delivered on his promise to you. It's nothing more than what he said. He's curious to see how things turned out is all."

Angela's sigh told him that she wasn't convinced but wasn't going to peruse the matter further. They spent the rest of the time in silence preparing for the mission. Kail finished tying her hair into a long braid before turning to finish getting himself ready.

Suki stood on the Canyamar jungle ground outside of the powered down *Snow Break*. Camden and Mr. Eleazar were having a quiet discussion about something she could not hear as they waited for Kail and Angela. Two volunteers of the crew were busy with light backpacks. They were checking and double checking that they had what they needed to help in case things went bad. She didn't even know their names. At one point that would have bothered her, but not now. She had long ago learned that the pain of loss was much less when there were no names to go with the faces. *When this is all over, I will change that*, she thought. *But not now.*

Kail stepped down the back loading ramp of the *Snow Break* with Angela right behind him. They looked the exact opposite of how she felt. Strong, confident, and determined to see this mission through. She could see no doubts or worries that they might not come home. *They looked like a pair of death cards the fortune tellers used,* she thought. She suddenly felt clumsy in her getup. The pack of medical supplies at her feet suddenly seemed huge and bulky. Fears of it getting caught up on things in the jungle and giving them away made their way into her thoughts. The pistol she wore on the side of her hip was the same. What if it snagged on something and went off? Or worse, she shot herself on accident.

"Do not worry, you will be fine," Mr. Eleazar's unexpected voice caused her to jump.

She had been so caught up in her own thoughts, she missed his approach. "It's not me that I am worried about," she admitted, looking at Camden, Kail and Angela as they talked to Harold, one last time before heading out.

Mr. Eleazar looked at her and followed her gaze. "Talented and powerful, all of us, including you. Together even more so. None of us can do this alone," he finished by walking towards the group.

Easy to say for someone who can walk through time, she thought, slinging her pack onto her back making her way to the others.

"Mr. Eleazar will take point in the jungle," Kail was saying as she approached. "I recall you seem to be able to navigate the area around The Gateway particularly well."

Mr. Eleazar nodded that the various enchantments around The Gateway did not affect him.

"Angela will keep to the tree tops and cover us from there," he said, looking at Angela.

Suki could see her nod. The hilts of her twin war blades stuck out on each side of her lower back. She had a full quiver of arrows and her bow slung over her shoulder.

"I'll follow behind Mr. Eleazar, then Suki and you two." He pointed at the volunteers. She felt better that he didn't seem to know their names either. She wasn't the only one who seemed to cope with all of the loss lately by distancing themselves from others. "Camden will bring in the rear," Kail finished.

She saw Camden wink at her and say, "There's a joke to be made there."

She just rolled her eyes at his antics. She wasn't sure of her feelings for the big man. There might be something there, but he never made a move towards her so her own feelings of being returned were in doubt. She missed what Kail said next but nodded like everyone else when they started to head into the jungle. *You need to focus more*, she berated herself. *I hope what he said wasn't something important.*

Camden stood in the shadows on the edge of the jungle looking at The Eternal Gateway outpost. Mr. Eleazar and Kail were assessing how they would approach, and he heard Angela land next to him and whisper to the group that the area was clear. He could tell Suki was nervous, but he didn't worry as this was as far as she had to go unless things went horribly wrong.

"Camden, you and Angela head towards those buildings there. Mr. Eleazar and I will skirt the jungles edge and approach The Gateway directly from the South," Kail explained. Angela looked at him and nodded her head. "Suki, you're in charge here, if you see my signal, then assist," Kail finished.

"Well Red, it looks like it's you and me once again," Camden said as Mr. Eleazar and Kail made their way through the jungle. "Suki."

"Yes Cam?"

"Nothing, just wanted to hear you say that," he said grinning. "Let's go Red. Your dirt farmer needs a distraction." Turning and keeping to the shadows of the cleared area around The Gateway, Angela followed behind him, her ability to fly would come in handy soon, but in the clear area, she would have stood out.

Camden and Angela stopped a hundred yards away from the first building. A barbed wire fence had been erected around the outpost. He saw Angela pull out one of her war blades to cut the fence, but he stopped her. Placing his hands on the wire his grip turned to metal and he easily snapped the wire without making a sound. He let the wire go slowly to make sure it didn't make any noise as it relaxed to the jungle floor. Camden brought his finger to his lips and signed a "shh" at her as he crouched through the opening in the fence. Angela returned her sword to its sheath and followed behind.

They made their way across the compound to an area of stacked equipment. Camden could hear soldiers talking as they made their rounds through the outpost. Holding his breath, he took a peek around their cover and counted two men. Looking back at Angela next to him he indicated that there were two headed their way. Angela's eyes had a deadly glint to them as she nodded in understanding. She un-slung her bow and held an arrow at the ready. Camden pulled a knife from his belt and counted down on his fingers from five. Stepping out from behind, he caught the first soldier under the chin with his knife driving it into his brain. With his other hand he pulled the second soldier around and Angela put an arrow through his eye before he knew what was happening. Both men were dead in his hands and he quickly pulled them back behind to where they were hiding. Angela pulled the arrow out of the man's head and looked at it before tossing it aside. One of the barbs had bent on impact at such close range.

Cleaning his hand on the dead man's uniform, Camden pulled a clockwork bomb from his pack. He looked at the time piece and set the timer for twenty five minutes as he set it inside the equipment. Angela took the lead and he followed as they made their way to the first building.

Kail and Mr. Eleazar had made their way through the fence and could see The Eternal Gateway in the distance before them. "Time?" he asked Mr. Eleazar after watching The Guardian look at his pocket watch.

"If everything goes well, we have less than twenty five minutes before it becomes distracting," Mr. Eleazar answered. "Let us not be late shall we?"

Kail nodded in agreement and made his way to the next hiding spot on the way to The Gateway. *There had been no sign of Therion, but that didn't mean anything. The man was either here or he wasn't*, Kail thought. They had little trouble avoiding the patrols as they neared The Gateway. "Looks like they have it pretty well guarded," Kail said now that they could see The Eternal Gateway clearly.

"This is more serious than I thought," Mr. Eleazar whispered, squinting at The Gateway.

"What is it?"

"It's locked for one, but The Eternal Gateway has been reset. I will have to unlock it and then synchronize with it." Mr. Eleazar said.

"What does that mean?" Kail wanted to know. Anything that Mr. Eleazar would label as 'serious' was something with which to be concerned.

"In short, it looks like when The Gateway returned, it had no guardian."

Kail could feel the blood drain from his face as he turned to look at Mr. Eleazar. "What do you mean no guardian? You are The Guardian," he said.

"Think of it like a normal door new from the carpenter. You pick out a lock, with that lock comes a key. Whoever has the key can open the door," Mr. Eleazar explained. "I have that key, but it won't work until I match it with the current lock."

"What else," Kail demanded.

"Well, there is a key already in the lock. Technically all one has to do is go and take it and well... like a door, they would have the key to open it."

"You're saying Therion could be in complete control of The Gateway right now and lock you out?"

"No, no. I can see the key from here. If he knew what he was looking at, he would have taken it long ago," Mr. Eleazar dismissed Kail's concern.

Kail shook his head at Mr. Eleazar's unconcerned words. "Let's get closer. The quicker you get in there and finish, the quicker we can leave."

Camden looked at his watch again before setting the timer on the clockwork bomb. On this one the fuse was set just under five minutes. "Last one," he whispered to Angela who kept watch as he set the explosive in place.

"They should be in place and ready," Angela spoke softly. "Let us move from here to the other side," she said pointing with one of her war blades.

Camden nodded in agreement and together they made their way quickly through the shadows. They stopped and hid where they could see The Eternal Gateway. He looked at his watch and held up two fingers for Angela letting her know when the bombs would detonate. "It looks the same to me. Just a pile of rocks," he whispered, nodding towards The Gateway.

"An empty stone archway for me. Same as before," Angela said, looking at The Eternal Gateway quickly before going back to keep watch.

"Think you can take out those guards around The Gateway when the explosions start?" he asked.

"Yes."

Camden held up one finger and continued to look at his watch as the time counted down.

Kail and Mr. Eleazar held ready when the first explosion erupted on the far side of the outpost. "Now," he said and together they ran for The Gateway. Three guards held their gaze on the billowing fireball reaching into the sky and never saw them. Kail brought his magic to him preparing to dispatch them, but all three fell dead with empty stares from Angela's arrows. He had to grin at his wife's handy work.

Mr. Eleazar rushed to the front of The Eternal Gateway and set to work. Kail turned and wrapped his magic around him in a protective barrier then took a defensive stance at the bottom of the small rise ready to buy Mr. Eleazar as much time as possible should anyone assault them. "Make it quick!" he yelled over his shoulder as the rest of the bombs Camden and Angela had placed threw the outpost into chaos.

Flashes of light pierced through his closed eyes. Therion had retreated from the outpost to a distant ridge to meditate. "Curious," he said to himself. He caught the last moments of a fireball explosion rise and disappear out above the outpost. Again there were flashes of light and more explosions could be seen. It took several more seconds before the first faint crack of the explosion reached his ears. "Unexpected, but fools none the less," he said, getting to his feet as his form dissolved into energy and he teleported to The Gateway.

Angela and Camden were making their way back through the outpost. Angela's bow felled soldier after soldier. The noise of the explosions and confusion made it easy for her deadly aim. Camden moved like a stalking Imaera though the shadows making one soldier disappear after another.

Bright flashes of light and the sound of clashing magic erupted from the direction of The Eternal Gateway behind them. Angela turned to see parts of wild magic cast into the air.

"Angela no!" Camden yelled at her when he saw her turn to head back to The Gateway. His words brought her up short. "We have to make sure no one else gets there. Stay focused!" He could see the struggle in her face, but she turned back to the outpost to quickly kill three more soldiers with her bow before discarding it as the last arrow was used before pulling twin blades of millennia old design cut down soldier after soldier.

Camden moved to her right flank and snapped the neck of a man who had brought his gun up at Angela. The surprise of their attack was wearing off as several of the soldiers were now firing in their direction. Bullets made things harder but not impossible. Camden picked up the dead man's weapon before moving away and fired back killing one man.

Suki and the two men with her watched in silence as the jungle night was lit up with explosions. The distant sound of gunfire could clearly be heard as the normal sounds of the jungle had gone silent after the first explosion. Her heart began to beat like a hammer in her chest when the exotic colors and flashes from fighting mages began to appear. "Therion is here," she said. She could see the cold sweats her words brought to her companions.

Mr. Eleazar stood in front of the closed Gateway looking at the clock that twitched. Pulling his pocket watch from his pocket he set it to match its time and locked it into place. Monitoring the results he began to slowly move the clock on The Gateway forward until he found the next snag.

"Step away from my destiny," cold hard words came from behind him. Turning Mr. Eleazar saw Therion step back into reality after teleporting. Wisps of magical ether were floating off of his body.

"Stall him Kail," he shouted, returning to work on The Gateway.

Kail heard Mr. Eleazar's shout behind him as Therion appeared in front of him. He didn't wait or hold back as he shot a bar of magical energy towards Therion that was hot enough to cut through an airship and punch out the other side. He didn't wait to see if it had any effect before teleporting himself to flank Therion.

Therion blinked away from Kail's attack before it reached him. He caught sight of Kail flashing to his left as he unleashed an attack of his own.

Kail barely dodged Therion's attack as it brushed past him to explode somewhere in the outpost. The Imaera hide armor took a glancing hit saving him from being badly burned. He could already feel the magic in the hide begin to creep as it slowly began to heal itself over the damaged part.

"Do you think you can take me head on, Kail?" Therion taunted after nearly cutting Kail in half with his first attack. "You're not a mage," he spat. "You'll be nothing more than a footnote in history."

Kail poured his magic into his muscles and closed the distance between them in half a heartbeat. His physical attack caught Therion off guard as his elbow connected with Therion's chest causing the magic between them to explode in a shower of colored sparks that sent Therion stumbling backwards.

Therion's shock lasted only an instant before he lunged back at Kail. Kail easily dodged the older man's attack, but had to bring his defenses up to block several smaller blasts of magic that left the air full of acrid smoke. Both men recovered from the exchange as they squared off.

"When I've killed you," Therion said, circling around Kail, "the first thing I am going to do is incinerate that city of yours."

Kail shot to his left with enhanced speed and let loose a ball of energy at Therion as he started talking. The older mage, un-amused, just swatted his attack away. The energy sailed upwards out of the outpost and lit up a distant part of the jungle as it returned to the ground.

"Then I am going to hunt down that pretty flying girl of yours," he continued.

"Not happening," Kail retorted back as once again he closed the distance between them. When it came to raw ability to throw magic around Kail was sure that Therion had him, but in close and physical he stood a chance.

Therion back peddled from Kail's assault. The younger man was faster, but very inexperienced. Several times he was able to push Kail back, but the man was right back in his face physically before he could charge up an attack large enough to cut through Kail's defenses. "Enough!" Therion yelled as he pushed his magic outward in all directions.

Therion's blast pushed Kail back and lifted him into the air. He landed on his feet, but the distance between them now gave the advantage to Therion. He could see the tendrils of magic gathering around the man's hands. He knew the next attack was going to be strong. Hot blue energy shot from Therion's outstretched hand at him. Kail blocked the attack with his own magic, but the force pushed him backwards across the ground. He could feel his magic failing quickly so he pushed out of the way and rolled across the ground as the remainder of the attack crashed into one of the outpost buildings.

"Pathetic," Therion said, advancing on Kail. "It's just one accident after another with you isn't it?"

Kail's head began to swim after blocking the last attack from Therion. *Damn that fight with Mr. Eleazar*, he thought. *I'm still weak from it.* Getting to his feet, he gathered his magic and sent it flying back at Therion. Therion pushed his own attack as the magic collided with a shower of light and explosions. He stole a glance at The Eternal Gateway to see that Mr. Eleazar had finished whatever he was doing and now stood in front of an open Gateway. "Hurry up old man," he cursed loudly.

Therion halted his attack as he turned to look at the open Eternal Gateway. "No!" he shouted, dismissing Kail as he advanced on Mr. Eleazar. Mr. Eleazar paid both men no attention as he focused on The Gateway.

Kail sprinted forward and teleported at the same time. Flashing out of and back into existence he collided with Therion as the two of them crashed to the ground. He heard Therion's gasp and grunt as he landed on top of him. Kail barely brought his magic up in time to absorb the brunt of the magic fired from Therion. Again his armor saved him as the blast sent him flying up into the air before he landed hard on the ground gasping for breath that rushed out of him.

Kail rolled to the side, but the attack never came. Therion clearly considered him no threat and had advanced on Mr. Eleazar. Kail could see Therion hesitate as he looked from Mr. Eleazar then back to the far side of the open Gateway. "Enough Guardian! The Gateway is mine," Therion yelled.

Kail fired with everything he had left, deflecting Therion's magical attack before it would have hit Mr. Eleazar in the back. The combined energy shot past Mr. Eleazar and poured into the open Gateway. The Gateway rumbled and flickered as the energy was sent through some unknown time. Mr. Eleazar flinched as his focus on The Gateway was broken. He quickly spun and at the same time The Eternal Gateway slammed shut.

Therion's shouts were incomprehensible as he started to run towards Mr. Eleazar. Kail watched as Mr. Eleazar swung his hand up, snapped his fingers and Therion disappeared. Mr. Eleazar ran to where Kail, exhausted, had dropped to his knees. Kail felt the magic wrap around him as Mr. Eleazar teleported the both of them away.

Kail collapsed onto his back when the two materialized several feet away from Suki and the others on the edge of the jungle. "We have to go back for them. Angela and Camden," he gasped.

"Don't worry my love, we are already here," Angela's voice said.

"Did you do it? Did you kill him?" he asked Mr. Eleazar.

"No, I simply sent him away, but we need to hurry. It will only take a few minutes for him to recover and return. We need to be leaving," Mr. Eleazar said. "Now," he emphasized when the group failed to move.

"Come on kid," Camden said, lifting Kail to his feet. "Plenty of time to lie around once we're back on the *Snow Break*."

"Is The Gateway yours?" Kail asked as they made their way quickly through the jungle.

"It is secure," Mr. Eleazar answered.

"That wasn't what he asked," Camden interjected.

"I need some time to sort out everything. We need to return to Silverton. I should have the answers by then," Mr. Eleazar said, stepping up the pace.

Chapter 15

"Whoa," Rhonin said as the *Snow Break* settled onto her landing zone at the Silverton airfield.

"No kidding," Rayne agreed, eyeing the plates that covered windows and the large crumple zone on the side of the ship.

"I'm not sure what caused that," he pointed. "There are no burn or shrapnel marks, but I bet the story behind it is going to be interesting," Rhonin added as the pair waited for the others to exit the ship. He flagged down a ground crewman to have an extra shift worth of repairs staffed to help with the damage. Everything was advancing fast and there wasn't likely to be time to do repairs in the future.

"They didn't report any casualties, and they said the raid on The Gateway outpost was successful," Rayne added.

"We will find out soon enough," Rhonin nodded as the back loading dock of the *Snow Break* was lowered allowing the ship's crew to exit. He heard his wife gasp next to him. The utter surprise on her face sent his heart racing. "What?" he asked, scanning the airfield.

"There," she pointed. "That's him."

Rhonin saw who his wife was pointing at after a few moments. He felt his stomach fall followed by calm resolve as he recognized Mr. Eleazar stepping off of the *Snow Break*.

"That explains why they radioed in Destiny instead of returning from Aldervale," he said.

"It's been so long I had nearly forgotten," Rayne said softly, looking from her husband to the mysterious man who years ago had saved them and their men during the War of Antiquities. "I figured that made us even with him after we were sent to help rescue Kail and Angela."

Rhonin put on his best poker face as the group slowly made their way over. "He looks the same as thirty years ago," he said quickly. Rhonin's mind quickly sifted through possible explanations. "Rayne, this might be before that. He obviously hasn't sent for us yet."

Rayne's eyes widened at the possibility, she hoped her husband was correct. Mr. Eleazar was clearly younger than he was that day five years ago. "Just-," her words were cut off with a wave of Rhonin's hand and a quick shake of his head.

"Rhonin, Rayne," Kail greeted, dropping his bags to the cement ground. "You remember Mr. Eleazar," he said, introducing The Guardian.

"We have met before," Rhonin said neutrally, taking the man's hand.

"Ah yes, the illustrious Mastersons," Mr. Eleazar greeted with a smile. "I trust everything has been going well for you," he added with a knowing twinkle in his eye while holding Rhonin's handshake longer than necessary before taking Rayne's hand with a bow.

"As well as one can expect given the circumstances," Rhonin answered.

"Yes, yes. To be remedied soon I think," Mr. Eleazar said. "Shall we convene in an hour? Is that enough time?" he asked, looking at those gathered. Agreements came from everyone as the group began to split up to change after the trip and deal with any issues that had arose while they were gone that needed immediate attention.

Once Angela and Kail were alone in their quarters onsite at the Silverton airfield he spoke his mind. "I know he did it on purpose."

Angela knew something was coming to a head. Kail had been in his silent mode assuring everyone that he was fine and nothing was wrong, but those who knew him better knew it to be untrue. "Who?" she asked.

"Mr. Eleazar," he said in a harsh whisper.

"Explain."

"The sparing match. The encounter with Therion," Kail started as he paced the room shaking his head. "It wasn't some test. He weakened me on purpose with that, that display," he said, becoming even angrier than before. "When Therion showed up at The Gateway, my magic was drained and I was tired after we barely started fighting."

Angela cocked her head to the side and watched Kail pace before answering. "Are you saying that if the two of you had not fought each other you could have defeated Therion?"

"Yes," he said quickly. "No, I don't know. It would have been different, that much I am certain, and yes I am sure that if it came down to it, I could have won," he finished by crashing onto their bed.

"It is a dangerous accusation," she said. "I do not see how letting Therion remain in power helps anyone's cause."

"Who knows," Kail said defeated. "The man has agendas inside agendas. If I ever find out that this could have all ended three days ago but he prevented it..." Kail shook his head. "I will probably kill him."

"Let us not speak about this again until you are sure," she told him. "It will do no good to put distrust among us."

"I'm not letting him out of my sight," Kail finally answered.

"Come let us get cleaned up before the meeting. It will wash away your anger," she said, holding out her hand.

Kail sighed and took her hand and let her help pull him up from the bed. "It's only going to get crazier isn't it?"

"It already has."

Kail walked with Angela into the crowded room. Mr. Eleazar sat at the end of the conference table cleaning his pocket watch. "Camden, Rhonin," he greeted as he sat in an empty chair at the table. Brom Carter of the *Odyssey* and Harold Riggins from the *Snow Break* stood next to their respective captains. Randal Wood and Duncan Deline were present as well to hear what The Guardian had to say.

"If you want to make enemies, the best way is to change something," Mr. Eleazar started casually while still focusing on his pocket watch. Snapping the watch closed he looked at Kail and then to Angela. "They also say that heroes die and become legends, or they live to become villains."

The room chilled with uncomfortable ease after the last sentence. "What point are you trying to make?" Kail broke the silence first. "That almost sounded like a threat."

"Not a threat, a fact," Mr. Eleazar continued unaffected by Kail's response. "Some of us are already legends," he said, looking at Angela. The pause stayed until all eyes in the room had shifted to Angela.

Angela met Mr. Eleazar's stare ignoring the attention focused on her. "Now is not the time for riddles Time Walker," she replied coldly.

Kail frowned and turned on Mr. Eleazar. "What game are you playing at our expense?" he demanded.

Mr. Eleazar leaned back into his chair before answering. "Your role is complete," he started while still holding Angela's gaze. "What you do now is of your own destiny."

"Explain yourself!" Kail said angrily, standing so quickly that his chair would have crashed to the ground if Angela hadn't been there to catch it.

"It's simple," Mr. Eleazar said unfazed. "She has played her part in this prophecy. There isn't anything left for her to do." He shifted his gaze to Camden and the Mastersons. "Others it seems still have roles to play."

Camden smirked and rolled his eyes. "Of course we do. Did The Eternal Gateway tell you all this?" he asked, laced with sarcasm.

"The childless one will decide the fate of all," Mr. Eleazar quoted. He pointed a finger in Kail and Angela's direction. "They are not exactly childless anymore, now are they?"

Kail felt his heart start to pound hearing Mr. Eleazar's words. He had never considered himself the childless one that the prophecy had spoken of, but to be flat out dismissed came as a shock none the less.

"Well you can stick your prophecy right up your nose. I'm not in this for deciding the fate of anyone. It's about money remember? That was the deal," Camden refuted while the Mastersons stayed silent.

"What can you tell us then?" Suki asked. "Honestly this time."

Mr. Eleazar looked at the medic for a few moments. "The Eternal Gateway is still vulnerable. I was only able to fix one of the disruptions while we were there. There are still two more that have to be corrected," he added, not counting the magic from Kail and Therion that had passed into The Gateway.

"What does that mean to us in non-Time Walker?" Camden sneered.

"Changes in time. Each one has to be addressed."

"And how are we supposed to do that?" Camden continued.

"We don't. I do."

"You're leaving aren't you?" Suki stated, meeting Mr. Eleazar's eyes. When he didn't answer she pressed. "When?"

"As soon as we're finished here," Mr. Eleazar admitted. The room broke out in confusion.

"What? You have been gone for five years. You show up with grand plans to save the world and as soon as you're back, you're leaving?" Kail said loudly after the noise died down.

"I have to try to fix the disruptions. It could take me a few days or a few years. Judging by your reactions when I arrived, I am guessing decades," Mr. Eleazar said. "Everyone here is capable of finishing what was started," he added with a touch of anger. "My role is no less or more important than any of yours."

"So that's it?" Kail questioned.

"No," Mr. Eleazar stated. "For this to work, for this all to come together, Therion must control The Eternal Gateway." The room fell dead silent at his words. "Only then can he be defeated. The final battle will have to be at The Eternal Gateway."

"Well, that's a relief," Camden said sarcastically, tossing his hands into the air.

Angela spoke next. "He can't control The Gateway as long as you are alive."

"As I said, some of us are already legends," Mr. Eleazar said with a smile.

"And how are we supposed to defeat Therion if he controls The Gateway? Have you not said that if someone else controls it, it could erase all of time?" Angela asked.

"There will be a sentinel to prevent that," Mr. Eleazar assured them.

"Guardians, sentinels, what's next? Are the King and Queen of Swords showing up next?" Camden sneered.

"Camden," Kail chided the big man before turning to address Mr. Eleazar. "There is something else you're not telling us isn't there?"

"You're getting better at this," Mr. Eleazar smiled. "You won't be able to defeat Therion alone."

"You said you might have to find another," Camden spoke up, remembering when he caught Mr. Eleazar in Kail and Angela's quarters on the *Snow Break*.

Mr. Eleazar shrugged. "In a way yes. They have what you need," he answered.

"Who are they? And have what?" Kail asked, getting tired of the run around.

"A small invention. One you use to possess."

Realization slowly came to Kail once he started to piece it all together. "My bindings. The ones that Therion tore out of me?"

Mr. Eleazar nodded.

"We don't have those," Camden objected.

"No," Kail answered still thinking. "Vincent and Bastiana do," he concluded.

Now it was Camden's turn to come out of his chair. "Are you all mad? That, that psycho woman has them?"

"In a demented time joking way it all makes sense," Kail said.

"The hell it does!" Camden argued.

"We get the bindings. We place them on Therion. Without his magic he is nothing. Then we can defeat him and end this," Kail summarized.

"Yeah, piece of cake," Camden continued.

Mr. Eleazar looked at his pocket watch again and stood. "Now that my guidance has been heard, it's time for me to leave."

"Wait one minute," Camden turned on The Guardian, but it was too late. Mr. Eleazar was gone.

Chapter 16

Vincent finished signing his name at the bottom of a document. Taking a pinch of sand he spread it across the wet ink and set the page aside to dry before moving to the next. The floor to ceiling sized glass windows behind him showed the ever growing metropolis of Cahir spreading into the distance. Dirigibles and the skeletons of several sky scrapers being constructed filled the sky. He paused his work as the sound of heels tapping on the marble floor grew louder. As expected the door to his office opened without a knock.

Bastiana closed the door behind her and leaned back against it. Vincent could see that whatever it was that had brought her to his office had her excited. He watched as she held her eyes closed and a shiver ran through her body before she stepped forward. *The black dress again*, he observed. *If it could be called a dress, a quarter of one or less is more like it. More expensive than its weight in gold too*. Gone was her childish nature, replaced by the more dominant and seductive personality that now showed through in her style of clothing and mannerisms. Dozens, which he knew of, had died in the first year after the protective staff had saved her from the encounter with The Guardian in the jungles of Canyamar. Now the runic tattoos that covered her dark skin seemed to be a source of pride instead of anger. Her left leg was bare all the way to her hip by the scandalous dress. The stomach and back of the dress were laid exposed as well. Only part of the right side of her body and chest were covered. *At least she grew her hair out again*, he conceded. Split down the middle, half of her hair was white as fresh snow that clashed with the other that remained dark. *The protection of the staff wasn't flawless*, he recalled, remembering the events that gave her the tattoos.

"Vincent darling, I have the most wonderful of news," she said while closing the distance between them.

"Unless Therion has died of unnatural causes, I cannot think of any news I would label as wonderful."

Bastiana sat on the front of his desk and leaned toward him. "I have a letter." She started pulling a folded piece of paper from the top of her dress.

Unfazed by her attempts to distract him, "All this for a letter?" he questioned, reaching for it.

"Not just any letter," Bastiana said, jerking the letter away before he had taken hold of it. Sitting back in his chair he let her play her game as she brought the paper to her nose and smelled it. "It's from them," she finished, tossing the letter to the desk.

Vincent held his tongue and ignored the now discarded letter in front of him. Bastiana slipped off of his desk and turned her back to him. Slowly she looked back at him over her shoulder and her bare arm began to glow with magic. Faint wisps of blue and red energy danced along her skin as she emphasized her next words. "All of them."

"Clearly whoever *they* are, have you excited," he said now reaching for the letter. Bastiana continued to entertain herself with her magic as he quickly read the letter. "Interesting."

"Entertaining," Bastiana corrected.

He pressed a button on his desk and spoke into the intercom. "Call the Mayor and have him report to my office, and the ambassador to Courduff as well," he said to the secretary on the other side before releasing the button. Returning to Bastiana he said, "It seems we have to prepare for guests."

Bastiana's eyes shone with agreement.

"I think I am going to buy you a helmet for your birthday," Camden told Kail. The *Snow Break* and the *Odyssey* cruised side by side on their way to Cahir.

"What would I need a helmet for?" Kail asked.

"To keep an idiot from hurting himself."

Kail shook his head. "I'll admit, I have no idea how we are going to get the bindings from them."

"How do we know they have even kept them in the first place? The whole thing gives me the willies," Camden shuddered. "I know things between Courduff and Cahir haven't been the greatest of late, but they are still allies. I sure can't picture them just handing them over for you to use on Therion."

"I don't know. Just be ready for whatever happens," Kail said, leaving the bridge to find Angela. Their quarters were empty so he made his way to the galley. Nodding to a few of the crew on his way he found the galley was also empty. *Maybe she's with Suki*, he thought. "Where is everyone?" he said out loud to an empty infirmary. He continued to wander the ship stopping by the engine room. He didn't bother to check inside because there were no sets of hearing protection missing from the wall.

"Like this?" Suki asked Angela, holding one of the red head's war blades in front of her.

"Yes but tighter so you don't let go of it." Angela swung its twin down on top of the blade knocking it from Suki's hand. The clattering of the blade hitting the metal floor in the cargo hold echoed loudly around them. "Are you sure you want to learn this? You cannot master the blade before we arrive in Cahir. It can take one's lifetime."

Suki shook the stinging from her hand as she retrieved the blade. "I am being silly," she said, moving to sit on a piece of cargo. She examined the runes etched into the blade as it lay in her lap. Forever sharp and indestructible, two things she wasn't.

"What is bothering you?"

"I don't know," she said without looking up. "I have this feeling that everything is going to go horribly wrong. No, more like it already has, but we just haven't noticed yet."

Angela took a seat next to her and waited a few moments before talking. "I remember when I was young, before the Time Walker brought me here. There was a girl who doubted. Every day when we were learning to become warriors she would let it be known to anyone who would listen, that she was no good at the tasks assigned: sword play, archery, even flying. When she did fail at these things, she was satisfied with the fact that she failed."

"What are you saying?"

"The girl failed because she believed she would."

"I don't go around hoping we fail so I can gloat," Suki countered.

"No, but you are already looking for it," Angela continued. "There is a saying among my people. Do not step quietly through life only to arrive safely at death."

Suki looked at Angela's face. "What is that supposed to mean?"

"It means that you have to take chances in life. Not recklessly or stupidly, but you can end up letting everything worth living for pass by you if you are too afraid to go after it."

"That is an interesting idea," she said, feeling a little better. "I don't think this is for me," she said, handing over the war blade.

Angela took the blade and held it in front of them. "Stepping quietly is something I have never done," she said. Both women started to laugh. Neither of them saw Kail quietly step away from the entrance to the cargo area.

Kail and Angela stood in front of the skyscraper in the heart of Cahir. "I shouldn't be surprised." He tilted his head to a placard on the side of the building.

"Hyperion," Angela said. "We should not delay. Vincent assured us we would be allowed to meet with him, but we are surrounded by enemies in this city."

"Agreed," Kail said, holding the door for her.

The lobby of Vincent and Bastiana's tower was pristine. Polished marble floors and carved stone columns lined the walls that held up the vaulted ceiling. Kail took a look around but didn't see anyone. Shrugging his shoulders at Angela, he took the lead and walked to the center of the room. Angela nudged his arm and pointed. A single woman stood behind a long counter.

Kail cleared his throat as the woman ignored that they were standing in front of her.

"Names please," the woman asked through painted lips without looking up.

"Kail Falconcrest and Angela Atagi, were here to--,"

"Weapons?" the woman interrupted finally looking up at them.

"Excuse me?" Kail asked.

The woman sighed, "All weapons need to be left here before continuing."

Angela took off the floor length duster she had worn to conceal her war blades, bow and quiver full of arrows. Hilts of knives were also visible tucked into the bracers she wore. The woman remained unimpressed. Kail held out his hand and produced a small ball of fire. "This isn't something I can just leave behind."

"That won't be necessary Tabea," a woman's voice said from an open elevator. The woman behind the counter went back to her work. The harsh ring of high heels on marble floor bounced off of the stone walls as Bastiana glided towards them. "It is such a pleasure to see you again Kail," she smiled. "And the woman who can fly," she cooed as she circled Angela, drinking in the sight of her.

"Bastiana," Kail greeted neutrally, keeping his eye on her.

"Come now Kail," Bastiana said, looking away from Angela finally. "Bastiana? We know each other so much better than that."

"It's been a long time Bas-," he corrected himself when her eyes glinted. "It's been a long time Tiana," her face relaxed. "It appears you have been doing well all these years."

Bastiana blinked slowly at him. "You're such a liar," she smiled. Grinding the stiletto heel into the floor she spun and made for the open elevator. "Come," she commanded loudly.

Kail looked at Angela, shook his head in dismay but followed after the tattooed mage. Bastiana had stopped at the elevator and offered for them to enter first. Kail and Angela stepped into the back corners of the elevator. Bastiana stepped inside, turned her back on them and keyed in the elevator. The tension in the elevator as they rode silently to the top of the tower could have been used to power an airship. Kail jerked when the elevator chimed and the doors opened.

Bastiana smiled but didn't turn around. She stepped off of the elevator into a long hallway that ended in large double doors. Grabbing both handles she swung them open wide and strolled into Vincent's office. Kail and Angela stepped inside together. Vincent sat behind a large wooden desk with the city of Cahir on display behind him. Bastiana turned to sit on the edge of the desk. She leaned back and crossed her legs, exposing herself more than was proper, smiling at the both of them.

Kail took a deep breath, eyeing Angela with a slight frown as he stepped forward.

Chapter 17

Three months ago...

Bright sunlight filled the room. White walls and the smell of antiseptic dominated the senses. Bandages covered every bit of his body that he could see, but it hurt too much to try to move to see more. The sound of a door opening drew his gaze. A nurse in a white uniform stepped into the room. She shrieked, dropped her clipboard and ran from the room when she saw him. Ignoring her reaction he went back to examining the room. *I must have been here for a while*, he concluded. The nurse returned with another woman. *A doctor by the look of her.*

"See, he is awake," the nurse said quietly, retrieving her lost clipboard.

"Can you hear me Mr. Ross? My name is Ari Ebonmore." Ari asked, examining his reaction.

Ross? He wondered. *The man in the jungle*, he remembered. He nodded at her question.

"This is Nurse Felicia Carlson," Ari said, indicating to the jumpy nurse from earlier.

"How?" his voice cracked.

"Felicia, water please," Ari said, sending the nurse away. "Take it slowly, you have been in a coma for over a month," she continued as she began to check his bandages to assess his condition.

The nurse returned with a pitcher of water and a glass. She brought the glass to his lips to help him drink. "Slowly," she told him.

"What do you remember Xavier?" Ari asked.

"Xavier?" he spoke. The two women passed looks of concern between them.

"Memory loss is not uncommon," Ari said kindly. "You were brought to the hospital after a battle in Canyamar. You had burns covering almost every part of your body. Several times we didn't think you were going to make but you did."

"I remember burning," Xavier said, pushing Felicia away.

"Slowly until we get a better idea of your condition," Ari said, placing his hand back. "These may help some." She grabbed a small box of items. "This is what you were wearing when you arrived here. It's not much."

He held up the identification tags from the box and read the name, Xavier Ross and an enlistment number. He sighed, dropping the tags back into the box.

"Give it some time," Ari assured him. "Now, if anything hurts too much or you can't move let me know." She took his arm and helped him lift it up. "Good, now open and close your hand. Any pain?"

Xavier shook his head. "It's numb, no feeling at all."

"There was a lot of nerve and tissue damage," she explained, moving to his legs.

"Mirror," he demanded, holding out his hand.

Ari looked at Felicia, nodded and continued her examination as Felicia left to bring him the mirror as requested. "Well, I am amazed that you are able to move everything," Ari concluded. "I had to get creative with your treatment."

"Here you are," Felicia said, handing him a small mirror.

Xavier looked at himself. His face was bandaged heavily on one side. "Remove them," he ordered, setting the mirror down on his chest.

Ari and Felicia looked at each other before they started to cut delicately at the bandages. Once they were removed he looked again at his face. Bright pink scars covered half of his face and up into his scalp. He was unrecognizable, even to himself. It was as if he had been made of wax and left to melt in the hot sun.

"It can be hard in the beginning," Ari consoled him as she watched him study his face in the mirror.

"When can I leave?" Xavier asked calmly, passing the mirror back to the nurse.

Ari frowned and shifted her weight on her feet. "You are in no condition to be leaving." Xavier's glare made her reconsider. "I will see about having you transferred to the recovery ward. It allows for access to the city park and market place."

Xavier's glare faded as he considered everything. *Rushing would only bring complications,* he reasoned. *They think I am dead and there is plenty of time, all the time in the world with The Eternal Gateway.* "Thank you."

Jessica Kelly quietly hummed to herself. Her kitchen had been kept busy with the addition of Amaya and Alyssa to the house. *Quite the handfuls, and totally the opposite of when Kail was a boy,* she smiled. The timer on the oven buzzed and she removed the freshly baked apple muffins. The farm still manned a stall at the city marketplace. Even though they did not rely on it for income anymore, it was nice to visit with people and stay busy. After placing another set of muffins into the oven, Mrs. Kelly looked out the window towards the barn.

Amaya and Alyssa were outside waiting. Royce was with them and was pulling the market cart out so they could clean and wash it. The first time her husband had to take the old cart to town after Kail had left, he bought a new one. *"How he put up with that piece of junk I will never know,"* she remembered her husband saying when he came home with it. Alyssa took to helping around the farm much more than her red headed sister Amaya. Not that there was a lot of work now that they had a dozen people working for them. Alyssa had marched over to point out the places that Royce had missed while Amaya was busying herself with the different flowers that had grown up along the edge of the barn. *So different, yet so alike*, Jessica smiled, wiping her hands on her apron.

"Amaya, what are you doing over there?" Royce called out, seeing her by herself next to the barn.

"Farming flowers," she answered without looking up.

"Ok. Are you going to have them ready for the market?" he asked her while Alyssa helped him rinse off part of the cart.

"Yup," came her simple reply.

Royce chuckled to himself and continued to wash the cart.

"Why don't you have an airship?" Alyssa asked. "This is small," she finished, giving the cart a disapproving look.

"Well, for one, airships are big and expensive."

"So?"

"I don't think the other people at the market would like it very much if we squashed their wares and food landing it," he said.

"Use that then," she said, pointing to one of the giant Hyperion tractors moving slowly through a distant field.

Royce considered it for a moment before answering. "Maybe, but it's still too big. It would run over everything once we got there."

Alyssa turned to give him a sour face.

Laughing he tussled her hair. "The market just isn't like that Alyssa. It's about getting to know your neighbors. Talking and meeting people. Finding out about all the things you didn't see or hear. Now maybe if we get this cart all cleaned up, you can steer the horses on the way to town." His words had the desired effect as she redoubled her effort to help clean the cart.

"Lunch time," they all heard Mrs. Kelly call to them from the back porch of the house.

Xavier sat on a metal bench just outside of the hospital. Bandages still wrapped his burned hand and his face. Some soldier who was also staying at the hospital had come to visit him a couple of times. The man apparently knew who Xavier Ross was and had spent several hours talking his ear off before the nurse had come by to tell him that he had problems remembering things. He had brought him several packs of cigarettes when the nurses and doctors weren't watching. He had to admit, they weren't as bad as he thought they were going to be. They took the edge off and helped focus his thoughts away from the parts that were missing. The challenges that were to come were going to require new ways of doing things. Old reliances had made him arrogant.

"I would think smoking would be the last thing you would want to do," a woman's voice said.

Looking to see who had spoken to him, he saw the nurse, Felicia, standing there. "Nurse Carlson, what do I owe this displeasure?"

"Your recovery is going well. We would like to see you get out a little bit more, perhaps actually making it to the park or the marketplace," she said, ignoring his attitude. When he didn't answer she continued. "You seemed eager to get out of the hospital when you woke up."

Xavier took a long drag from his cigarette and let the smoke drift out of his mouth. "I'm planning what I want to do next. A lot of loose ends need to be dealt with."

"Well this might help you decide," she said, pulling an envelope from her pocket and handing it to him. "It's from the military. If it's anything like the others that I have seen, it will be the start of your discharge."

Giving her a sour look he took the envelope.

Ari sat behind her desk at the hospital. Paperwork had piled up while she had helped with the emergency when the *Lotus* had arrived with wounded men. She was finally getting caught up now that most of the injured had either been treated, released, recovering at their homes or in the hospital. A light knock at the door broke her focus. "Enter," she said a bit harsher than she had intended.

Captain Bailon tentatively opened the door to enter. "If I am disturbing you, I can return later," he said.

"No, no," Ari said, standing and running her hands over her hair. "Just some minor paperwork is all."

Bailon looked at the pile of papers on her desk. "The unglamorous side of the profession that no one tells you about," he said.

She looked back to the paperwork and sighed. "Isn't that the truth," she laughed lightly. "So, what do I owe this pleasure?"

"I have some papers for a Mr. Xavier Ross. I understand that he is up and about now, and I wanted to deliver them in person."

"Yes, he woke up from his coma a few weeks ago. He has been moved to the recovery ward on the other side of the campus," she informed him.

Bailon nodded his head and hesitated for a moment.

"I could take you there if you like," Ari quickly added, seeing the opening he had provided her.

"I would appreciate the company." He smiled, holding the door for her.

"How has your command of the *Lotus* been?" Ari asked as they strolled through the hospital on their way to the recovery wing.

"About what I had expected. I have good people with me. Especially Cid," he answered. "Combat with airships can be quite scary."

"I can't imagine. They scare me, I don't ever want to fly on one of them."

"It's not unlike the Navy. One wrong hit or lucky shot and it could bring the whole ship down," he emphasized with his hand as a gun.

"That's horrible," she replied.

"Ari, have you ever considered marriage and starting a family?"

The sudden change in subject threw her for a loop. "I, I can't say that I have," she floundered.

"Why not?"

"Well, I went to school, then when Sarah left and I graduated I came back here to be with my father. Now the hospital... I guess I have been so busy that I never thought about it," she reasoned as they made their way across the courtyard.

"A career woman then."

"I guess you could say that. More like this is where events led me," she countered. "What about you Captain?"

"More now than I had in the past. I have a feeling that in this time of war, starting a family is the most irresponsible thing one could do. But each passing day I believe more and more that if it is important, then you make the time."

"I can see the merits of both of those philosophies," she said. Trying to raise children during a war would be very difficult. War has a way of reaching its hand to places where or when you least expect it.

"I don't want to wake up one morning when I am in my forties or fifties only to find that such opportunities have long past me by," he said.

"I'm not sure I can help you, these are all things I haven't thought through before."

Captain Bailon stopped as they neared the entrance to the recovery wing. "Actually Miss Ebonmore you can," he said nervously. "With your permission, I would like to enter into negotiations with you and your father for your hand in marriage."

Ari's ears were ringing as the blood rushed to her face as her mind raced to recover from what he had just asked her. "I'm sorry," she said.

Backpedaling his words almost immediately from her rejection, "I apologize Miss Ebonmore. I was unaware that you-,"

"No no, that's not it," she assured him. "You just caught me by surprise is all. Captain Bailon, I would like it very much," she said unable to contain her smile.

"Ahem," he cleared his throat doing the best he could to keep from grinning. "Thank you ma'am. I will speak to your father soon and I will write to you. Unfortunately duty calls," he finished by holding up the papers for Xavier Ross.

Now it was her turn to watch him flounder. "Of course Captain," she smiled. "I will leave you to your duty and await your letter," she finished, letting him escape the situation gracefully.

Excusing himself from her company, Captain Bailon continued into the recovery ward alone. A nurse at the front desk gave him Xavier's room number informing him that if he wasn't there to check the commons room or check outside facing the park and marketplace. He found Xavier outside sitting on a metal bench doing a good job of creating a pile of ash and cigarette butts. "Private Ross?"

Xavier eyed him up and down without answering, calculating him before going back to his own thoughts.

"On your feet Private," Bailon ordered.

Xavier slowly put his cigarette out before rising to his feet. "Something I can help you with... Captain," he finished after looking for Bailon's current rank.

"I hereby formally issue you a medical discharge," Bailon said, presenting the papers to Xavier. "Due to the nature of your injuries, they have been found to be primarily cosmetic, your benefits will continue at twenty percent. Sign and submit the discharge at the local garrison," he instructed, walking away.

Xavier didn't even bother to look inside the envelope that held the discharge papers. Sitting down on the bench, he lit another cigarette and used it to set the envelope on fire. He watched as the flame grew and consumed them.

Chapter 18

"You two are getting good at this," Royce complimented Amaya and Alyssa. The two girls had easily charmed their way into the hearts of everyone that stopped by to purchase food from the Kelly Farm market stand. "We might just have to buy a couple of new carts for each of you."

"Everybody likes food," Alyssa commented.

"Flowers," smiled Amaya.

"It's a powerful combination, I will say that much. I think it has more to do with two little girls who can't keep from smiling at everyone though," Royce said, turning to inventory the remainder of the produce. They were selling at the market three times a week now instead of once. Alyssa had taken charge of helping him sell the produce, and Amaya gave away ten flowers for each one she actually sold. He had to admit, the flowers brought in people, and they were dazzling. The whole area next to the barn had flowers growing on it. They seemed brighter, larger and lasted much longer once picked than any he had seen before. *She has a green thumb that's for sure.*

"At least one of your girls isn't trying to rob us Mr. Kelly," Mrs. Wilson said.

"Good afternoon Mrs. Wilson. How's the gout?" Royce asked with all sincerity.

"What's 'the gout'?" Alyssa asked while bagging Mrs. Wilson's order.

"Yes Mrs. Wilson, tell her what it is," Royce said with a smirk.

Mrs. Wilson's glare matched her retort. "It's the price for dealing with robbers like you my whole life," she grumped while slapping down a few coins then hesitated before kicking the leg of the cart.

"Steel is harder than wood," Royce mentioned, causing the older woman to frown.

Amaya gave Mrs. Wilson a puzzled look. "Don't kick the cart," she said while looking through her basket of flowers. Pulling out a daisy she smelled it and frowned putting it back. "This one," she said, settling on a purple phlox. She held it out to Mrs. Wilson.

Mrs. Wilson slowly took the gift Amaya was presenting. Looking back and forth between the twins she turned to Royce. "One of them has a real future," she said stiffly, marching away.

Royce shook his head. "The more things change, the more they stay the same."

Xavier Ross slowly made his way through the marketplace. Customers as well as merchants were keeping their eyes on him. The look of resentment he had wasn't helping his cause. Thinking back, he shouldn't have burned the discharge papers. Securing money had been more difficult than he had thought. It simply wasn't something he had to deal with in the past. After the hospital had kicked him out, he had been staying in the back alleys.

"I don't have any work for you," the fat merchant told him.

"How about a donation so I don't stand here all day scaring away your customers," he countered.

"How about I get the constable, and he makes you leave."

"He can't, because standing here isn't doing anything wrong and even if he does, it will be better than the last few days," Xavier sneered, holding out his hand.

Scowling the merchant handed over a few coins telling him to get away from his market stall.

Looking at the coins, Xavier added them to the rest he had managed to gather. *In a month I'll have enough to buy a train ticket out of this place*, he thought, meandering through the market again. Ice filled his veins and his breathing stopped when his eyes passed over her. A little, red headed, girl handing a purple flower to an old woman. When her black haired twin came into view, it confirmed it. Grabbing the first stranger in reach he pointed and asked, "Who, there, those two girls." The stranger looked at the girls from the Kelly farm and gave him a disgusted look and shrugged him off without answering. Again he couldn't get someone to tell him about the girls. Finally calming down he took note of the sign above the stall that read "Kelly Farm Produce," before leaving the market.

His mind was racing as he made his way randomly through Aldervale. *I'm going to need help*, he concluded. The possibilities that this presented were mind boggling. *Falconcrest's kids, here for the taking.* He saw the answer in the window of a nearby shop. A wanted sign that had Kail, Angela and Camden's faces on it as well as a list of other known terrorists. Twenty five thousand coins for their capture and up to five thousand for information leading to their arrest and prosecution. The money was meaningless to a point, but it would be motivation for others that needed it. Swiping the poster from the window, Xavier made his way to the garrison near the train station. The type of people he wanted would be there.

"Come now," Xavier said, sliding the reward poster forward. "You know the type of thugs I need. If I am right, we all win and if I'm wrong, well... It's a filthy job and no one would look past them to us."

"I might know a few people," said the broken man, sitting behind the desk at the recruitment office. "There's been a lot of wash outs and plenty of ex-military that would be happy to get their hands on something like this."

"These traitors and sympathizers don't need a trial, but don't give me psychopaths that don't have enough self control that they ruin this."

"Don't worry, I have a guy in mind and he's got some friends," the recruiter said, scribbling down a note. "Be here at midnight in four days," he finished, handing the note to Xavier.

Treylane Armstrong looked over the Kelly farm house. All of the lights were off as expected for this time of night. He and a small crew of three other men had received a tip regarding the terrorist that ran Silverton. Hyperion Industries put them on an airship and sent them straight to Aldervale. The information had to have been credible for them to send them as they had. He wasn't one to question an assignment, but there were certain things that crossed his mind as being odd. Hyperion seemed to have a curious infatuation with the outlaws that seemed counter to their business model that war was good for business. Next came the scarred man that accompanied them. Credible did not define this man, and lastly was the strange part of the order. *Act on any opportunities and deliver to a high security military research center in Courduff, eliminate all witnesses.* Standard enough but hand written at the end was the words, *Xavier Ross is in charge, do not eliminate, his death will be yours, give him anything he wants.* The man had friends in high places, but he clearly didn't seem to be aware of it.

"Arson will be best," Xavier whispered.

"Agreed, there are massive amounts of kerosene and exotics in the shops over there." Treylane pointed out.

"After we secure the two girls, we burn one shop and the home."

The group headed towards the farm house. Treylane nodded to one of his men to make for the shop. The lock on the back door of the Kelly's house was easy to pick. It was intimidating to look at, but the lock itself was so simplistic that it was useless. He reset the lock once the door was open as to not arouse any suspicions when the authorities came to investigate. Keeping to the edge of the stairs along the wall to avoid any noise, he made his way upstairs. The twins' room had the door open and a soft light glowed. Jerking his head, the other two men silently stepped inside. A loud snore came from the Kelly's bedroom further down the hall. He saw Xavier grin like he had just cheated the devil and escaped from hell.

The two of them stepped inside. Xavier took the initiative and went to the side of the bed with the wife. Treylane took the man's side of the bed. Royce's snore was cut short as he punctured the man's brain though his ear with his thin stiletto knife. Quick, bloodless and the man never made a noise. "Son of a bitch Xavier," he whispered harshly as he watched the man wake Jessica Kelly only to slice her throat open. The woman wasn't able to scream, but she thrashed around in panic as Xavier just watched with that grotesque melted grin. He hadn't cut any of the arteries in her neck so she was going to die by suffocation, a death that can take several minutes that they didn't have. The damage was done though and Treylane quickly put her out of her misery with a quick stab to the heart. "Do something stupid like that again, and you die next," he threatened.

"Don't threaten me pawn," Xavier said as the life faded from Jessica's eyes. "This game is beyond your station."

Alarms went off in his head. *This man knows exactly where he stands*, he corrected his assessment. He had never been afraid of anyone his entire life, but right here, right now, Xavier Ross scared him.

Wilhelm Bailon stood up from the small dinner table when Ari walked into the room. Her father had arranged for a modicum of privacy in the dining area of the Ebonmore Inn. "You look stunning Miss Ebonmore," he complimented her.

Suppressing her blush as much as she could, she took the chair he held out for her. "Thank you." Her black dress flowed like it was poured from liquid silk just for her. Light makeup accented her face, and her hair was curled up behind her ears to reveal her shoulders and slender neck. "You're looking quite debonair yourself Captain," she replied, giving him an approving glance.

"Please, call me Will," he said as he smiled and sat down after her.

"Will it is, if you call me Ari. Miss Ebonmore makes me sound ten years older," she said, bringing her hand to the back of her neck nervously.

"Some wine?" he asked, pulling a bottle of wine from a pail of ice.

"Yes please."

Removing the cork from the bottle he poured her a glass. "That is a curious necklace you are wearing," he said as he filled his own glass.

Ari quickly swallowed the bit of wine already in her mouth and looked down. "This? I had it made several years ago before I went to Courduff."

Will also felt the heat rise in his face and quickly swallowed some wine to cover it. The necklace rested on her chest and it made it difficult to not notice other things. "Before you left for studies correct?" he recovered.

"Yes, that's right. I found a large stone one night on the shore of the lake nearby while collecting moon moss. It stood out because it seemed to hold on to the light. If that makes any sense," she finished looking up. She caught him looking at her and she smiled. "The jeweler hadn't seen a stone like it before, and I remember him saying it was the worst thing he had ever worked with."

"It looks enchanting, but I think it's the woman that is making it shine," he complimented.

Ari smiled again. "He was able to make matching earrings and the rest of the stone was set into a bracelet," she said, sipping her wine.

Nodding he poured some more wine for her. "I hope you are hungry. Your father has fixed us, how did he put it? A visceral appeal that you can't help but fall in love with it."

Suppressing a chuckle Ari shook her head. "I see my father is doing his best to influence our date."

"Don't be too hard on him. It's a father's duty to look after his daughter," he said. The smile on his face faded when he noticed Cid enter the dining area. Staying on the far side of the room Cid nudged his head in the direction of the door. "I apologize Ari, but can you excuse me for a moment," he said, standing from the table before she had a chance to answer.

"Sure," she said curiously, watching him cross the room to talk to an officer.

"Sorry to interrupt your evening sir," Cid said, reaching for a paper under his jacket. Handing it to Captain Bailon he continued, "we received immediate orders to take the *Lotus* to Cahir. It seems the rebel group from Silverton is on their way there for some meeting with Vincent."

Bailon looked over the orders and muffled a curse while glancing back at Ari at the dinner table. "Get the *Lotus* flight ready, and I will be right there," he ordered and turned to break the bad news to Ari.

"She already is and sir," Cid stopped him, "there's more."

Bailon turned to listen.

"There is a fire crew and investigation team at the Kelly farm. We don't know if it was accidental or intentional, but the house and farm have been burned. The owners Royce and Jessica Kelly are dead. As you know the farm supplied most of the food for the military in this area."

Bailon closed his eyes and sighed. *There would be retaliation from Silverton for this*, Bailon knew. Only a handful of people knew the connection between the Kelly's and the most wanted man, Kail Falconcrest, who commanded Silverton. "Alright," he said turning.

"Sir," Cid stopped him.

"More?"

"Intelligence that crossed my desk at the same time talks about an override for a train leaving Aldervale to Courduff. An override that can only come from someone very high up. Also it listed the override was from Therion, as we know he is in Canyamar and none of these men matched his description. Also the report lists they had two female children with them. I recall you mentioning that the Kelly's had recently taken in some relatives, two girls."

"That's right, Miss Ebonmore knows the Kelly's well. Nieces if I remember right," Bailon said with a frown knowing where the conversation was going.

"The Kelly's bodies were found sir. But there is no report of children being found at the farm."

"Alright," Bailon said thinking. "Give me two minutes," he said, returning to Ari still sitting at the dinner table.

"It's alright Will. I know that look," she said, getting up from the table.

"I sincerely apologize, but the *Lotus* has been called away. We leave immediately," he said.

"I had a wonderful time."

"Thank you Ari. I will make it up to you next time," he finished by kissing her hand and then left with Cid.

That moment her father came into the dining room with two culinary masterpieces. "Where is the Captain?" he asked confused.

"Called away," she sighed. "Looks like it's the two of us for dinner tonight," she smiled.

Chapter 19

Vincent eyed the pair standing in his office. "Curious, you send a letter stating your intention to arrive in Cahir. And now that you are in my presence, you are dressed and armed for battle," he said.

"I think they want to play," Bastiana spoke.

"Why are you here? I do not believe that you are slow minded enough to think you can simply walk out of here." He watched as Kail and Angela exchanged looks.

"We're here for the bindings," Kail said. "The ones that you helped Therion tear out of me."

"I see. And what makes you believe that I have these bindings?" Vincent asked.

"We have it on good authority that you possess them," Kail answered.

"Do not evade my question."

Kail looked at Bastiana before answering. "The Guardian of The Eternal Gateway said you had them."

The smile slowly slid from Bastiana's face. "The Guardian is dead. I killed him," she said venomously.

"Maybe, but not yet for him you haven't," Kail countered.

Lust returned to her face. "I know that he is dead. I expected more from you two. Lies and more lies."

Vincent turned his eyes from Bastiana's outburst and focused back on Kail and Angela. "It seems plausible. The Eternal Gateway has returned. It's guardian has returned with it." Bastiana's eyes grew dark as she looked over her shoulder at him. Ignoring her he continued. "What do you want with the bindings? What is your purpose for them?"

Angela spoke first. "Our purpose is not your concern. You either have them, or you do not."

"She can talk." Bastiana smiled and slipped off of the desk.

Angela placed a hand on one of her war blades but eased off after a quick glare from Kail. "Step in range of my blade. I beg you."

Bastiana's shrill laugh filled the room. "Begging? You have taught her better than I ever imagined Kail. I didn't think she was capable of such training," she taunted while moving closer. "Trust me, I tried."

Ignoring the taunt Kail kept his eye on Angela. Her breathing had increased and a fight seemed likely to break out. "She will kill you Tiana," Kail stated. "She's right though," returning to Vincent, "you either have them or you don't."

"And what are you prepared to give for them?" Vincent asked.

"You will give them nothing!" Bastiana yelled, facing Vincent.

Ignoring Bastiana as if she were not in the room Vincent continued. "Well?"

"What do you want for them?" Kail asked, seeing that Angela was leaving her hand on the war blade now.

Vincent was losing patience. "You come here, desiring to repossess the bindings removed from you and you have nothing to offer for them. Yes, I have the bindings, but there is nothing you have that I want Kail Falconcrest," he finished, standing up from behind his desk.

"Therion," Kail said quickly to stop Vincent from leaving the room. "Give me the bindings and I will get rid of Therion."

"Now you are just insulting. Courduff and Cahir are allies," Vincent said as he made his way out of the office. "You have a few minutes before the authorities arrive to arrest you. I suggest you use them well."

Kail turned back to Bastiana and Angela.

"Play?" Bastiana asked with a smile.

The look in Bastiana's eyes made Kail bring his magic to the ready. "Don't start something Tiana," he said, hearing Angela remove her war blades.

Bastiana looked at them. "Look at the two of you. You're so cute and so clueless." When neither Kail nor Angela responded she continued. "Of course I am going to start something. Your coming here is a golden opportunity that can't be passed by."

Kail gave Angela a look and the two of them began to make their way out of Vincent's office while keeping Bastiana in front of them.

"Haven't you wondered why you are allowed to play in Silverton? With all the might that Cahir and Courduff command, that your pathetic little town is allowed to exist," Bastiana said, halting their cautious retreat.

Angela shook her head at Kail, not wanting him to rise to her bait.

"What are you going on about?" Kail asked.

"You're the excuse."

Angela continued to urge Kail. "Enough of this Kail, we leave or we fight."

"Excuse for what?" Kail wanted to know.

Bastiana matched each backward step. "Your existence is the excuse for our war. Rouge mages, terrorists, and outlaws. You are what everyone fears thus allowing us to control them in exchange for our protection."

"You're crazy. People are not that stupid," Kail countered.

"People are very stupid and even more stupid when they are frightened. When you and your friends attacked the old Mage Council tower all those years ago, you cemented yourselves in the hearts of everyone as the most evil people on the planet. Two airships firing cannons into the building trying to assassinate Therion," she said with a smile. "And you're little stunt down in Canyamar. Hundreds wounded or killed in an unprovoked attack and a second follow up attack in the middle of the night. With each failed assassination attempt on the benevolent ruler of Courduff the whole world fears you and your little band of outlaws Kail. The best part is they love us because of it."

"That's not what happened, and you know it," Kail hissed.

Bastiana let out a laugh. "No one cares what really happened." A look of mock regret slipped over her face. "Today is going to be but another tragedy for the world as well. Kail Falconcrest and his brutal wife, personally attack the upstanding citizens of Cahir."

The door to the elevator at the end of the hall opened with a ding. Glancing back, Kail saw several men exit and take up position against them. Angela turned to put her back against his to stare down the newcomers while Kail kept his eye on Bastiana.

Chapter 20

With a loud crack and flash of light Bastiana summoned her rune covered staff while advancing on him. He gave Angela a quick elbow in her back signaling her to leave to take care of the men who had gotten off the elevator behind them. He didn't try to say or reason any longer with the insane mage. Their focus must be on getting out of the tower alive. Bringing up his hands up he channeled his magic into his attack. A scalding bar of magical energy shot from his hands, racing towards Bastiana who stood grinning at him from Vincent's office.

Side stepping the attack, Bastiana let it fill the hallway in front of her and watched as Kail's attack destroyed Vincent's desk as it exploded out the back windows of the tower. Seeing that Kail's magic continued to shoot out over the city Bastiana let out a laugh. "Thank you Kail," she called to him. "You make it so easy sometimes."

Kail slapped his hands together causing the beam of energy to collapse into a thin blade of searing heat. He focused the magic to slice into the walls in the direction that Bastiana had leaped out of the way.

Bastiana saw the flattened magic quickly slice towards her as it cut through the wall. Ducking she centered herself and in a flash of blue magic, teleported under Kail's attack to the other side of the office. Rematerializing she threw ball after ball of magical energy back towards the doorway, curving in their flight to shoot down the hallway back at him.

Kail hadn't seen Bastiana teleport to the other side of the office and almost caught the full force of her attack. The first ball of energy forced him to abandon his assault as he brought up a barrier of magic around him. Still the concussive force of magic hitting him sent him slamming shoulder first into the wall of the hallway. His ears rang with the explosions around him as he scrambled to block the rest of her assault.

Angela sized up the five men who had stepped out of the elevator. Two of them were on their knees on either side of the hallway. All of them brought rifles up to bear on them. *Guns were the weapons of the weak and skill-less*, she thought. She heard a loud crack at the same time she felt Kail elbow her. She was not about to give them the chance to reload and fire twice. Sprinting down the hallway towards the men she waited until they had her in their sights. Seeing the first of them start to pull the trigger she angled the direction of her run and relied on her ability to fly to save her.

All of the shots had missed her as she ran up the wall and continued to run at them sideways. *Know your enemy*, she chastised them as they were caught dumbfounded by her ability to run on walls. Two of the men simply froze with wide eyes as she closed the distance. The others hurriedly tried to reload their guns. *No training beyond being shown how to point and shoot*, she could see. Leaping from the wall feet first she caught one of the standing men full in the chest sending him backwards off his feet. Spinning she brought each of her blades down before landing onto the two men who had been kneeling in the hallway. One of the other guards swung his rifle at her like a club. Blocking the man's attack with both blades, she shifted her hip to catch the remaining man with a side kick to the neck, collapsing his esophagus.

Forcing her war blades forward then downward she stabbed into the man who had tried to hit her with his gun cutting him down the middle as he collapsed dead on the floor. The man she had kicked in the throat thrashed around defenseless as she advanced on the first guard she had knocked down. Seeing the fear in his eyes as she advanced on him, she granted him no remorse other than to end his life quickly. Explosions rocked the far end of the hallway as she turned to see Kail and Bastiana. Slapping the button on the wall to call for the elevator she called out. "Finish it Kail."

Hearing Angela call his name, Kail glanced down the hallway to see her standing among the guards' bodies as the elevator door opened. Kail shot a blue ball of energy towards the office room where Bastiana was attacking. As soon as it reached the center of the room, he let it explode. Random tendrils of energy crisscrossed, filling the room with a web of chronomancy. Anyone touching the web would be held frozen in time until it dissipated. Sprinting down the hallway towards Angela he continued to channel the time stopping spell allowing it to fill the hallway behind him.

Bastiana recognized the characteristic color of time magic as Kail's attack shot into the room. Even with that warning, she was unable to get away as it struck the side of her leg before she could teleport, freezing her into place. If she had not been able to manipulate chronomancy she would have been captive until the spell faded, or Kail came in to kill her. Immediately she began to weave her own magic against his to free herself.

Kail grabbed Angela holding her close as he pulled the both of them into the elevator and hit the button for the lobby. "Stay close so if I need to teleport us," he told her, "this elevator is a deathtrap."

"We cannot leave without the bindings Kail. You heard what the Time Walker said."

"How about we survive this first and worry about the details later," he smiled. The elevator slowed and Kail quickly lifted a magical barrier in front of the elevator doors. "This isn't the lobby."

The elevator doors opened to reveal Vincent standing on the other side. "What?" was all Kail managed to get out before Vincent simply walked through the magical barrier as if it wasn't there. The act caught them by surprise and with the back of his hand Vincent caught Angela on the side of her jaw sending her to the floor of the elevator. Kail lashed out with a blast of magic to the center of his chest. The attack burned a hole in Vincent's shirt, but once it made contact with his skin it simply did nothing.

Vincent grabbed Kail by the throat then lifted him off of his feet, pinning him to the back of the elevator. Kail felt all of his magic simply vanish as if it had never been there. The man's strength was unreal for his build and age. Pulling a gun out Vincent pointed it at Angela. "If either of you move she dies, then you," he said calmly.

Kail struggled in Vincent's grasp, "What are you?" he managed to get out.

"Now there is a question worth asking. If you ever find your father, you can get the answer from him," Vincent said. "Stand up Keratin." He motioned with the gun.

Angela eyed the burned hole in Vincent's shirt and slowly got to her feet as she wiped a line of blood from her lip. Although she still had her war blades in her hands, she did not bring them to bear. "What do you want?" she asked with steel in her eyes.

"Step out of the elevator," Vincent demanded. He watched her comply before continuing. "The bindings are there on the table next to you," he said, watching her glance quickly to the side before meeting his gaze once again. Vincent tossed Kail like a toy into the hallway next to her.

"Now, this is my elevator, and I will not be taking the stairs," he said, pressing a button as the doors closed.

Kail felt numb all over. He could feel his magic slowly starting to return now that he was no longer in the man's grasp. "What the hell was that?" he said, rubbing his throat.

"An enemy we do not understand," Angela answered. Grabbing the bindings from the table she held them out to Kail. "Are these what he says they are?"

Kail could feel the bindings' ability to block magic as she presented them. Involuntarily he took a step backwards. "Yeah, that's got to be them. I think you should carry them though. They make me feel strange and smothered."

She nodded and stuffed the three rings of runes into a secure pocket of her vest. The building shook with the sound of a muffled explosion from somewhere above them. "That would be Bastiana if I had to guess," Kail said, looking upwards. "Let's get moving before this day gets any crazier."

Chapter 20a

Vincent stepped out of the elevator into the hallway leading to his office. Frowning at the dead bodies as he passed, he entered what was left of his office. First order of business was to replace the shirt that Kail had so rudely burned a hole in and then to the securing yardarm on the roof where the *Colossus* waited.

When she heard Vincent walk in, Bastiana stopped trying to divine where Kail and Angela were and opened her eyes. "Where are they?" she demanded.

"On their way to the lobby I would imagine," he answered, making his way to the wall that held the closet.

Bastiana frowned as she moved to where Vincent was changing his shirt. Seeing the burned hole she rounded on him. "You saw them, and you let them go, didn't you?" she accused. When he didn't deny it she stopped him. "There is more isn't there?" Grabbing his wrist she brought his hand to her nose and smelled it. "You gave them the bindings."

Vincent gave her hand a cold look where she had grabbed him. Knowing how his touch affected mages he frowned at her. "I did," he said as she let go of him. "And now they will rush back to Therion's waiting arms."

"You fool," Bastiana spat.

Vincent ignored her tantrum and continued to dress himself. "Fools do things without reasoning past the obvious. The bindings will give them something to pin their hopes on and blind them from the truth."

Bastiana turned to look out across the city of Cahir. The sky was filled with airships transporting materials to the Hyperion factories and passenger ships ferrying workers from the canyon mines. "Their ships are coming for them aren't they?" she said.

"I assume as much," Vincent said, surveying the state of destruction in his office. "I doubt they missed the show you two put on here."

"I will kill them."

"Understandable," he said, looking at the tattoos that covered her skin. As much as she now tried to flaunt them, they were still a source of deep inner pain for her. "Do not underestimate them my dear. They said it themselves that The Guardian had returned," he said to remind her of who it was that gave her the markings. "Now to maintain the illusion of an upstanding citizen, I have to meet them with the *Colossus*," he finished, stepping away from the closet.

Angela had returned her war blades to their sheaths, but held her bow at the ready as she followed Kail. So far everything seemed to be going in their favor as they searched for a stairwell or another elevator.

"I would have thought stairs would have been near the elevator or the edge of the building," Kail muttered as they half ran half walked the halls. People who worked in the building were starting to notice the armed pair. It was only a matter of time before they alerted the guards.

"It would not be a surprise if they are setting a trap for us now. Vincent was the one who stopped us on this level of the building," Angela said.

Her words put voice to some of the thoughts in his head as he nodded. "Let's try over here," he said, pointing towards a new hallway as a pair of shocked employees pressed themselves against the walls as they passed.

Quickly the two made their way into the hallway. Kail gave a start when from behind Angela let an arrow fly past his head. Before he could say anything the body of a dead guard slid into the hallway from a nearby room.

"I saw him spying on us through the door," Angela answered Kail's startled look. "His gun was sticking out." Instantly Angela let another arrow fly as gunfire filled the hallway.

Kail wrapped himself with protective magic as he pulled Angela into the room where she had killed the first guard. The barrage of gunshots made it hard to think straight as bits of wall shattered by bullets sprayed around them, magnifying the danger of the situation.

"Arrow!" Angela shouted as she pointed at the dead guard. Kail gave her a confused look, but at her insistence he reached over to pull the dead man into the room with them. Angela pulled the arrow from the body, wiped off the end and gave it a nod. "I'm going to need more than I brought. It is still good for another kill." Kail understood.

A lull in the gunfire told him the guards in the hallway were probably reloading. "Let's move." Peeking into the hallway he was greeted with another volley of gunfire. He wasn't the only one who had dared to peek into the hall. Several employees were sent back screaming into their rooms. Nodding to Angela he quickly stepped into the hallway, sending several blasts of magic towards the attackers.

Angela was right on his heels. Several places in the hall were smoky from gunfire, and the floor was littered with debris. Kail's attack had worked. They made it several doors down before bullets started flying again. "Behind," Angela called out as a group of guards filled the hallway where they had just been a few moments ago. Two of the guards fell to her arrows before they had a chance to bring up their guns.

Kail rammed the door forcing it open causing them to fall into the room. Three women shrieked as the gunfire pierced the frame of the door and walls around them. A door on the opposite side of the hall was jerked open by a guard who had been hiding in the room to fire a quick shot at them. It missed Kail and Angela, but one of the other women in the room was not so lucky. The screams renewed as Angela put an arrow into the man at the same time Kail sent a bar of energy into his chest. His dead body fell into the doorway.

Kail wrapped his magic around the man to pull his body into the room, removed the arrow and tossed it over to Angela.

Angela wiped off some of the blood then snapped the tip off easily with her thumb. She shook her head as she discarded the broken arrow. She saw Kail look towards the wounded woman. Again she shook her head, telling him they could not spare the time.

Angela was right, Kail thought. *We don't have time to worry about anyone else.* "Stairs," he yelled at the women. His words were of no use as they were beyond reason with shock. Shaking his head he let a dozen balls of magic float out of the room to shoot down each direction of the hallway. After the magic exploded they tried to make a run for it, but as soon as he stepped into the hall, several bullets impacted the magical shield he held around him. Shoving Angela back into the room he continued across the hall to where the guard had tried to surprise them.

The hallway now separated them, and Angela was yelling at him over the gunfire. Pointing to the floor he heard her shout, "Down." Waving her out of the way he focused his magic and sent a wide blast of energy into her room that burned a hole through the floor. As soon as he finished, he saw her step into it and disappear. Quickly cutting one for himself he also descended to the floor below them.

Landing in the room below brought startled cries and frightened looks from people who were already scared from the noise of the fight that had gone on above them. Angela was already in the hallway shooting arrows. Stepping into the hall to join her, he could see several dead guards on the floor and several more guards trying to set up a position around the corner. "They weren't expecting us to go through the floor," he said. Angela didn't answer him while keeping the guards pinned down. Glancing at the terrified people in the room he remembered the woman from the floor above that had been shot, a clammy chill filled his stomach. Bastiana's taunt, *"You're what everyone fears,"* echoed in his mind.

"We have what we came for. Get us out of here," Angela shouted as she shot another guard with an arrow.

Kail couldn't agree more. Stepping up behind her he grabbed her and focused his magic on them to teleport away. An uneasy feeling crept in and in a flash Kail found himself tumbling backwards outside onto the street as he rematerialized. "Angela? Angela!" he called out. When she didn't answer him, "the bindings..." Kail cursed.

Angela heard the snap and saw the flash as Kail teleported away behind her. When she was not pulled along with him, the first slivers of fear started to creep into her consciousness. She suspected the bindings she carried had prevented him from taking her with him. Years of training took over. There was nothing she could do about it now except push everything aside and concentrate on surviving. Sighting down the bow she let another arrow loose. At the same time she caught sight of another guard dropping down from the floor above into the room next to her. Without breaking her motion she gripped one of the knives from her wrist and sent it flying at the new guard while grabbing another arrow, pulling it back, and letting it fly into a second man dropping from the hole. Spinning in the other direction, Angela took off at a dead run as more guards arrived on this floor of the tower.

The elevator shaft was her only hope for escape she reasoned. The hallways were clear now that the people working in the building were keeping their heads down or had already fled. When the elevator doors came into view she slid one of the runed war blades into the seam and forced the door open. The elevator was not there and a quick glance showed it to be several floors above her. Stepping into the shaft she let herself float before turning back to shut the elevator door. *It wouldn't fool a real enemy*, she thought, *but it might just buy me a few extra moments.* She quickly dropped through the air.

Kail felt rage starting to build. He had trouble finding the correct floor when he teleported back inside the building. He had tried to use divination to find Angela, but was unsuccessful. Again he suspected the bindings to be the culprit. It also explained why Bastiana hadn't shown up once she was free from his spell. He had been expecting her to attack at any moment, but when it didn't happen he figured she couldn't find them. Regardless the building was full of guards and soldiers. Vincent and Bastiana had no intention of letting them leave, even though Vincent did give them the bindings. Without Angela he was getting reckless, but he didn't care. Life without her would be empty. Both of his arms were giving off fumes of magic as he searched floor after floor. Anyone that got in his path didn't stand a chance. His magic protected him from anything they could do, and they were helpless against him.

Angela quietly crept into the lobby of the Hyperion Tower. All of her instincts told her it should be full of guards or soldiers, but it was not. Just as when she and Kail had arrived, the lobby was empty. She had known that Bastiana and Vincent were arrogant, but the amount of planning to have the building filled with soldiers to stop them had her doubting that they would leave an easy exit for them.

Sticking to the edge of the lobby and pausing behind the marble columns, she made her way to the front entrance. A peek around the second to last column however revealed the worst possible outcome. Bastiana was there waiting. Angela was still undetected as the insane woman had not seen her. Bastiana's eyes were closed. Angela had a chance, if Bastiana was trying to divine her location, she might get off a shot and put an end a to great threat once and for all. Angela cleared her thoughts and settled her heart. If there ever was a chance of missing, this would not be the time to do it.

Spinning around the base of the column she took aim and almost let the arrow fly. Bastiana was not there. Coldness gripped her stomach as she caught movement to her left. Dropping to one knee as she fell to her back she brought her aim around at the same moment as Bastiana brought her rune covered staff around to hit her. The arrow missed, and Angela caught Bastiana's blow hard on the shoulder. The magic that flowed through the staff ricocheted off her sending her sliding across the polished floor with a grunt.

"Found you," Bastiana chimed.

Angela quickly pushed herself up off of the floor. The Imaera hide armor had done its job of softening the blow. The bindings may have helped too, because it should have been much, much worse. She was still outmatched, but it wouldn't be completely one sided. "A great man once said, 'Never catch something you cannot kill,'" Angela taunted.

"Ooh, I like that."

Angela pulled each of her twin war blades from their sheaths. The silvery runes of indestructibility shone in the light. They reminded her of her twin daughters Alyssa and Amaya as she squared off with Bastiana. *If there ever was a time for a rescue Kail, now would be it,* she thought.

Angela sprinted towards Bastiana with both blades. The grin on the psychotic woman's face only reinforced her resolve to end this feud. Reversing her grip on one of the war blades she brought it up to catch the rune staff as Bastiana swung it at her. Ancient magics collided between the artifacts as Angela leapt up and around the mage. The angle left her free to stab downward with her other blade. Bastiana's quick movements blurred her body. It was all Angela could do to bring the blade back to a blocking position as the staff came around from an impossible angle.

Gravity did not hold Angela to the same standards as everything else. Using the momentum of the staff to help her she flew tightly around the column to catch Bastiana in the back with a hard kick from both feet. She heard the mage's surprised cry as Bastiana was sent sprawling onto the floor. Pressing the advantage, Angela came down from above to stab her. Like before Bastiana teleported away as Angela's missed attack sent cracks through the marble floor from where her blades had came down.

Blinking herself back into existence, Bastiana brought the rune staff down trying to catch Angela across the back, but the red headed Keratin was quick to roll out of the way. Still the magical blast that erupted from the staff meeting the floor sent Angela tumbling through the air. Bastiana watched and timed her next attack precisely.

Angela fought to control herself in the air and landed lightly on her feet facing Bastiana. An instant later a red bar of magical energy slammed into her. Luck had been on her side when she instinctively had both war blades in front of her as the magic hit. Protected by the blades that would never break, the magic resistant Imaera hide armor, and the binding runes she carried, the magic hit her with about the force of a hard kick. *A very hot kick.*

Anger and rage crawled across Bastiana's face when her attack failed. "You did not think we would walk into the lion's den unprepared did you?" Angela bluffed.

"What is this trickery?" Bastiana shouted.

"That's my wife," an angry voice answered.

Bastiana and Angela turned to see Kail approach. A scream of rage came from Bastiana as she channeled her magic against him. Kail met her attack with one of his own. The colliding magic shook the foundation of the building. Unfazed, Kail continued to advance on her. Knowing this wasn't a fight she could win, Bastiana sent a slicing blast of magic through the building that severed the majority of the support columns. "Die together," she spat, teleporting away.

"My heart sings at your sight," Angela said to him.

"Let's sing when we're out of here," he replied with a grin. Grabbing her as the ceiling crumbled above them they ran for the exit, not risking teleportation again with the binding runes.

Chapter 20b

Camden slowly rose from the command chair of the *Snow Break* as a line of magical energy exploded out the back of the tower and shot across the city where Kail and Angela had traveled to recover the bindings that Therion had melted out of Kail's skin. "Not exactly a subtle signal," he said to no one in particular. He looked to the communications officer and nodded. He could hear the officer relay the order to the *Odyssey* that hovered in the sky next to them.

"I hope they are ok," Suki said as the airship started to move forward. "This doesn't bode well that they were able to get the bindings."

"They better have gotten them before all this. It's going to be bad enough getting out of here, but worse if it was all for nothing. Harold, keep an eye out on this traffic. Last thing we need is to collide with some freight hauling blimp."

"Aye sir, eyes out," Harold joked as the *Snow Break* picked up speed.

The *Odyssey* fell in behind them. They had been watching the *Colossus* all afternoon in the distance as it floated moored to the top of the building. No other warships had been spotted, but that didn't mean they were not out there. *Maybe luck will be with us and I'll get to knock it from the sky*, Camden thought.

The radio clicked off and Rhonin gave the order for the *Odyssey* to move forward. "Let her get a head of us and fall in behind."

"Yes sir." Brom Carter confirmed from the helm.

"Ready for this?" Rhonin asked his wife.

"No, but what choice is there," Rayne answered.

Rhonin hit the intercom button. "Everyone man your stations," he announced to the crew. "Be ready for combat when the signal is given," he finished, clicking off the feed.

Rayne surveyed the busy sky above Cahir. A line of luxury sky-ships glinted on the horizon as the massive lines of rail track spread out on the ground below them. Everywhere she looked there was movement. Trains paralleling each other and freighters carrying materials to the clockwork factories that churned out everything from airships, weapons, whatever their designers could program them to do. "The city itself has become a giant machine," she stated.

"What?" Rhonin asked.

"All these moving pieces, instead of gears and steam, it is people supplying the energy."

Vincent stepped onto the bridge of the *Colossus*. The crew had been readying for several days by running drills. When your enemy tells you when they are coming to visit, it changes the dynamics of battle. "Release the moorings and bring us level with the traffic lanes," he ordered.

"Sir, two enemy airships are on approach," an officer reported.

"That would be the *Snow Break* and *Odyssey*," Vincent replied.

"Confirmed sir."

"Switch to battle stations and order Alpha Squad to the outer deck."

"Aye sir."

"Tell the gunners to use a two one proximity firing solution," Vincent continued. Every third shell was a fuse-less round with the potential to cause heavy damage on the ground if it misses its target. *Damage that can be blamed on the Silverton terrorists and their unprovoked attack on Cahir*, he mused.

"Cannon decks confirm a two to one firing solution, sir."

Vincent stood watching as soldiers manned the outer deck of the *Colossus*. Two against one were not the best of odds, but the *Colossus* was no ordinary factory made airship. The near limitless power output of the rune furnace at the heart of the ship allowed for speeds that were unmatched. Reports had come in about refits done on the *Snow Break*, but they gave him no concern as the *Colossus* had the very best available from Hyperion Industries.

"Sir."

"I see it," Camden answered as the *Colossus* rose above the tower. "Suki, I think you better get below to the infirmary. We don't know what condition Kail or Angela might be in when they arrive," he said, looking back at the *Colossus* as it positioned for a fight. "We're going to have wounded of our own," he finished softly.

The hardened resolve mask that Suki had come to hide behind slid over her face. "Keep us in the air, and I'll keep the crew together," she said while leaving the bridge.

"Hang on!" Harold yelled as the *Snow Break* jerked hard to starboard nearly rolling the ship onto its side. Ground fire from anti-air cannons lanced into the sky towards the ship passing through the air where they had just been.

"Close one there," Rhonin's voice crackled over the radio.

Too close, Camden thought. "Bring us higher. It should give us better distance against those ground guns." Flashes erupted along the length of the *Colossus* as they closed the distance. Camden hit the incoming fire warning light to let the crew know that at any moment things could get bumpy. "Give us a firing angle," Camden ordered.

Without answering, Harold brought the ship up as he angled their approach towards the *Colossus*.

"Take us in the other direction," Rhonin ordered when the *Snow Break* pulled away.

"Aye sir," Brom confirmed.

The *Odyssey* began to shake as explosions from ground fire, and the *Colossus* reached them. Shrapnel from missed shells and flak bounced off of the hull but scored no direct hits. "Keep us as steady as you can," Rhonin reassured.

Camden cursed as a series of sharp impacts traced down the hull of the *Snow Break*. "Careful," he called out. Quickly glancing at the indicator board every light was still green. No crew had reported any injuries or damage; yet.

"*Odyssey* is breaking to port sir," an officer reported.

Camden hovered his hand over the firing light for a few more agonizing moments. "Fire!" he called out, pressing the button on his chair.

Suki not only heard but felt the *Snow Break* fire its main cannons in quick succession. The repeater guns never let up their fire as she felt the deck floor tilt as the ship turned.

"Hold," Rhonin ordered as the *Snow Break* opened fire at the *Colossus*. The *Odyssey's* range was not that of the *Snow Break*. The bridge crew watched as the two ships fired upon each other. The *Colossus* was at a disadvantage by remaining stationary, but it had less to worry about from stray ground fire than they did. "Fire at will," he ordered as the sounds of the cannons echoed through to the bridge.

"Release counter measures," Vincent ordered. The incoming fire from the *Snow Break* and *Odyssey* wasn't enough to threaten them. Small cannon fire came from every direction of the *Colossus*. Charges detonated magnesium sand filled payloads as a ring of white fire erupted around the *Colossus*. Almost all of the heavy cannon fire from the Silverton terrorists' ships detonated at a harmless distance from them. The smaller gun fire punched through causing little damage. Vincent smiled at the effectiveness of the invention. "Helm, bring us around and start pursuing the *Snow Break*. Let the gunners know they can fire at their leisure," he finished, settling into his captain's chair.

"She's moving," Harold called out as most of the *Snow Break's* attack was neutralized.

"Where are they?" Camden asked frustrated, about Kail and Angela. The situation had moved from insane at best to flat out idiotic when the *Colossus* simply rendered their attack harmless. Camden watched as a blue streak of energy shot into the sky and impacted the bottom of the *Colossus*. "Get us out of here, go now!" he ordered. "If that's the magic of Vincent's crazed girl then we're all done for without Kail."

Harold heard stories and had witnessed firsthand at The Eternal Gateway how battles change in an instant when mages get involved. Remembering the final moments of the

Wind Runner before it was annihilated, he didn't need to be told twice to run. The whine of the *Snow Break's* turbines screamed as he pushed the power to the limit.

Camden felt his stomach drop as the ship lunged forward. What made him hold tighter was the top of the Hyperion Tower sinking away from them. It was like the ground opened up deciding the building shouldn't be there anymore. Quickly the top of the tower disappeared into a cloud of dust and debris as it collapsed.

Rayne's sudden intake of breath that she had been holding seemed to bring everyone on the *Odyssey* to their senses. The tower's collapse was out of place for any part of the recent engagement. "I think they have the right idea," she said, pointing to the *Snow Break* as it picked up speed.

Rhonin didn't argue. "Take us out away from the *Snow Break*, they can't follow us both."

Brom nodded his head quickly.

Bastiana materialized on the bridge of the *Colossus*. The look on her face spoke volumes, and Vincent didn't even bother to ask. It was all he could do to keep his fury in check as he watched the tower fall. "Destroy them," he ordered.

Chapter 20c

The sound of the empty train car's rhythmic clacking made it hard to talk. Escaping from the tower on foot had not been difficult for Kail and Angela. The collapse of the tower had provided excellent cover. They were not the only ones who had been in the crowds running away from the scene.

"That's something new," Kail said, referring to the recent events. "We need to signal them."

"Agreed. Events are out of control," Angela answered, resting against the side of the car. "But we have the bindings."

"How are you doing? That was quite the blast you took from Bastiana back there."

Angela examined the war blades. Their condition was still pristine. "Luck and being prepared," she answered, rubbing the Imaera hide vest.

Kail looked away as he stood at open door of the train car watching the *Snow Break* and *Odyssey* battling the *Colossus*. Raising his hand he let a bright ball of red magical energy launch into the sky. "The bindings are a bit of a problem."

Angela got to her feet to take Kail's hand in hers and gave it a squeeze. She didn't have to express her thanks or feelings with words for showing up in the lobby. "Maybe, but they helped as much as hindered."

Bastiana watched the magical signal float skyward. "Taunting me now are you?" she hissed.

"Signaling their allies for a retreat," Vincent said. "Redeem yourself and finish them Bastiana."

Anger filled her. Vincent only on rare occasions called her by her name and even less often ordered her to do something. It had been a long time since she had his disapproval, and she had forgotten what it felt like. She was *darling*, to him. Not Bastiana. She responded with a feral growl as she teleported away.

"Go!" Kail shouted when they saw the magical trail of Bastiana teleporting towards them.

Angela gripped the top of the doorway to swing herself onto the top of the rail car. Eight lanes of train tracks paralleled them. The wind whipped and threatened to blow them away whenever another train traveling in the opposite direction raced past. Kail appeared next to her gesturing towards the front of the train, and she started running. At each boxcar junction she easily used her powers of flight to glide over the gap.

Kail turned back and fired three small blasts of magic in the direction of Bastiana hoping to get her attention before teleporting several tracks over to another train.

Bastiana flashed back into existence on top of the train leaving a deep dent lined with scorch marks. She had seen Kail's feeble attempts to distract her, but the focus of her wrath was in front of her running away. Still, she sent looping balls of destructive energy in his direction before she started running after the woman who could fly.

Kail escaped the explosion by teleporting further down the train. Rematerializing inside a passenger car he was knocked off his feet as the rest of the train impacted the damaged section in front of it. Startled shouts filled the car as people were tossed forward with more than one of them landing on top of him. Tearing metal and screeching overwhelmed everything else when bodies started to fly about the car as it left the tracks.

Turning Angela saw a train derail behind her. Bastiana was following her along the top of the train. She did not see Kail anywhere. She knew that she would not be able to outrun her and that the mage was simply toying with her. Pulling the war blades from their sheaths she turned to face Bastiana and waited.

Bastiana couldn't help but smile when the red head caught sight of her and posed for battle. Closing the distance she finally stood on the same train car with Angela. "Round two?" she shouted over the noise of the trains and wind. Her rune staff materialized with a flash in her hands, leaving a trail of magical particles behind her.

Angela's answer was to raise the war blades.

Bastiana charged Angela bringing the rune staff around towards her knees. Angela sent the staff back with a swipe of her blade then blocked the follow up that came at her head. Seeing a hole, Angela spun through the opening to come around behind Bastiana.

Bastiana was faster as she caught Angela across the shoulders sending her tumbling across the top of the rail car. Bastiana delighted at the sight of her foe going down.

Angela recovered quickly making a quick leg sweep that sent the mage landing hard on her back and was rewarded with a cry of surprise. Using the momentum of her attack, she rolled backwards landing on her feet at the same time Bastiana picked up herself. This time Angela pressed the attack by bringing her blades around on top of Bastiana.

Bastiana was driven back by the flurry of blows from Angela's twin swords. Catching sight of the edge of the train car she quickly teleported the short distance across the gap and raised her hand to fire a blast of magic at the red head.

Angela brought her blades up to take the brunt of the attack. Still it was enough force to send her off of her feet, tumbling across the top of the train car.

Bastiana hopped back as Angela tumbled off the back between the two cars. "Too easy," she smiled and peered over the edge where Angela had fallen. Bastiana screamed in pain as two blades sliced across her back bringing her to her knees.

Angela had flown around the edge of the train car coming up behind the mage. Bright light flared across the wounds she had created as the cuts were sealed by the protective magic of the rune staff.

Bastiana blindly swung the staff behind her forcing Angela back. "I will skin you alive," she screamed, advancing on her.

Angela quickly stepped inside the wild attack to lock her arm and blade around the staff while securing the grapple with her other arm. Bastiana's spit landed on her face as the two fought each other for possession of the staff. Pulling the crazed mage around, Angela backed her up against the edge of the train car. She was stronger than the mage and more agile. The look of horror was satisfying when she brought her foot up between them and shoved. The rune staff went sailing into the air behind her as Bastiana was sent flailing off the train. Angela winced when she saw the mage hit the ground in a cloud of dust. Without the staff she hoped the mage would stay down this time.

Dropping to her knees on top of the train car, she took the moment to catch her breath. "Come on Kail," she whispered.

Kail regained consciousness to the noise of crying passengers and dust filled confusion. All limbs seemed to be still attached and unbroken although sore including some deep scratches. Exiting through a broken window, he crawled on top of the wreckage where in the far distance he caught the silhouette of someone on top of a train. Taking a deep breath, he teleported.

Angela stopped to bring her blades around in hearing the familiar snap and discharge of someone teleporting. Relief ran through her when she saw that it was Kail and not Bastiana.

Kail smiled. "We need to move," he said as the pair started to run up the train.

Chapter 20d

"Hang on!" Harold yelled, turning the *Snow Break* almost on its side. A slow ore hauler traveling deeper into the city tried to avoid a collision by turning away from them as Harold brought the nimble airship around. The slower dirigible had been built for one purpose, performing evasive maneuvers was not it. Its only defense was to sound warning klaxons. Harold managed to avoid a direct collision with the hauler, but the wash of the *Snow Break's* turbines sent it out of its traffic lane drifting towards other ships.

Camden gave Harold a sideways glance and a small shake of his head after the near miss. "Too close," he said. As much as he hated it, the heavy traffic in Cahir was going to be there best defense. "Keep around the traffic lanes to keep them from getting a clear shot!" Camden slammed his hand on a button on the console to let the rest of the crew know to expect more heavy evasive maneuvers and to secure themselves. "If you get a shot, take it," he ordered into the ship's intercom.

The *Odyssey* was faring only a little better. Rhonin hissed through his teeth as Brom Carter directed the ship in a twisting pattern through the heavy traffic away from the fallen tower and the *Colossus*. The *Odyssey* protested as the drive fans were forced back and forth to keep them from smashing into other airships.

"They are going after the *Snow Break*." Rayne pointed at the *Colossus*.

"Bring us around behind," Rhonin ordered as he held on tighter.

"Trying sir," Brom grunted as he maneuvered the *Odyssey* through oncoming air traffic.

"There!" Rayne shouted with excitement as she spotted a red magical flare launched from the train system below. "They are alive."

Rhonin frowned at Kail's signal. Everything was getting out of control, but destiny at least had the *Snow Break* headed in the same direction as the trains. "Keep an eye on the ground for them," he said. He hoped that his friends had managed to secure the bindings.

Vincent watched the *Snow Break* avoid a mid air collision. *What an unsatisfying end that would have been,* he thought. The rumors had been true about the refit of the *Snow Break*. Any other ship would be a burning wreck of twisted metal having tried the same maneuver. "Pursue them and give us a firing solution." He made a mental note to increase the funding for espionage. The decades of research and development by Hyperion Industries shouldn't be supplanted by the enemy.

"Aye sir," the helmsman replied, increasing the speed of the *Colossus*.

Bastiana seems to have found her prey, he thought when one of the trains derailed in the distance. She would blame the tower's collapse on them, but he knew better. It was one thing to hide the bodies of the people she killed when she was younger to avoid his displeasure. Her emotional control had matured over the years as had her tastes. However the loss of the tower was not as forgivable. The collection of artifacts that had been held there were irreplaceable.

"Whoa, whoa, whoa," Rhonin shouted as the *Odyssey* came about only to find a large ore hauling dirigible plowing its way through traffic, barreling right down at them.

Two smaller airships were already tumbling out of the sky after colliding with the massive ship, their wreckage adding to the chaos on the ground. Brom managed to avoid colliding with the hauler. Crew from both ships could see each other as the *Odyssey* passed by only a dozen feet away.

"We've got more trouble," Rayne said, looking through binoculars. "There is a warship approaching. Looks like it wants to try to cut off the *Snow Break*," she finished, pointing in the direction of the *Snow Break*.

"Make for that ship," Rhonin ordered.

"Aye sir," Brom acknowledged, turning the ship. "It's going to be a minute, that freighter cut us off."

"Incoming fire!" Camden yelled as the new airship angled in on its attack run. Unlike the *Colossus*, the captain of this ship was not willing to use the larger cannons over the city. Tracer fire from two high caliber repeater guns raced towards them.

Harold brought the *Snow Break* into an evasive climb causing the ship to buck and vibrate with the power of the new turbine engines. The streaks of enemy fire passed missing the ship. Nevertheless, the gunners on the new ship were doing a good job adjusting and kept the *Snow Break* in their crossfire. Harold had ideas of his own as he twisted the ship around providing their own cannon crew a full broadside attack.

Camden smiled as the familiar ear splitting cracks of the ship's cannons opened fire on the new vessel. Explosions filled the sky as the *Snow Break's* cannon fire detonated around the enemy ship. The warship broke off its attack as it retreated with several sections of its hull billowing black smoke. "Fuel fire, she's going down," Camden said as the crew cheered watching the crippled warship loose altitude.

Pathetic, Vincent thought as the Cahir defense ship did nothing but let itself be shot from the sky. *The least its captain could have accomplished was delaying them.* The billowing ship convulsed once before the rest of the burning fuel ignited. The ship exploded, raining debris and fire on the city below them.

Chapter 20e

Kail stopped to watch as the Cahir warship crashed out of sight in the landscape of the city. Black smoke billowed into the sky as the fuel continued to burn as well as catch surrounding buildings on fire. The trains Angela and he were crossing were beginning to pick up speed as they approached the outer edges of the city. The wind buffeting against them was starting to become a problem. Once Angela had moved the bindings away from him the nagging sense of danger filled him. Again he had to yell her name several times before she heard him. He furiously pointed to one of the trains paralleling them.

Angela nodded in understanding and leaped from one train to the other with her ability to fly. She looked back to see that Kail wanted her to move one more train over so she glided the distance to the next train. She followed his next signal to continue up the length of the train but this time from the inside.

Once Kail saw Angela disappear inside the train he turned his attention back towards the city behind him. Bastiana was coming, and he readied himself for her arrival.

Bastiana didn't bother to dust herself off. Her magic had kept her from becoming a broken ball of meat and bone when the red headed freak had knocked her off the top of the train. Her dress was frayed, filthy and torn in a dozen places, and her black and silver hair whipped wildly around her face from the wind of the passing trains. She could feel the fresh tattoos from the rune staff tingle across her back where it had protected her from what would have been a fatal blow.

She teleported to the top of the noisy train, and in the far distance she could see Kail smugly waiting for her. Her fury began to build as it bled into her magic. Wild magic began to arch and jump from her onto the train leaving lines of melted metal in its roof.

Kail watched with apprehension as Bastiana gathered more and more magical energy around her. The air surrounding her began to crackle and distort. Showers of sparks were beginning to flake off of the train where the uncontrolled magic discharged. He recalled stories Angela had told of one of her first encounters with the mage all those years ago aboard the *Colossus*. He wasn't going to be so lucky as to get away without a fight.

"Do not look at me!" Bastiana yelled into the wind. Bastiana's scream turned into a guttural growl as she blinked out of existence crushing the top of the train car in her wake.

Kail's eyes were wide with disbelief. He reacted quickly as Bastiana teleported the distance between them. She reappeared in front of him tossing out blasts of magic, one after another. He was thankful for the protective Imaera hide armor that he wore, as it took the first attack leaving only a burned welt. Using chronomancy he went into a chaotic dance as he blocked and parried her magic with his own.

Bastiana's face was fanatical as she laughed, sending another handful of magical balls spinning towards Kail.

His body was a blur as he countered her attack, catching some of the balls and deflecting others, causing them to sail into the sky or explode around them. He couldn't keep up with her assault and was forced to retreat backing along the roof of the train as it fled the city. *Too much, too fast*, he thought trying to get in a moment of concentration to focus on his own offense. Kail spun out of the way of a ball of magical energy as it sizzled by just inches from his head. Losing his balance he landed on his back, tumbling across the top of the train.

Bastiana leapt forward to land in front of him. "You will never win," she promised, bringing her hands to bear.

Kail's own magic flared to teleport him down the train just as her attack blasted through the roof of the train where he had just been. The train car bucked but managed to stay on its track even though the explosion of energy caused the sides to be blown out of the car. Kail managed to get to his feet as Bastiana slowly turn to look at him over her shoulder. *Running would be a good option right now*, he concluded.

Kail took off down the length of the train. He caught a glimpse of her attack through the magic of divination only a split second before it happened. Diving low, he caught Bastiana just below the waist as she teleported in front of him, diverting the blast of destructive magic over his head. The physical attack caught her off guard and when he slammed her down, was rewarded with a satisfying cry of alarm.

Bastiana didn't relent, but Kail was faster. Pressing her down he wove a shield of magic that held her tightly against the roof of the train. He traced a holding rune to keep the shield in place so he would not have to sustain it. Hopefully it would keep her there for a while.

"I will melt the skin from your body!" she cursed at him. Her magic shoved against the shield, but it held.

Kail sighed exhausted, "I'm getting sick of this."

"Finish it now," she taunted. "I will make you watch her die."

Kail left her and her screaming rants behind him. Crossing the gap to the next train car he severed the connection between them and watched as the rest of the train slowed. She was probably right, leaving her alive was dangerous. As the train she was pinned to began to sink in the distance he turned to find Angela.

"Angela," Kail called out in relief when he found her in an empty passenger car.

"You let her live?" Angela asked, eyeing his cuts and burns. The look of hesitation before he answered was revealing enough. "Why?" she wanted to know angrily.

"I don't know," he said. "It was different or something. I can't explain."

"This is war. A wounded enemy is the most dangerous," she scolded, pushing her finger in front of his face.

"I know that," his protest was brought up short when she thumped him on the head with her finger.

"You seem to forget quite often."

He just looked at her with a frown, rubbing the spot where she favored driving in lessons. He knew it had been foolish. There were few enemies as dangerous or as unpredictable as Bastiana. Kail felt the faint release of magic in the distance. "She's free," he said, moving to the window.

Bastiana didn't care anymore, defeated at the top of Hyperion Tower, defeated again in the lobby, and Vincent's disapproval. Tossed from the train by a woman with no race and no magical ability. Then the final humiliation, pinned and sent away by Kail as if she was no longer worth his time or effort. Tears were leaving muddy streaks down her face as the train slowed.

Closing her eyes, magic burst into colored flames around her. The flames rose higher until the steel beneath her feet began to sag and melt. She shot forward with fury and rage towards the distant train.

Chapter 20f

Vincent watched as the *Colossus* gained on the *Snow Break*. The air traffic was starting to thin, leaving the smaller ship more exposed. Bright light shot along the rail lines followed by an eruption of flames that rolled as high as they were into the sky. Every crew member on the bridge leaned away from the direction of the explosion and some cried out. Vincent frowned as he held his hand in front of his face. Even at this distance through the glass he could feel the searing heat as the rolling flames slowly turned into a black smoky trail more than a mile long.

When the sound of the explosion reached them the ship shook like a toy instead of a massive warship that ruled the sky. "You have seen firsthand what ruthlessness they are capable of. Remember this day and focus on the enemy in front of us," he said to rally the morale of the bridge. Inside he knew that the destruction was caused by Bastiana. *This time, for her sake, it had better have produced results.*

The crew responded well, and for the first time since the chase began the *Colossus* opened fire on the *Snow Break*. Vincent watched with a smile as the agile ship reacted to the explosion on the ground. The distraction proved useful as the *Snow Break* flinched after taking fire and scrambled back into the traffic lanes to avoid more of the *Colossus's* attack.

"Did you see that?" Rayne asked, watching the distant line of fire and smoke fill the sky in front of the *Odyssey*.

"How could I miss it," Rhonin quipped. "Get us in range to support," he ordered, frustration seeping into his voice.

"On it sir," Brom answered.

Rhonin tightened his grip on the command chair when he saw the *Snow Break* take fire from the *Colossus* and retreat into traffic. He knew Brom Carter and the rest of the crew were doing everything they could and more, but it wasn't enough. He cursed once again as they were delayed from air traffic scattered by the *Snow Break* and *Colossus*.

"She'll be alright," Rayne said. "She's the best ship there is and there is no way Camden would go down without swinging."

"Kail and Angela seem to be swinging quite a bit," he remarked, glancing back to the wall of smoke. "Come on!" he said exasperated as another ship blocked their path, forcing them to swing around.

"Report!" Camden shouted. Several of the lights on the status board had switched to yellow after the *Colossus* had caught them with their cannons.

"Several wounded, but no one has called in a fatality yet," a voice answered.

"Have the heavy cannon crews report to those sections to help with the wounded," Camden ordered, pointing to the status board. He held the button down on the intercom to the infirmary. "How are you holding up Suki?"

"We're fine, the first of the wounded have just shown up," her voice crackled over the speaker.

"Help has been dispatched. Expect more."

"Tell me something I don't know," she barked and cut off communication.

"Hang on!" Harold yelled from the helm.

Camden managed to slap the collision alarm only seconds before a small luxury airship crossed in front of them. He hoped the warning was enough as he was tossed forward when Harold brought the *Snow Break* into a steep climb as the bottom of the ship collided across the back of the smaller ship. Screeching metal echoed throughout the ship as Harold opened up the power to the turbines.

The *Snow Break* jumped forward as soon as it cleared the other ship. Camden got back to his command chair assessing the ship with wide eyes. Everything seemed to be making normal enough sounds. "Have one of the engineers check that collision. Last thing we need is to find were bleeding out."

"Yes sir."

Vincent watched as the *Snow Break* seemed to stumble as it tried to scramble away from them. *Next they will be begging for mercy*, he thought, frowning after the *Snow Break* crossed over the top of another airship. The damaged airship sailed right into their path. He felt the helmsman begin to veer out of the way. "Fly straight helm," he ordered. "Destroy that ship."

"Sir?"

"It is going to crash regardless. It will cause less damage if it is destroyed now than if it smashes intact to the ground. If we don't, the enemy will get away," he said to ease the crew's discomfort about firing on a civilian ship.

"Yes sir," came several replies. He smiled as the forward cannons responded.

The smaller ship disintegrated as four explosive shells from the *Colossus* impacted its hull and detonated. Vincent stood at the front of the bridge as the *Colossus* emerged from the debris cloud like a demon just released from hell. The *Snow Break* came into view in front of them like a sacrificial animal trying to escape.

Harold let up on the throttle, pushing the helm forward as the *Snow Break* began to dive towards the ground.

"Make a run for the canyon." Camden pointed in the far distance. The canyons of Cahir were famous for their heavily mined rich ore veins. The majority of the incoming air traffic had all been coming from the mines carrying ore for the clockwork factories as well as transporting workers. "We're running out of city."

"You got it sir," Harold said, excitement creeping into his voice. Cannon fire from the *Colossus* screamed over their heads as Harold's diving maneuver sobered him as it saved them from another direct hit.

"We're not out of this yet," Camden said dryly.

Harold saw an opening in front of them. Four large cranes sat in a group waiting to load and unload train cars from the mines. A pair of large ore hauling dirigibles was moored above them as well.

Camden saw what Harold was planning to do, and he felt the blood drain from his face. Opening the ship wide intercom Camden ordered everyone to hang on.

Again Harold's piloting skills kept them in the air as several cannon shells exploded near them with others whistling through empty air.

Camden held on as the *Snow Break* rolled onto her side to pass between the ore haulers and cranes. They were only feet above the ground and he flinched as they shot by in a blur.

"Don't follow them you fool," Vincent shouted when the helmsman seemed too caught up in the chase. The *Colossus* pulled back and had to slow down to avoid the ore haulers that came loose from their moorings. He let a sigh of disappointment escape him as the *Snow Break* shot forward out of cannon range.

Chapter 20g

"I definitely made a mistake," Kail admitted.

"Do not make it a habit," Angela said, folding her arms. The scene of destruction they were paralleling was unnerving. "Why do the trains not stop? People are scared and in danger."

Kail glanced at the locked door to their cabin car. The commotion on the other side was frantic, and had not let up since the train several rails over exploded. "If I had to guess I would say the train is automated. I don't see how a conductor would keep going either."

Angela sat on the bench deep in thought and continued to watch the smoke rise into the air as the train continued. "Was it the Time Walker?" Angela asked out of the blue.

"Mr. Eleazar?"

"He said we would need their help. We assumed he meant they had bindings, but what if it was more? You said you did not know why you let the dark skinned mage live."

"Vincent and Bastiana?" Kail asked confused.

"Vincent is a man of many unknowns," she recalled when Kail's magic had no effect on him. "Bastiana is the living vessel of chaos. Maybe the reason you did not kill her was because they are still needed," Angela said.

Kail took in a deep sigh as he mulled over Angela's insight. "It might be possible, but I know this much, I won't hesitate next time, and I am not about to go asking for their help again either."

Angela smirked. "That did not go so well did it? It does not lend itself well to this theory."

"Let's live through this first, but you do have some valid points," Kail said, unlocking the door to peek out into the hall. "Rest time is over. We need to move."

Bastiana found what she was looking for in the fifth private passenger cabin she checked. The first had been full of men. The second one was empty. An old fat couple had been in the third and the fourth was simply too small. Ignoring the protests of the young woman in the corner she went through the luggage for something to replace her tattered clothes.

"Absolutely no sense of style," she muttered, tossing one unsuitable garment after another onto the floor. This had been the first time she could remember using so much magic that she actually felt tired. With the bindings in their possession, she wasn't able to use her powers of divination to find them. Still she was able to smell him. Magical power like Kail possessed left a trace. Even when she first met him, and he was still bound, she could smell it on him. The same smell she now sensed. It was faint, but she knew he was on this train.

"Do, do you have something to do with what's going on?" the woman finally squeaked out after seeing Bastiana's condition.

"Well, of course I do." Bastiana smirked at the woman. "Give me your dress," she demanded, finally settling on the clothes the woman was wearing.

"My dress?"

Bastiana brought her hand up covered in magical flames. "Don't make me ruin it."

The chaos on the train made it easy for Kail and Angela to move unnoticed. The crossing area to the next train car was locked, but a tiny push of magic fixed that and they found themselves in a cargo car.

"This is better now that there are not crowds of people," Kail said, hustling to the next train car.

Angela followed close behind. "The train is slowing down," she said, feeling the change of momentum. Cargo creaked and shifted around them as they crossed to the next train car.

If Angela had been anyone else she would have fallen onto the tracks. As soon as Kail had crossed over, the two train cars had separated. Only her ability to fly had saved her from being run over and killed.

"You ok?" Kail called out.

"Fine." She replied. "I am going to see what is happening," she said, pointing upwards.

Kail nodded, giving her a thumbs up.

The top of the train revealed a change in scenery. Behind her on the horizon large black columns of smoke were rising from Bastiana's attack on the trains and the Hyperion Tower. In front of them, all of the train's cars were detaching from each other to be sorted. Their rail car was now slowly coming into a line with dozens of others like it. Passenger cars were funneled to another area. "We are at the Canyons of Cahir," she called down to Kail.

The train car shuddered as improperly greased gears began to turn. "What's going on?" Kail shouted.

Angela watched as half of the train's metal wheels rotated out from under the car and off the track. "I do not know," she shouted back over the noise. She waved to Kail to come see for himself.

She watched with Kail as theirs and the train cars in front of them, continued to move some of their wheels to the top of the cars. Kail shook his head at her not knowing either what was happening as their train car continued to move forward towards one of several hangar buildings.

Angela went back into the train car after Kail. "What do you think of that?"

"I'm not sure, but for right now I think we should stay low."

Angela nodded and secured the door behind her.

Chapter 20h

The *Snow Break* stayed low to the ground as it pressed its engines hard to put distance between the *Colossus* and themselves. The bigger ship could not match its agility, but it had the power source that in a flat out speed race, it would win.

Suki wiped hair out of her face with the back of her hand as she sent one of the mechanics back to duty. Considering all they had been through, there had been no injury more serious than a broken leg. Using her ability to heal, it had taken her only a few minutes before he was back on his feet. Serious injuries could take much longer, but she was more than happy if she only mended bumps and bruises.

"Everyone is back on duty," she reported to the bridge as she rested against the bulkhead.

"Good work," Camden's voice scratched back over the speaker.

"You're welcome," she replied softly with her finger off of the transmit button. Her thoughts returned to the advice Angela had given her about everything passing you by if you don't take the chance to grab it. She hoped that wasn't the case now.

"Sir," the helmsman of the *Colossus* spoke up.

"I see it helm. Give it everything she has and catch them. If they make it to the canyons we will lose our advantage," Vincent stated. The *Snow Break* had managed to put some distance between them with their little stunt, but that was soon to change. Vincent took a deep breath, straightened his shirt, and sat back down in the command chair. His thoughts were on Bastiana while his eyes kept track of their prey. The trains she was playing on were most likely at the gondola monorail stations. *She had better control herself*, he thought. It had taken over three years and millions of man hours to construct the conversion stations that sent materials, supplies, and equipment on their high speed journey through the canyons on the way to Courduff. Loosing that supply route would be disastrous if they had to go back to hauling by air, or use the slower winding land rails that went around the canyon system.

Camden shoved the random thought to the back of his mind. Right now wasn't the time to be concerned with what was bothering Suki. *It was probably part of the intercom system anyway that made her sound resigned*, he dismissed, focusing back on the situation of escaping from Cahir. "How are we doing Harold?"

Harold quickly checked all of the gauges in front of him. Everything seemed ok, but the nagging feeling that there was something wrong ate at him. "Everything checks out sir..."

"I hear a 'but' in there," Camden said.

"I don't know sir. Just a feeling. The airspeed indicator seems a little slow, but everything reads ok."

Camden double checked all of the readings before calling down to the engine room. It took a moment for them to respond because someone would have to leave the room to talk over the noise. "Everything alright down there? We have lost a little bit of speed."

"Everything's good here captain," came the static filled reply.

"Bridge out," Camden said, closing the connection. "Maybe we have some hull damage that is causing some drag," he said, turning back to Harold.

"Maybe," Harold agreed. "The controls seem fine."

"Keep an eye on it anyway," Camden said, returning to the command chair. "Last thing we need is something else going wrong."

"Time to firing range?" Vincent asked as the *Colossus* chewed away the distance between them and the *Snow Break*.

"Twenty seconds sir," an officer called out from behind binoculars after repeatedly checking the *Colossus's* flight speed.

"Give the signal when we are in range," he ordered, keeping a mental countdown in his head. The *Snow Break* had an infamous reputation, one that would grow after the events of today. The damage and destruction caused in Cahir with the loss of Hyperion Tower, a defense airship and the chaos with the train systems would not be forgotten. Combine that with the *Colossus* shooting down the *Snow Break*, and this would indeed be a day for the history books.

The officer at the front of the bridge turned to look at him and nodded. "Fire," Vincent ordered with a smile.

The first shell exploded wide off of the port bow in front of them. Even its miss sent shockwaves through the *Snow Break* and kicked up shrapnel and debris from the ground into the air that bounced across the hull. "Can you get to the canyon?" Camden called out.

"I don't know..." Harold grunted as he began to juke the airship to make it harder to shoot at as another shell rocketed past them. "Maybe... Yes, yes we can make it."

Camden was rocked in his chair again as an explosion detonated in the air above them. Tearing metal followed by a loud crash echoed around them. "Do I want to even know what that was?"

"We're still good here sir," Harold called white knuckled from the helm as the rate of fire increased from the *Colossus* behind them.

"Come on," Camden urged as the canyon came closer and closer hoping that the power of wishful thinking might make it happen.

Vincent watched with satisfaction as the *Snow Break* tried to escape its doom. Explosions erupted all around the smaller ship as it tried to evade being knocked from the air. Each near miss forced the *Snow Break* in another direction. The gunners on the *Colossus* were herding them for a fatal blow, and they didn't even know it. "Predictable," he said, making his way to the front of the bridge. Without disappointment the next cannon shot sent the *Snow Break* end over end and over the edge of the canyon rim with a trail of dark smoke.

The cheers of the crew broke through all tension and anxiety that the day's events had piled up when the *Snow Break* was shot down. Normally he would have said something, as some of the more junior crew jumped up and down and even grabbed the nearest person next to them, punching their fists into the air, but there was good reason to let them celebrate.

"Take us over the remains," Vincent ordered as the crew settled down.

"Aye, aye sir," the helmsman answered proudly, guiding the *Colossus* to the rim of the canyon where the *Snow Break* had disappeared.

"All cannons prepare to fire!" Rhonin shouted. The *Odyssey's* engines were pushed to their maximum as it raced through the sky. Countless delays had them playing catch up the entire time the *Colossus* chased the *Snow Break*. They were too late to help the *Snow Break* when the *Colossus* opened fire, but now the *Colossus* was left exposed as it approached the canyon.

Vincent was thrown forward across the bridge when the first explosions rocked across the *Colossus*. "Return fire!" he commanded. "Lock that leak down," he yelled while dragging a fallen officer away from the superheated spray that filled the bridge.

The *Colossus* came around to engage the *Odyssey* as it opened fire. The speed of the *Odyssey* out ran all of the return fire from the *Colossus*. A line of repeater cannon fire from the *Odyssey* traced across the outer deck of the surprised ship then punctured the lower decks.

"Swing around for another run," Rhonin urged.

"There!" Rayne called out, pointing out of the front view port. The *Snow Break* crested the rim of the canyon. Its turbines clearing the smoke around it as repeater cannon fire launched from the ship, cutting into the side of the *Colossus*.

Vincent had a hard time believing what he was seeing. The *Snow Break*, like some sort of demon from the depths, rose out of the canyon and opened fire on them. Combined with the *Odyssey*, they were caught in a perfect

crossfire.   "Fall back and launch countermeasures," he
ordered.

Chapter 20i

Angela leaned back against the cool metal wall of the train car. She rubbed at some of the sore spots and shook her arms and legs to keep them from stiffening up after the day's exertion. It would be disadvantageous to be caught with slow reflexes. She watched as Kail paced about the equipment filled train car. She held no doubt that the Time Walker's words weighed upon him as well as his concern for their friends on the *Snow Break* and *Odyssey*.

The train car jarred to a stop as the secure cargo shifted and groaned in their securing belts and harnesses. Both Kail and she held quiet as the sound of machinery rumbled outside of the train and banged noisily across the top of the train car.

"What do you think is happening?" she asked as the train car was once again jostled forward.

"I don't know," Kail said. "It sounds like little ones are eating the big ones."

Angela shook her head and smiled at the description of Kail's words. She had to admit it did sound like a mechanical monster eating something metal. Smiling was something that seemed to be happening less and less these days.

"What?" Kail asked, looking at her.

"Nothing," she said, unable to suppress the smile. A small laugh escaped her lips.

"What?"

"The little ones are eating the big ones," she repeated, as the laughing took hold of her.

Kail smiled. "Yeah, well what else could make a racket like that?"

Kail was quickly knocked to the floor of the train when it violently jerked. Angela managed to stay on her feet only by grabbing onto something secure. The absurdity of it all caused her to laugh even harder.

"That wasn't funny," he protested. "I think something picked up the train car."

"Maybe we are about to be eaten," she joked. Shock and surprise replaced humor when the train car lurched with a deafening screech and accelerated forward. Kail went sliding out of sight to the far end of the car as if an invisible hand had grabbed him. If she had not been already holding on, she would have been the second thump and yell.

Bastiana stood on top of a detached train car as it entered one of the monorail stations. She used her magic to hold herself in place as the train car bumped and jostled its way along. The monorail wheels had already rotated into position around her. Somewhere amongst the chaos, there was a car that held Kail and the flying woman who continued to defy her.

She let her stare linger from one train car to another. She had lost his trail once the cars had become separated. All she knew was that he had moved from the passenger cars to cargo. One private cabin literally reeked with his presence.

"You down there!" someone yelled, interrupting her thoughts.

Bastiana looked above her and saw a monorail technician trying to get her attention. The man was clearly upset that she was standing on top of one of the train cars. The monorail through the canyon wasn't built for transporting people. It was dangerous, fast, and anything not secured often ended up on the other side smashed to pieces. Suicide would be the word you would use if you tried to ride the monorail outside of the train car.

"You can't be down there," the man yelled sharply, rudely was more accurate. "Get off of the train!"

Frowning Bastiana turned to face him with fire in her eyes. Cheap ugly clothes was bad enough but now someone was yelling at her. It was only a slight burst of magic, but it made the unnecessary noise stop.

A giant crane swung down to grab hold of the train car she was riding. Quickly and efficiently without regard to her presence it secured the car to the monorail track as a giant chain began to pull the car forward.

Bastiana held her hands to her eyes as bright sunlight washed over her as the train car exited the darker hangar. Smiling as the wind blew against her the train car shot forward hanging from the monorail track above her. The Canyons of Cahir sprawled out in front of her as cargo cars were sent speeding down the lines. *This was better than an airship*, she thought as she blinked and teleported to one of the rail cars in front of her.

Kail slid a couple of dozen feet, slammed into the back of the train car, and let out a curse of pain. Before he had a chance to get to his feet he was sent bouncing against the side of the compartment as the train car dropped and swung to the side.

Angela had managed to make her way to him to ask if he was alright.

Finally securing himself to the side of the train car he felt the back of his head. "Bumps, but nothing broken or bleeding," he answered.

"What---," Angela's question was cut off as the car was tilted over and it felt like as if a giant hand was pressing down on them. "This is worse than Camden's flying," she said.

"I don't know!" Kail called out. "Want to take a look?"

Angela nodded her head.

Kail tied himself to a piece of securing strap and jerked on the lever on the back of the train car. He heard Angela protest, but it was too late. The doors flew open, one instantly snapped off its hinges from the inertia, and the other swung open wildly then slammed back almost taking off his hand. As the wind rushed in he was nearly taken off of his feet.

"Get rid of it," Angela shouted through the noise.

Hanging onto the strap, he blasted at the door hinges until it finally tore free. The wind let up substantially once the drag was gone. The both of them watched as the door sailed through the air to disappear into the bottom of the canyon shooting past below them.

"Holy crap!" Kail cursed, moving further into the train car to get away from the edge.

Angela thumped him in the exact same spot where he had hit his head. "There is a hatch," she finished, pointing to the top of the train car.

"Just put it on the list of things not to do again," he retorted right before an explosion filled the back of the car.

Bastiana held herself forward on the front of her train car letting her mixed colored hair billow behind her. Another train car, one line over and about four ahead of hers had suddenly blown open losing one of its doors. The unmistakable use of magic flashed, and its twin was severed and sent to the distant canyon floor. *Still a child*, she thought as she caught the sight of Kail and his chosen wife backing into the train to get away from the edge.

Raising her hand it erupted with energy as she sent a small blast of magic into the back of their rail car. The following explosion was satisfying even with its ineffectiveness. It would be far too simple for her to just destroy them inside the car. This rivalry demanded a more intimate end.

Kail wove a barrier of magic that he tied off with a rune at the back of the train car.

"She is playing with us," Angela said sternly.

Kail had to agree. Bastiana could have easily just snuffed them out of existence with a surprise attack like that. "We can't stay here forever," he said. "Time for that hatch." Climbing on top of the cargo, he twisted the wheel that pulled down, opening the hatch. "I'll go first."

Angela nodded. *If the mage tried anything, Kail would be the better one to defend us*, she thought, watching him exit the rail car. Flashes of light and the hiss of magic quickly started. Peeking out, she saw Kail block and bat away the magic that Bastiana sent towards them. Exiting the container, she made her way to the front. She was used to heavy wind when she flew, but the sudden changes in direction of the track forced her to be careful. Looking back she saw the glow around Kail's feet as he secured himself while battling the mage.

Angela assessed the racing train cars. It would be very interesting if they had to abandon the cargo container. They were traveling faster than she could fly so the only way to go was backwards. Back is where the mage was.

The *Odyssey* swept over the top of the *Colossus* as it retreated. "Kail is on the monorail," Rayne called out, spying the magical exchange in the distance with Bastiana.

"Head for them Brom," Rhonin ordered. "Get Camden on the radio."

The *Odyssey* dipped into the canyon to start after the racing cargo containers. The *Snow Break* rotated around starting to follow while continuing to fire on the *Colossus*.

"Sir, I can't reach them. Their radio must be out," the comm's officer guessed.

"Rayne," her husband called.

Rayne nodded as she headed off the bridge. Before the luxury of radio, they had had a visual method of communication. As inconvenient as it was when radios and other equipment failed it was put into use. She grabbed a high intensity lantern and made her way to the back of the airship to signal the *Snow Break*.

Chapter 20j

Another grating squeal echoed through the *Snow Break* bringing a wince to Camden's face. He saw Harold give the same look of concern. For the entire time that Camden had owned the *Snow Break*, the noises she made now were ones he had never heard before, and ones he never wanted to hear again. When the *Colossus* had nailed them dead on with their last attack that sent the *Snow Break* end over end into the canyon, it was only luck the new turbine engines had saved them from being nothing more than a scattered debris field.

"How are we looking?" he asked Harold.

"Controls seem to be responsive. Engines as well," the helmsman answered.

"Put some distance on and head into the canyon. We need to get Kail and Angela and get the hell out of here," Camden ordered. "If we can get out of here without another fight, all the better, if not, at least the canyon will even the odds.

Harold nodded his head, the thought of navigating a canyon system wasn't one that he enjoyed though Camden's words made sense. Maneuverability of the *Snow Break* seemed intact and the Canyon's of Cahir was their best hope until Kail was on board and able to use his magic.

"What have the reports been?" Camden asked, looking at the damage board. Several of the indicator lights were off. They were probably damaged in the last exchange, but a good number of them were still lit green indicating everything was ok. He expected them to be red after the ship had been flipped in the air.

"Nothing major so far, but only a few stations have reported. The intercom system is down on most of the ship," the comm's officer reported.

"Keep at it. Have repair crews focus on the electrics. I want to know how badly we're really damaged," Camden said as another rumbling groan ran the length of the ship.

Vincent ignored the rest of the damage report, he had heard what he needed to know and that was that the ship was more than capable of continuing. "Bring us about and follow them," he told the bridge crew. "We will have our justice done today," he added after seeing some of the crew's concerned looks. Only a few moments ago the scene on the bridge had been one of celebration. Then the impossible had happened, not only the *Snow Break's* survival, but the *Odyssey* as well had caught them in a deadly crossfire.

The *Snow Break* once again came into view in front of them. Aside from the visible damage the ship had taken, there appeared to be nothing wrong with the defiant ship as it veered along the vertical walls of the canyon. Their target was now in sight, and the *Colossus* began a full out pursuit.

Repeater cannon fire shot forward from the *Colossus*. Visible tracer rounds left coils of smoke trails as the cannons chewed across the rock of the canyon walls, but missing the *Snow Break* as it turned full speed around a slight outcropping of canyon and out of sight.

Vincent sucked in his breath when the *Colossus* swung around the turn in the canyon. A large natural rock bridge filled the space as it had for thousands of years before they arrived. It was where the *Colossus* was headed. The *Colossus's* maneuvering fans roared as the helmsman brought the ship up in time to avoid a collision. The smaller *Snow Break* had punched through underneath the rock formation, putting some space between them.

Explosions shook the *Colossus* as three cannon shells slammed against the port side. Vincent growled with frustration as the *Odyssey* shot past them in the other direction. The sudden attack had caught the gunners of the *Colossus* by surprise, and they had not even fired back. "You!" Vincent yelled, pointing to a bridge crewman. "Watch for that cursed ship. If that happens again, you will be held responsible."

The first few blasts of magic enraged Bastiana. The next one nearly took her off of her feet despite her own magical energies holding her into place. It seemed that Kail was finally starting to put some muscle into his attacks. She batted away the next two attacks sent at her before launching a blinding bar of magical energy at Kail from both hands. She felt her blast collide with one from Kail. Straining she pushed harder and felt his magic begin to waiver. Rage then turned into pleasure as she poured more of her will into the attack.

Kail had had enough and pushed Bastiana's attack downward. Cursing himself for not doing it sooner, her attack slammed into the rail car below them. Acrid smoke from steel being vaporized billowed around them as the magic tore apart the bottom of the rail car. Thousands of pounds of equipment that had been secured inside now spilled out, raining down onto the canyon floor below.

"Hang on," Kail yelled back towards Angela. The damage to the train car plus the loss of its cargo weight had caused it to slow down. The next rail car was coming at them fast. "Get ready to jump."

Angela nodded as she continued to hold on tight.

"Now!" he shouted.

Angela let go and sailed onto the incoming rail car. Kail sliced through support arm of the old rail car where it suspended itself from the monorail track. As it fell away he made a quick teleporting hop and snapped back into existence on the rail car next to her.

"The *Odyssey* is coming up behind us sir," the officer called out across the bridge of the *Colossus*.

"Use the main cannons and convince them of their errors," Vincent barked as cannon fire quickly sounded below them. They did not score any direct hits, but the *Odyssey* was forced to back off and abandon its planned attack.

Repeater cannon fire again shot forward towards the *Snow Break* as they closed the distance. This time the *Colossus* was rewarded as a line of high caliber rounds punched into the side of the *Snow Break* before it was able to evade the assault.

Suki stared in horror. Several rounds of cannon fire had pierced through the walls of the infirmary causing glass to shatter as medical supplies ricochet throughout the room. She held her hands up in front of her. Blood covered. She tried to understand as her body chilled. She looked down to see that her chest was covered in blood. Dropping to her knees her she began to relive the horrors of the day she had been stabbed in the back by a trusted friend, Xavier.

Her breath came in labored gasps as she started to understand that it wasn't her blood that covered her. The source was the nameless crewman she had been helping to heal who now lay dead. The wave of relief was so much that she let out a crazed laugh before breaking down in tears, realizing that it wasn't her that had been shot as her body trembled as the adrenalin drained from her system.

Chapter 20k

Kail held one hand out towards Bastiana. In front of him a group of three large runic circles spun absorbing or deflecting the attacks she threw at him. The cannon fire from the *Colossus* hadn't gone unnoticed either. Summoning several large balls of magic that crackled and snapped with energy, he concentrated on floating them into the sky as he pictured his target. Flashes of divination raced through his mind as he sent the magic to where he had seen the *Colossus* would be.

Bringing his full attention back to Bastiana, he let loose several dozen lines of magical energy. He needed to distract her from destroying the attack he had set for the *Colossus*. The web of energy rained down on Bastiana, punching holes through the train car upon which she stood.

"We cannot stay here," Angela yelled as the wind whipped her fiery colored hair around her.

Kail knew she was right. These magical exchanges had been going on for far too long. Eventually they had to get back to the ships and get out of here. How many times had they cheated death today? How many more times would they before their luck ran out? "Stay here. If you get the chance, get to airship," he called out over the wind. He saw her frown, but nodded her head that she understood.

Kail turned away from Angela, took a running start, leapt off of the back of the hanging train car, and teleported three cars behind.

Bastiana saw Kail teleport behind her. She wrestled with the idea of going after him, or staying to kill the Keratin. Ducking a blast of energy, she had her answer. The woman who could fly could wait. Kail was the only real threat.

Camden watched several orbs of magic pass by as the *Snow Break* continued up the canyon after Kail and Angela. He gave a cheer when they detonated around the *Colossus* following behind them forcing the larger ship to back off and halt their cannon fire. "We just might make it through this," he said. "Harold, get us up there," he finished, pointing to where Kail and Bastiana now battled in front of them.

"All stations report ready sir," Lieutenant Cid called out.

Captain Bailon nodded. Standing on the outer balcony of the *Lotus* he peered into the canyon through binoculars at the *Colossus* giving chase to the *Snow Break*. The *Odyssey*, clearly the inferior of the ships, trailed behind and struggled to keep up like a younger child chasing after older siblings.

"Everything in order?" Bailon asked.

Cid glanced around before answering. "Yes sir. Everything is in place as instructed. Are you sure about this?"

Bailon felt a twinge of regret when his trusted friend brought up his concerns. "You don't have to worry about yourself Cid. As Captain, I am responsible for everything and everyone on this ship."

"I don't doubt your conviction to take responsibility sir. Only concerned about how this will be taken, if it becomes known is all."

Bailon wondered how he had been gifted with someone who never doubted or questioned his motives. Anyone else would have taken word to his superiors if ordered to send a message to the enemy. Treason would be the easiest of charges brought against him. Getting word to his half sister, Suki, on the *Snow Break* about the loss of the Kelly farm was just the right thing to do. He understood war and believed that in the end the side he was fighting on was the right one. However, he did not believe that Silverton was the real enemy. There were other armies in the east that were more powerful and aggressive than Kail and his group of labeled terrorists.

"I couldn't ask for anything more Lieutenant," Bailon said. "Inform the crew that we will be assisting Cahir and the *Colossus* shortly," he finished, returning to assess the conflict below them.

Bastiana came at Kail hard and fast. She had teleported closer and the two of them battled it out above the Canyons of Cahir. Both of them were starting to look battle worn, with burns and cuts starting to cover Kail's body. The Imaera hide armor absorbed the majority the magical energy that slipped past his defenses. Bastiana's tattooed runes were fresh and sore.

"Come on!" Kail taunted.

Bastiana's answer was to send a ball of energy into the cargo container on which he was anchored. Billowing smoke and heat began to radiate from it as he was forced to abandon it to one further down the monorail. The flaming cargo car came loose from its connection with the track and sailed to the bottom of the canyon, exploding as it shattered among the rocky floor below.

He was now in sight of the *Snow Break* and he waved them forward to continue after Angela. It wouldn't do anyone any good if he teleported to the airship only to have Bastiana focus her deadly rage upon them. The *Snow Break* gave a small wobble letting him know that they understood and Kail watched as the *Snow Break* screamed forward pressing her engines to the limit.

Bastiana teleported across from him to take a shot at the passing *Snow Break* with her magic. Kail blasted the connection of the train car from the monorail sending Bastiana and the train car towards the bottom of the canyon. Without skipping a beat, Bastiana teleported away from the doomed car to materialize onto the train car behind him, and they continued their assault on each other.

Without warning the metal roof of the train car was ripped apart by repeater cannon fire. Kail protectively pulled his magic around him as the *Colossus* had come in range and opened fire on him. Several rounds pushed him back as the magic blocked the attack, but the force and mass of the projectiles still thudded around him. He wasn't going to be able to take cannon fire and magical attacks from Bastiana at the same time. Gritting his teeth, he blinked out of existence and instantly reappeared next to Bastiana. His hope was that by using her as a shield like this, the *Colossus* wouldn't fire on them both.

Chapter 201

"The *Colossus* is firing on Kail!" Camden heard the comm's officer call out.

"Damn it," he cursed. "Anyone see Angela yet?"

When no one answered him he slammed his fist against his chair in frustration. *The dirt farmer is trying to get himself killed*, he thought. A crazy plan filled his head when he saw the curve of the canyon in front of them. Quickly he stood next to Harold and pointed. "There, do you think you can pull the ship in a roll and come up behind the *Colossus*?"

Harold gave Camden a look like he had sprouted a second head. "You want me to roll the ship over?" he asked.

Without answering Camden shouted to the comm's officer. "Tell the crew to hang on, and prepare to open fire with everything we got."

The officer nodded and set about relaying the information to the rest of the ship.

"Slow down. Let her get in range," Camden said, sitting back securing himself in his command chair.

Harold eased off of the throttle as they approached the curve of the canyon wall. Steeling himself he slammed the engines forward again as he pulled the flight controls back causing the *Snow Break* to climb. When they were almost vertical he the cut power to the port turbine and feathered the starboard side turbine as the ship turned on its side. Shadows walked across the bridge as the momentum carried the ship onto its back. Everyone was looking upwards, which was now downwards, as the airship reached the peak of its climb. The mighty *Colossus* quickly passed beneath them as the *Snow Break* started to fall back into the canyon.

The hull of the *Snow Break* groaned in protest at the maneuver. Harold had the turbines maxed out as they finished the roll and continued to drop in behind the *Colossus*.

"Fire!" Camden commanded.

Disappointingly only two deep thuds of cannons let loose. *We're worse off than I expected*, Camden thought. A single repeater cannon lanced out from the *Snow Break* and began to tear at the hull of the *Colossus*. One of the gunners must have moved to the other gun after firing one of the main cannons.

Bastiana hesitated for only a second when Kail teleported in front of her, and then, suddenly, she rushed ahead, her arms glowed with her magical power as she swung wildly coming down for Kail's shoulder. Kail managed to block with an explosion of clashing energies, but Bastiana simply spun around swinging along the other side.

Kail was momentarily stunned at her choice to attack more physically. This was the last thing he would have expected from her. "I won't stay my hand this time," Kail said.

"You are weak," came Bastiana's retort, her mixed colored hair billowing around her face matching her insanity. There came a flash as her blast of sizzling energy sent Kail stumbling backwards to the edge of the train car as it raced through the canyon. "Know that when you die, I will hunt her down, and break her body," Bastiana shouted sending another power blast into Kail. "Her mind," another blast, "and lastly her soul!" the final blast erupted around him. He felt his stomach lurch as the back part of the train car disintegrated.

Kail panicked as he tumbled through the air, but a small rational part of his mind told him that he had been in worse situations several times today. Bastiana's words had stabbed him in a way he couldn't grasp. His mind froze as he fell and the world swung around him. His nightmares from earlier gripped him. Flashes of memories from that day so long ago, when he had recklessly teleported from the *Snow Break* to safely steal Angela from the sky.

"*It's not hard if you're a chronomancer,*" Kail flinched as Bastiana's words from so long ago snapped him out of his doubting thoughts. The floor of the canyon raced to embrace him. Not being able to see where he was he didn't try to teleport normally. His power flared as a dark tear appeared to swallow him.

"Nothing fancy, helm. Just put us between the *Snow Break* and the *Colossus*," Captain Bailon ordered after the *Snow Break* had performed its aerial stunt. "Prepare to open fire." The *Lotus* descended from the sky with practiced skilled precision that he had come to expect from the crew. Airships had the reputation of being slow clunky vessels, but anyone who would had witnessed the *Snow Break* and the *Lotus* would know the lie of that reputation.

The *Snow Break's* guns continued to chew away at the *Colossus*. While faster, there simply was not a way for the *Colossus* to shake the more maneuverable *Snow Break* in the confines of the canyon. Bailon wondered if there was more to the situation or if the *Colossus's* captain, Vincent, was just that arrogant.

Lieutenant Cid checked the readouts and gave him a nod. The nod held a double meaning that no one, but they knew about. "Have they noticed us yet?"

"It doesn't appear so sir," Cid answered.

"Flak cannons first," Bailon said. "Fire when ready." He stood and listened to the bridge chatter as Cid followed through with the orders, then he felt the vibrations through his feet and heard the muffled thuds as the cannons fired. It was a fine line to walk, stopping the *Snow Break* without destroying her or his half sister.

"Break off!" Camden yelled as they flew through heavy flak raining from above. The hardened metal in the turbines had been designed to tolerate flak, but not excessively as the *Snow Break's* engines protested. "Damn it," Camden cursed as the *Lotus* cut them off. There was no way now for them to get to Angela with a fresh enemy between them. "Where is my radio?"

"Radio's still offline sir," came the reply.

Bastiana waited until she lost sight of Kail before teleporting on ahead. She was determined to deliver on her promise to Kail. She knew that there was little chance that he had simply let himself fall to his death, but for now she moved forward as if he had. Angela, the focus of her fury, was somewhere ahead of her. *That woman, that freak*, who at every turn defied her. So mundane was her one ability to fly, it was insulting that she continued to not only survive, but to best her as well.

Teleporting from one suspended rail car to another she continued her search for the red-headed Keratin. The bindings she carried hid her from her divining powers which only compounded the spite she felt.

Angela could sense that danger was getting closer, and she shifted her twin war blades for easier reach. Years of living in the future, and more than decade of warrior training from her past had prepared her well for these moments.

"Interesting turn of events," Vincent said to no one as the *Lotus* dropped behind them effectively ending the *Snow Break's* attack. "Status?" he ordered. The damage report added to the long list of frustrations and failures of the day. The interference of the *Lotus* grated on him. The events of the day would now bring doubt to Cahir and its ability to defend itself. Loss of Hyperion Tower, a defense airship, and now an airship from Courduff arrives to save the day. Repairing the damage to the city was nothing compared to the political fallout with which he would have to deal.

Chapter 20m

The moment had finally arrived. Even through the noise of the wind rushing around her she heard the familiar snap and recoil of magic when someone teleported. Stepping out from behind the steel arm that held the train car to the monorail track, Angela saw Bastiana. The dark skinned mage stood stiffly, magic holding her in place against the pushing winds.

"Are you ready to die?" Bastiana shouted through the wind.

Angela drew her twin war blades, set her feet but did not reply.

Bastiana rolled her eyes and smiled her customary grin. "Why, oh why, do you make me desire you so?" Bastiana went on, soaking in the sight of Angela.

"I will not leave you to live, you can count on that," Angela promised, keeping a watchful eye as the mage casually stepped towards her. Bastiana had yet to summon her staff; this did not sit well with Angela. If the mage intended to fight with magic, there would be little she could do to counter it. Provoking a melee fight is what she wanted, but perhaps the mage had finally learned that she was outmatched when it came to armed combat.

"Come now, wouldn't it be better if you stayed with me?" Bastiana asked, holding her hands out to her side.

Angela already knew the woman to be insane, but it was simply impossible to try and figure out the method behind her madness. Bastiana came at her suddenly, insanely, and Angela reacted with warrior instincts and training. It was the slightest use of her ability to fly, just lifting herself the smallest bit off of the top of the speeding train car. Angela saw the confusion flash across Bastiana's face as she closed the remaining distance between them without taking a step. Waiting until the last moment when Bastiana brought her hands around to attack, Angela touched back down, sticking her front foot, she pivoted and rolled to the side. Both blades passed through the air. Bastiana teleported at the final second to avoid having both of her legs cut off.

It was a bold move. Unlike Kail or the mage, Angela did not have magic to hold her to the speeding train car. As the back edge of the train came closer, she jumped and shot into the air.

Bastiana bit back her desire to blast Angela from the sky. She watched as the red-headed flying angel spun in mid-air then looked back before coming down on the next suspended train car.

Angela pushed her flying abilities as hard as she could. The train car came into range quickly. Stabbing both of the twin war blades into the roof of the car she held on as they cut through the steel while she matched its speed. The right war blade suddenly jerked from her hand as it encountered something it could not cut through. Her left arm felt like it was about to be yanked from her shoulder as she held on to it. Flailing about she saw the right war blade bounce free and sail into the air before falling away. Her first reaction was to go after it, but the snap hiss of a teleport brought her head around. Bastiana stood looking down on her with a wicked grin. A second flash and the rune staff was in the mage's hands as she brought it down on her.

Frustration had Rhonin out of his command chair. The situation had gone from worse to whatever word there was after worse. "Starboard, target the *Colossus*, Portside on the new ship," he ordered. Only now when the other airships had come to a standoff had the *Odyssey* been able to catch up. "Punch it!"

The *Odyssey* roared up the canyon towards the *Snow Break*, *Colossus*, and the *Lotus*. The *Odyssey's* cannons, port and starboard, thundered away. The repeater gun fire tracked perfectly as they passed over the top of the three ships. "Get the hell out of there Camden," Rhonin cursed as the Odyssey bombarded both enemy vessels.

Cannon fire cut across the deck of the *Lotus* tearing the hull in more than a dozen places. Secondary explosions followed as the shells exploded inside the ship. Rayne gave a cheer then relayed that the *Lotus* was disengaging and pulling out of the canyon. The amount of smoke billowing from her would keep the crew busy putting out fires to prevent loosing the ship.

The *Colossus* as heavily damaged as it was, was like a giant that refused to die. The Odyssey's cannons tore at the hull, and some of the tracer rounds from the repeater guns punched out the far side, yet the ship somehow managed to stay airborne, although it made no move to follow or retaliate.

"Find them Rayne," Rhonin called out, wanting desperately to put an end to the day's events.

Time slowed for Angela. She could let go abandoning her remaining weapon to avoid Bastiana's attack, or she could hold on hoping for a miracle. Either way she would be defenseless against a superior opponent, one that frankly should have beaten her at every encounter. The choice was easy, die with weapon in hand.

Bastiana slammed the rune staff down. The force of the blow echoed through the canyon as the magical staff struck Angela across the back of her shoulders.

Angela hung on with all of her might and cried out from the staff's blow. As noisy as the impact was, the blow was light in comparison. The Imaera hide armor and the binding runes she still carried absorbed all of the magical power behind the attack. The hit was simply the force of the swing as if the staff were but a mundane practice weapon. She could hear the mage's laughter as she brought the staff down again. The explosion of magic flashed between them echoing again and again.

Angela finally managed to get her feet under her. Disbelief and rage filled Bastiana. "Impossible!" she screamed, renewing her attack with fury.

Angela blocked and parried the staff with her war blade. The clash of unbreakable blade and magic fueled rune staff sent sparks of errant magical power arching around them. Angela went on the offensive, her blade flowed around her like a silvery line that promised death to anything that was foolish enough to get in its way.

Bastiana was forced backwards, confusion, doubt, and for the first time a trace of fear crept through her. Death glinted at her through the red-headed eyes. One of them was going to die. "Surprising as always," she shrilled. Bastiana pressed forward, staff swinging low then arching high. Angela twisted her body, the first blow was knocked aside with her sword, the arching second swung harmlessly high. Angela brought her sword around and pinned the rune staff down.

"Fancy, but to no avail," Bastiana cried as she caught Angela in the side with a blast of scorching magic.

"Burn that son of a bitch!" Camden commanded, pointing to the vulnerable *Colossus* in front of them.

Harold held with fierce determination and followed his captain's orders, swinging the *Snow Break* around the bow of the larger ship.

Camden could see Vincent standing on the bridge of the *Colossus* as the *Snow Break* maneuvered for the killing blow. "Fire!" he ordered. Moments passed and nothing happened as he stared down the man.

"Sir, we've got nothing left. Main cannons are down. The repeater guns have exhausted all of their ammunition," the communications officer announced.

Camden bit down to swallow the frustration and rage that threatened to undo him. "Get us out of here," he snarled, eyes locked on the captain of the *Colossus*. "Comms, order everyone to assist with the injured."

The *Snow Break* shuddered as Harold brought the ship about leaving the canyon system.

"Have them focus on emergency repairs as well," Camden added, shaking his head. *An opportunity lost, one we won't have again*, he thought, leaving the bridge to assist as he could.

Bastiana's shrill laughter pierced Angela's ears. The Imaera hide armor and the bindings had helped, but not enough. A smoking hole was left in her side where the armor had been seared away. *There was nothing more painful than a burn*, Angela winced as fiery pain stabbed through her. Her breath was a short shallow pant as she finally managed to take a look at the wound. The skin had been burned away leaving scorched muscle twitching and deeper organs that were never meant to see the light of day. Her legs started to give out, but she managed to keep from slipping off of the train car by leaning against the support beam. Tears began creep from the edges of her eyes as she fought to remain on her feet in spite of the pain.

Bastiana, smiling in victory, raised her face to feel the warmth of the sun. Bringing the staff back to deliver the final blow, she paused for one final taunt. "Now you die my pretty angel."

"I agree," Kail's voice came from behind. Kail grabbed the end of the rune staff that was near him easily yanking it from Bastiana's stunned hands. Spinning and swinging the staff around with every fiber in his being, he smashed it across Bastiana's chest. The percussion of exploding magic sent the dark skinned mage flying through the air like a marionette with cut strings. He didn't stop there. Focusing his magic he sent blast after blast that exploded around her as she fell, not letting up until she had reached the bottom of the canyon.

With the rune staff in hand he turned to Angela. "No," he cried, cradling her in his arms.

"You are late," she gasped between each word.

"Shh," he tried to stop her from talking. His eyes bouncing to the gruesome wound on her side then back to her face.

"Promise me you will sing songs of me?" she asked.

"No," he refused much to her chagrin.

Smiling, "We all die some day. Here now with you instead of alone a thousand years ago," she said, trying to soften the coming moment for him.

"No!" Kail yelled, grabbing the war blade from her weak hand before she could protest. He wasn't going to allow her to just give up and die. He would rip apart the world, undo all of time to keep her with him. Thrusting the rune staff in her arms he slid the war blade across her arm in an act of desperation.

The shock of painful betrayal crossed Angela's face as he cut her with her own blade. Kail prayed to every deity he knew that this would not be the last image he would remember of her. He was forced to hide his eyes as blinding light flared along the rune staff in Angela's hands. The scream he heard tore at his heart and stabbed his soul.

Angela lay on top of the train car gasping for breath and cried through tightly shut eyes. Kail looked back with desperate hope. A line of black tattoos crossed her arm where he had cut her, and hope almost caused his heart to burst from his chest. The fatal wound on her side was no more, replaced by pink tender looking skin with a circular pattern of runes.

"I love you so much," Kail said, holding her to him, unable to keep his own tears at bay, as Angela embraced him back. He could see the *Odyssey* approaching rapidly from behind. He kissed her fiercely. "Ready to get out of here?" he asked her, as they watched the *Odyssey* pull alongside of them.

Chapter 21

Camden slowly made his way along the catwalks and corridors of his ship. Each groan from the hull or unfamiliar sound the ship made reminded him of how close they had come to being destroyed. He told Harold to keep the ship as steady as he could as they made their way away from Cahir. In-flight repairs were not the easiest, but they could not afford under any circumstances to land. The risk of being caught on the ground was too great and if they were, they would not survive. The crew was in good spirits despite the state of the ship and the number of casualties. He couldn't blame them as having Suki on board to heal wounds meant that the infirmary was empty with no one suffering on a bed somewhere. Even with the death of some of the crew since they were out of sight they did not seem to weigh on their minds in the same way.

As he neared the weapons deck, Camden noticed some holes in the bulkhead where repeater guns had punched through. Circling the damage with a stick of chalk, he made a mental note to make sure it was put on the list of repairs. Diligence to repairs and maintenance was something a friend had taught him years ago. He hadn't thought about Ellenore Black, the first pilot of the *Snow Break*, in a long time. He could hear Lawrence Burke's loud voice reach him, snapping him out his wandering thoughts. He couldn't help but smile at the man's devotion, even now with the cannons in such bad shape.

"No. Move this one here, then replace it with the coils from that one," Lawrence's voice echoed.

"How are the weapon systems?" Camden asked, stepping onto the weapons deck to see Lawrence and two other crew members struggling with the cannons.

Lawrence gave him a look of resignation. "How do they look to you? Because this is fantastic compared to what they were an hour ago," Lawrence said mockingly. "In another hour, this one might be able to fire one shell before it retires on a sunny scrapheap beach somewhere."

"One shot might be all we need, you never know," he said, looking around the deck.

"Yeah, if we had any shells to shoot," Lawrence added, becoming more frustrated. "I don't trust the ones we have anymore after all that fancy flying you guys on the bridge like to do, and the repeater guns don't even have that much."

Camden had to concede the point brought up by Lawrence. Enemy fire had done its share of damage to the ship, but having the ship flip over in flight either on purpose or by accident wasn't something she was designed to do. The ship was designed for bumpy rides, but upside down was not part of the definition of a bumpy ride.

"Do what you can. I don't believe we will get time for proper repairs any time soon."

Lawrence's experience made him suspicious, he wasn't born yesterday. "What is that supposed to mean?"

"It just might be a while is all," Camden said, satisfied that in Lawrence's capable hands the weapons deck was in as good an order as it could be. Making his way to the infirmary, he needed to talk with Suki about her brother. His decision was pretty much already made, but he wanted her input as well.

Camden looked at the securing leaver on the door to the infirmary. He took a few deep breaths before pulling it to the side with a metal clunk as he stepped inside. Suki was busily scrubbing down one of the walls with a wet rag and a ruddy bucket of water that smelled strongly of cleanser and sterilizing agent that caused his eyes to water.

"Suki," he coughed, adjusting to the smell. "We need to talk," he said, sniffling as his nose started to run as well.

Suki put down the rag and looked at him. Her hair was sticking out in odd places and her eyes and nose were red from the solution. "What is it?" she asked, wiping her hands dry on her bloody uniform she had yet to change.

"Your brother," he started, blinking his stinging eyes. "Got enough in there to kill a horse," he complained.

"You get used to it," she explained softly. "Wilhelm? What about him?"

"When your brother dropped down on us back there, the running lights were configured for a meeting."

Suki's expression did not change. "You want to meet with him before going to Silverton," she stated.

"Yeah. It must be something pretty important. If I didn't know better, I would say he let us get away on purpose," he said, frowning as he saw holes in the walls caused by the repeater gun fire.

"Seems like a good idea to me. We are closer to Aldervale right now than Silverton. If it's that important, it would be good to know before we get home," Suki replied. She locked his eyes with her gaze.

Camden furrowed his brow. "What is it?"

Suki looked away shaking her head as she bit her bottom lip. "I just want to get cleaned up," she said finally in a different tone.

Camden suspected that wasn't what was bothering her, but he didn't press the issue. "Looks like it got dicey in here," he said, pointing at the line of holes.

Suki looked to where he pointed, then quickly looked away coughing as she wiped her nose with the back of her hand. Camden noticed her trembling. "Yeah," she said, taking a deep breath. "I was helping one of the crew when it happened. That's what did this," she said, pulling on her blood stained shirt.

He knew it was a taboo subject for her, for all of them really. He couldn't help but remember that day long ago when he found her stabbed through the back, laying in a pool of her own blood. Focusing back on the holes in the wall, "When we get back, I'll have them weld some additional plating around the infirmary," he said.

"Cam," her voice quivered, turning him around.

Camden draped his strong arms around the trembling woman and held her close as she broke down. "It's going to be ok," he soothed, holding her tight. Concern crossed his face, as he continued sooth her. It bothered him more than a little that she was this shaken.

"I'm sorry," she said, pulling away after a few moments.

"Hey, don't worry about it," he offered. "When we get home we can talk about it if you want."

Suki gave a half smile and sniffed. "Sure."

"The intercoms are all working," he said, pointing. "If you need anything, just let me know, ok?" he said, looking at her with concern.

Suki didn't reply but nodded her head.

"Get some rest too. I'll let you know in plenty of time when we get close to meeting with your brother," he finished, making his way out of the infirmary.

"I will," she said. "Thank you," she added.

Camden nodded his head in understanding and exited the room to head back to the bridge. *Suki, fragile and strong, with the power to heal wounds. Perhaps her gifts were starting to weigh on her*, he wondered. He could make his body transform into other materials, useful in many situations, but his limited magic did not force or funnel him into a role he did not desire. He would have to make sure that she didn't feel she was wanted solely for her ability to heal the wounded.

"Change of plans Harold," Camden said, arriving on the bridge.

"Sir?" Harold questioned.

"Our return to Silverton is going to be delayed," he answered. "I need you to take us to these coordinates," Camden said, pointing to a location on the map.

"Aye sir," Harold acknowledged, adjusting their heading. "Deeper into the dragon's cave aye?"

"Nothing that grandiose. Just a quick stop to pick up a message then we will be heading home."

"Understood sir."

"How is the radio coming along?" Camden queried the comm's officer.

"It has to be replaced. We won't be able to repair it until we get back," the officer replied.

Camden nodded his head in understanding. Whatever it was that Bailon wanted to tell them, they would find out soon enough. If it was as important as he suspected, they would just have to make do until they got home. There was no use worrying about it now.

Chapter 22

"Do you think it will stitch itself back together?" Kail asked after returning to their quarters. He held up Angela's Imaera hide tunic, looking through the hole that Bastiana had burned through it with her magic. The same attack that would have instantly killed Angela if not for a combination of factors, both the Imaera hide's natural ability to resist magic and Angela's possession of the bindings created by Kail's father to block a mage's magic.

Angela stepped closer to examine the black leather as she towel dried her red hair after a much desired shower, "I do not know. There is new growth around the edges here and here," she pointed, examining the tunic. The other ability the Imaera hide had was to grow back or heal after being damaged. "It was a lot of magic, and the burn is large. It may take some time."

"Yeah, we will just have to wait and see," Kail concluded, setting down the armor. "Take it off so I can see," Kail said, pointing to her side.

Angela turned, opening the towel to reveal the large circle of runes that were now tattooed on her side. The burning wound that matched her armor was gone. Kail got closer to study the magic of the rune staff that had saved her life.

"How does it feel?" Kail asked, glancing up at her.

"It is hard to explain.   There is no pain or discomfort," she answered.

Returning to the runes, Kail softly ran his fingers across them. "But you feel something?" he quizzed.

"Yes. It feels the same as the skin around it, but the sensation changes," she tried to explain. "When you touch your own skin, you feel it one way, if someone else touches the same skin, it feels different," she finished.

Kail raised a concerned look at her words. "So you can't feel this?" he asked, drawing his fingers across the runic tattoos.

"No, I can feel your touch," she corrected. "It is the same as I feel here," she said moving his hand off of the markings. "But at the same time, not the same," she added, moving his hand back.

Kail moved to the smaller line of tattoos on her right arm just below the shoulder. The place he had intentionally cut her with her own blade. When he had pushed the rune staff into her arms, nothing had happened. Its magic was still a mystery, but they had both witnessed its protective healing abilities. It was a desperate attempt to save her, and he knew it was something else that would haunt his dreams.

Angela saw the sorrow in his eyes as he examined her arm. "You did not hurt me. Never forget that."

Kail tried to blow her statement off with a half smile. "It doesn't matter. It was just the way you looked at me when I let go of you."

"Stop," she demanded, thumping him on the head. "The situation was dire, and you reacted quickly. If you had taken the time to give a speech, I would not be standing here."

"I'm going to need that staff soon if you keep thumping me there," he said jokingly. "Still, we will need to keep an eye on it," his voice returned with a serious tone. "When we meet up with Camden and the others in Silverton, we should have Suki take a look at it first thing," he said, kissing her on the arm.

"What?" Angela asked after seeing him make a strange face after kissing the tattoos.

"There is still magic here," he said, moving his face closer to the markings. He brought his lips close to the tattoos again, but didn't kiss them, "I can smell it too. It's faint, but definitely something."

Angela brought her arm up to her nose to smell. "I do not smell anything."

"It's magic. Maybe Suki will know more," he shrugged, rubbing his hand across his mouth in thought, eyeing the rune staff in question that stood in the corner across the room.

The *Lotus* rested on the ground next to the *Colossus*. Captain Bailon had just finished reading the damage assessment from the *Lotus*. The fire had quickly been put out, and the damaged systems were already being repaired. The majority of the smoke had actually been caused by the paint used on the ship. Walls covered in a flammable paint was a serious defect that was at the top of his list to have corrected when they returned to Aldervale.

Cid stood next to him as they waited for the commanding officer of the *Colossus* to meet with them. It should be Vincent from Cahir, but until he saw the man in person, he wasn't going to assume anything. Cahir and Courduff were allies, but they were still in Cahir's sphere of influence. Proceeding from here was at the *Colossus's* discretion; however it was a formality, nothing more.

"Sir?" Cid questioned, catching him looking once again at the timepiece on his wrist.

"Ten more minutes and this formality ends," Bailon replied tartly, annoyed at being kept waiting. "We are good to return to Silverton are we not?"

"Yes sir. The damage to the ship is only cosmetic at this point in relation to its functionality," Cid replied.

Captain Bailon nodded his approval in response.

"About time," Bailon said, biting back a curse as a short portly man descended from the *Colossus* followed by a pair of other men. "That," Bailon started, "is not the man described to me as Vincent."

"Agreed sir," Cid said.

Bailon waited until the men were near before offering a salute. "I am Captain Bailon," he said. "This is my first officer, Cid Daltry. Can the *Lotus* or the people of Courduff offer you or your crew assistance?"

The man looked them both over glancing at the *Lotus* several times. *Was that jealousy he saw in the man's face?* he wondered. Given the state of the *Colossus*, he did not blame the man. The *Colossus* was heavily damaged, where as the *Lotus* had taken only a few hits.

"No, no, that won't be necessary," the man answered.

Bailon and Cid exchanged looks before continuing. "Are you the captain of the *Colossus*?" Bailon asked firmly when the man did not introduce himself.

"Sorry sirs. No, but I am the ranking officer right now," the man managed to get out.

Bailon's patience was wearing thin. "My understanding was that Vincent is in command of this vessel."

"Yes, yes sirs. That he is," the man answered quickly.

"Has he been wounded or killed?" Bailon asked.

"No, not at all, he left and is in the canyon somewhere," the man said not bothering to elaborate.

Both he and Cid shifted their stance after hearing the man tell them that the captain of the ship was not on board, but in fact had left some time earlier. It sounded like desertion regardless of the reason. Bailon nodded to the man. "Good luck sir."

It was clear that the man did not know how to respond as Bailon and Cid turned to make their way back to the *Lotus*.

"Interesting turn of events," Cid remarked when they were out of earshot of the man.

"Indeed. Cahir seems to be in worse shape than it lets on," Bailon added. "Let's get back to Aldervale as quickly as possible. I don't imagine my sister will wait forever."

Cid glanced back at the *Colossus* to examine the damaged ship for a moment. "No, I don't believe they are the type, sir."

Rhonin looked apprehensively at the three silvery rings of runes that were on the middle of the table. They were the source of all the frustration, death, and destruction of the day's events. "I hope they are worth it," he said, looking at Kail and Angela.

"Of course they are," Rayne said next to him.

"Regardless," Kail brought the conversation back on track. "We have them. How we use them can wait. After what happened in Cahir, we need to do everything we can to prepare Silverton for attack."

Rhonin silently agreed as Angela nodded her head in response to his statement. "How did the tower go down?" he asked, watching as Angela and Kail glanced at each other.

Angela started. "We were separated. Vincent had given us the bindings so Kail tried to teleport us away," she said.

"Angela had the bindings on her, and I found myself outside without her," Kail finished for her, pointing at the bindings. "They block magic. I couldn't find her at first. By the time I did, she was in the lobby of the tower fighting Bastiana."

"They just gave them to you?" Rhonin backed up the conversation.

"No they didn't and that's not the weird part," Kail continued. "They refused. The place was full of guards and soldiers to take us. Vincent left and Bastiana started a fight."

"Ok, so they didn't give them to you?" Rhonin asked again confused.

"He did. We were leaving down the elevator when Vincent stopped us. Bastiana wasn't there, I left her tied up," Kail said, pointing upwards. "He kicked us out of the elevator and gave us the bindings."

"Ok..." was all Rhonin could reply, trying follow out the events.

Angela chimed in next. "Our information about Vincent is incomplete. Kail hit him with his magic, and it did nothing."

"What do you mean nothing?" Rayne asked this time.

"Like the hide of a living Imaera. The magic did nothing to him," Angela said.

Everyone exchanged concerned looks. "I know," Kail said. "Unexpected doesn't quite cover it."

Rhonin didn't know what was worse now, a man immune to magic, or trying to take a mage's magic away from him with what amounted to jewelry.

"When I found Angela in the Lobby, Bastiana was there. When she fled from us, she took out the support columns of the tower before teleporting away," Kail said.

"You're right," Rhonin said wearily. "They will blame that on us, and everyone will believe them. There is no way they will let it go un-retaliated."

"The *Snow Break* shot down another airship too," Rayne added.

"Let's not forget the destruction to the trains and everything else," Kail added to the list.

Rhonin sighed. "It's good to see that we're all in agreement with something. Cahir and Courduff will be coming. Even if we are the 'excuse' now, they will find someone else to be their poster child when they are through with us."

No one wanted to admit it, but none of them could see a way for Silverton to survive an all out attack from both Cahir and Courduff.

Angela caught Rhonin looking at the single war blade. She had modified the sheath so the hilt now stuck out from behind her shoulder, prior she had kept both of them at the small of her back. "I lost it in the canyon," she stated.

"Are you going to replace it or go look for it?" he asked.

"Neither, it is only a weapon," she said.

Rhonin wasn't in agreement. Only a weapon or not, it was unbreakable and he had never seen her without them. *Then again, who knows what is important to a Keratin and what isn't,* he thought. "Speaking of weapons," he said, pointing at the runic tattoos on her arm. "What are you going do to about that?"

"I don't know," Kail said. "Bastiana could summon the staff at will. Personally I don't trust it."

Rhonin and Rayne nodded in agreement. "Something to worry about I guess if we survive all this," he said. "The mage, Bastiana, did you kill her?"

Angela nodded at the same time Kail shook his head.

"We don't know, do we?" Rhonin assumed, seeing their disagreement.

"If a fall into a canyon and a dozen magical hits do not kill, then I do not know what can," Angela said. "The mage is dead. She did not have the staff to save her."

"I hope so," Kail said. "But after everything I have seen. I would need to see a dead body. Even then I would still have doubts that she was really dead or not."

"I am sure we will hear about it over the wire. If Vincent's companion is dead, it will rile the peasants even more," Rhonin sighed. "We came out ok, not even a scratch on the ship, but the *Snow Break* was in pretty bad shape when we last saw her."

"They are probably already back to Silverton by now," Kail said with optimism.

Vincent squinted against the sunlight as he surveyed the desolate terrain of the canyon. The monorail tracks above him still had cargo shooting through the canyon. There were very few animals or any life in the canyon anymore. The noise of the monorail had displaced them elsewhere. He recalled the complaints some people had brought to the city about it. A pair of mysterious deaths by the same wild animals they wanted to protect had quickly quieted them. The message was clear about what he thought of animal rights as were the people who put a priority on them.

He finally found what he was searching for; melted sand and shattered rocks. Ahead of him about fifty feet he away could see tiny wisps of smoke from a burned out impact crater. At the center lay his darling Bastiana. Nothing was left of her clothing but tattered rags and once again her hair had all been burned off. Reaching her side he carefully rolled her over to assess her condition. Scrapes, cuts and a few minor burns seemed to be the worst of it. Although one large gash still trickled blood from her forehead. He took a clean handkerchief from his pocket to stem the bleeding. No bones appeared to be broken, and he was satisfied that she would survive.

"Bastiana, Bastiana my impulsive," he shook his head, covering her with his shirt. He pulled out his gun loaded with a special round in the chamber and fired it into the sky. The flare would signal the *Colossus* to come pick to them up. "Don't worry my dear," he said. "Don't worry."

Chapter 23

"Feeling any better?" Camden asked Suki as he scanned the perimeter of their camp once again.

"Yes, thank you," smiling as she answered.

Several hours ago the *Snow Break* landed in a clearing. Aldervale was a couple of hours away by air, and Silverton lay a few of days at top speed to the southwest. Camden had ordered the crew to focus on as many repairs as possible while the *Snow Break* was on the ground.

"We have more people than cannons," Camden said with a sigh. He sat next to her with the grace of an elephant, revealing the trip's toll on the big man.

Suki wasn't surprised he was worn out, she too looked forward to a week of sleep, but deep down knew that it might not ever happen or at least not for a long time.

"I hope your brother hurries. We can't stay here much longer," Camden said, "too dangerous."

"I'm sure Wilhelm will show. If not, whatever it was will get to us," Suki said.

"That's something I never understood," Camden started. "He helped us once before, but why now? Why would he help the enemy?" Camden asked.

Suki gave him a frown. "Does that make me the enemy?"

"No, you know what I mean. I just can't see any reason where I would do the same thing," he explained. "There is good and bad. Them and us. What is an *us* doing with a *them*?"

"It's more complicated than that," she said with a touch of anger.

"Don't get angry with me. I know it's more complicated than that. That is why I don't understand it," Camden countered. "We sure could use more like him," he mumbled.

"There is more you want to say, isn't there?" Suki said, sensing his mood.

Camden took a moment to rub his hands over his face before replying. "What happens next time?" he said, looking at her.

"What next time?"

"The next time we're on opposite sides, ships face to face with cannons ready to fire. There will be a next time, and someone is not going to back down. So what happens next time when one of us dies?"

Suki digested what Camden had said. She hadn't given it much thought, but until recently her brother had not been a captain of an airship that had been ordered to hunt them down. "War is ugly. It makes people do ugly things," she said.

"Isn't that the truth," Camden agreed, standing back up. "I don't want to be an ugly person, but it might too late for that."

"It's never too late," she disagreed.

Camden laughed. "Now you sound like Mr. Eleazar."

"Uh, no," she denied. "Don't compare me to him. Do you even remember what his clothes looked like? Not in a thousand years," she said flatly, swiping her arm.

"Hello ahead," a voice called.

Suki was quickly on her feet, and Camden had already shouldered a rifle as he stepped in front of her. His skin was beginning to turn a dark color to match the metal of the gun.

"Hello," the voice came again.

"Show yourself," Camden called back.

They watched as two riders on horseback came into view.

Suki recognized the first man as her brother, Wilhelm. "It's my brother," she said, stepping around Camden.

Camden stopped her and pushed her back. "Who's the shadow?" Camden called out, keeping an eye on the both of them.

"This is Lieutenant Cid Daltry, my first officer," Bailon said, motioning to Cid.

"Can we trust him?" Camden asked, still holding the rifle on them.

"I trust him," was all Bailon said as he got off of his horse and moved closer. "Suki," he greeted. "Are we good here?" He nodded towards Camden who still had the rifle still pointing at them.

"Yes, were good," she said, elbowing her way past Camden. The metallic clink from her elbow hitting his arm produced a quiet apology from him as he lowered the rifle. "It's good to see you," she said, smiling as she gave him a big hug. "Captain, it suits you," she said, looking over his uniform.

Bailon seemed to unwind and change from a stiff backed captain to a real person, a brother, Camden noticed. The other man, Cid seemed wound tighter than one of Angela's bow strings.

"I would say it's nothing like you could imagine, but you beat me to the skies little sister," Bailon said, nodding at the *Snow Break*.

"Camden," Bailon greeted, holding out his hand.

"Captain," Camden said, shaking Bailon's hand. Camden's hand was still metallic and gave him a little squeeze.

Bailon didn't flinch, but Suki saw what Camden was doing and slapped their hands apart angrily. "Stop that," she chided Camden.

"Sorry," he apologized to Bailon to appease the glaring look from Suki.

"No harm done," Bailon accepted, turning back to Suki. "Where to start?" Bailon said, deciding that the news for Kail could wait since he did not see him present. "I am getting married."

Suki's face lit up at the news. "That's wonderful!" she congratulated him.

"Yes, to Ari, Ari Ebonmore. You remember her from the Aldervale Inn?"

"Yes, I remember Ari," she said. Camden's snicker was not earning him any points.

"I fail to find the humor," Bailon stated.

"It's just a little clichéd," Camden explained. Bailon's questioning look asked for an explanation. "The innkeeper's daughter."

Bailon rolled his eyes. "Yes the innkeeper's daughter," he confirmed. "She happens to also be the director of the Hospital in Aldervale," he finished. "Now what?" he continued when Camden seemed even more entertained.

"Oh, nothing. The innkeeper's daughter, who has a staff of nurses," he said. "I've always pictured myself with a nurse one day," he finished, grinning at Suki.

Suki's pondered the comment but filed it away for later while trying not to blush when her brother gave her and Camden an odd look. "I am happy for you Will. But catching up isn't the reason you are here."

"Yes, quite to the point as always. I have news for Kail Falconcrest," he said, looking around once more for Kail. "May I speak with him?"

Camden and Suki glanced at each other. "He isn't here," Camden said.

Bailon knew better than to ask his whereabouts. It was information he did not need nor want to know if this meeting ever came to be known to anyone else. "I feel honor bound to tell him in person, but I can see that simply will not be possible," Bailon said.

"We can take whatever message you have to him," Camden said as Suki nodded her head in agreement.

Bailon held his hand out, and Cid handed him a folded letter. "Two weeks ago, there was an incident at the Kelly farmstead."

Camden stopped Suki before she could demand more information. "What kind of incident?" Camden said coldly.

Bailon handed over the letter. "There was a fire. The house was lost, and the Kelly's were found inside," he paused. "They did not survive."

"Oh god," Suki managed to get out before her breath failed her.

Camden's blood turned to ice as he carefully asked the next question. "Was anyone else hurt?"

"No," Bailon answered much to their relief. "But, to my knowledge there were other family members living there as well, the two nieces of Jessica Kelly," he added.

Camden nodded not trusting his ability to keep his voice in check. Suki had moved behind him with her face buried in his shirt and had started to hit him lightly with her fist.

Cid let Bailon continue to talk, but their reaction to the news spoke volumes and as far as he was concerned, confirmed all of his suspicions about the unusual activity surrounding the event, as he handed Bailon a new set of documents.

"I thought as much. We don't have too much information on their whereabouts, but there is no evidence that they were in the fire. Only the bodies of the Kelly's were found," Bailon said.

"But," Camden stated coldly.

"But there was some high level security activity at the same time," Bailon continued, handing Camden the documents. "I know things can be difficult when friends or family die," he said concerned with Suki's reaction to the news.

Camden couldn't think enough to make sense of what the documents were telling him. "Just tell us," he managed to say, indicating to the documents.

Bailon turned to Cid and nodded.

"The night of the incident, intelligence reports a group of people leaving Aldervale by train. By itself this is not news, but the description of the party along with its timing with the Kelly fire makes it stand out," Cid explained. "Two of the people are described as children, girls to be exact. Next is the security access levels used to commandeer transport to Courduff," he pointed out on the document.

Camden didn't say anything but shook his head.

"This," Cid showed Camden, "is Therion's level and his access code."

Camden crushed the document in his fist as Suki let out a choked sob, starting to hit him harder.

"Clearly this is disturbing news for you, however all reports have Therion still in Canyamar at The Eternal Gateway outpost," Bailon responded to their reactions.

"Two weeks," Camden's voice trembled. "Where are they now?" he asked, keeping his eyes on the crumpled document in his hand. Cid pulled out a small folded map.

"There is small detainment center here," Cid said, pointing to a spot marked on the map. "The last of the reports place them here, but they are several days old. I can't vouch for their accuracy at this time."

"These girls," Bailon said. "Who are they?"

Camden hesitated before telling him. Each time Suki used his back as an outlet for her emotions he could see Amaya and Alyssa's face's flash through his mind. His voice started to betray him when he answered. "They are-- Kail's. Kail and Angela's daughters," he said. "Twins," he added.

Bailon and Cid exchanged very concerned looks.

"I told you," Suki hissed at him.

Camden ignored her words even though they stung like a knife. He took a deep breath to clear his thoughts while he pushed his emotions away. "We have to go get them," he said. "We can't wait. It will take just over three days to get to Silverton, if they are even there," he said, referring to Kail and Angela.

Bailon nodded in understanding then motioned to Cid, who once again produced another set of papers.

Camden couldn't help but cough then laugh at the man who seemed to be a filing cabinet.

"This is the patrol route of every ship from Aldervale to Courduff," Cid said hesitantly before handing them to Camden. "They will not be valid at the end of the week."

"I had Cid gather this information on the chance that Kail was not here. His abilities would have made them unnecessary," Bailon said.

"Thank you," Camden said.

"If you leave now, bypass Aldervale and go straight to Courduff," Cid said, "you can land here. There will be a four hour gap for you to get in and back out before the next patrolling warship passes."

Camden nodded.

"Suki?" Bailon asked, approaching his sister.

"No!" she yelled at him as tears rolled down her face. Crying she made her way back to the *Snow Break*, leaving them standing there.

Bailon turned back to Camden. "If we had known."

"You weren't supposed to, that was the point," Camden said. "Nobody was."

"I can't help you any further," he finished, nodding to Cid who left to get the horses. "Tell Kail I am sorry for his loss."

Camden nodded.

"Tell my sister good bye as well. I don't know when we will be able to meet again," Bailon said, turning to leave with Cid back for Aldervale.

Camden stood for several minutes before the gravity of everything hit him. He felt his emotions detach and his mind clear to concentrate on rescuing the twins. Turning, he ran back to the *Snow Break*, rushing onto the bridge.

Slapping on the ship wide intercom he commanded the crew to prepare for immediate take off and man the battle stations.

"Sir?" Harold asked confused as he brought the turbines online, causing the ship to vibrate.

Camden knew Harold wasn't the only one who deserved an explanation. "We are going to Courduff. Information has been given to us that Kail and Angela's twin daughters have been abducted," he said into the intercom.

"The information is time sensitive and requires immediate action."

Camden shut off the intercom to face Harold. "These are the patrol routes for Courduff and Aldervale. We need to get to this location here," he said, pointing to the map.

Harold nodded. "Yes sir."

Suki had made her way to the armory trying to find the right bullets to go with the gun she had randomly picked up. Taking out her frustration, she slammed the gun down and swept the counter top, sending everything crashing to the floor.

"Suki, are you ok in there?" Camden asked after a long search.

"We got them killed, and now they are gone as well," she snapped.

"It's nobody's fault Suki," Camden said, lifting his hands in the air.

"It is your fault and their fault," Suki growled at him. "And my fault, I said it was a bad idea, and I went along with it anyway."

"We all agreed, and it was their choice in the end, not yours or mine," Camden retorted, reminding her that they had not come to the decision to take Amaya and Alyssa to the Kellys without a lot of thought and argument.

Suki clenched her fists, glaring at him. She was unsure if she should take it out on Camden now or push it aside until the danger to the twins had passed.

"We can't blame what happened on one decision," Camden said, shaking his head. "I know how much they mean to you, they mean a lot to everyone."

She admitted to herself that he was right, but it didn't do anything to make her feel better. "How long until we get there?" she asked.

"Not long, the information your brother gave us is accurate," he answered.

Suki turned back to the guns in the armory. "I'm going with you on this one," she said in a tone that left no room for argument.

"I wasn't going to stop you," he said, moving over to help her get armed. "Actually it's going to be just you and me on this one."

Suki's glance told him to continue.

"Like the time at the gateway. A small force. Get in, find them, and get out," he explained. "We will need everyone on the *Snow Break* ready to go the moment we have them."

She didn't like the plan, because they shouldn't be in this trouble to begin with, but she couldn't find any real fault with it. The success they had as a small force at The Eternal Gateway proved that.

Camden handed her a rifle. "It's loaded and ready to go," he said. "These are the bullets for it," he finished, handing them to her.

She looked at the bullets in her hand before placing them into her pocket. The question that had been nagging her since her brother had told them about the Kellys surfaced again. "What if we don't get them? What if they are not there? What if--," she rambled.

"No 'what ifs'," he cut her off. "We find them, we bring them home," he said firmly, sliding a pair of pistols into their holsters and shouldering a rifle. "We bring them home."

"War is one thing," Captain Bailon said to Cid as they approached the Ebonmore Inn. "Murder and kidnapping children, that's not war," he finished.

"You try to bring honor to a fight that does not respect it. I hope for both of our sakes you don't regret it," Cid said.

Bailon gave Cid a hard look. "What is that supposed to mean?"

"Regardless of the reason, what we did was treason at the highest levels."

"Thank you Cid, but I am well aware of what we did and the consequences that it may bring," Bailon said curtly. "At least I can say with dignity that I died for doing what I felt was right."

"Understood sir," Cid said, letting the argument drop. "Looks like someone might still be waiting up for you," he added, pointing to the lights on at the inn.

"Possibly, care for a nightcap? I'm buying," Bailon offered.

Cid considered the offer before answering. "Knowing that there will be a paperwork mess from hell if they shoot up Courduff, this might be the last time for a drink in a long while."

Bailon agreed at Cid's assessment. The next few days were going to be interesting. He hadn't thought how the higher-ups would respond to back to back attacks by Silverton. First Cahir then Courduff. They entered the Ebonmore Inn after securing their horses out front.

Ari quickly greeted them with a smile. "Hello fiancé," she said.

"Hello dear," he greeted back, kissing her hand.

"Come, there is someone waiting to see you," she said excitedly, pulling him forward to the dining area of the inn.

Bailon glanced back at Cid who gave him an understanding shrug as he was pulled away by Ari. Cid walked to the bar area to order himself a drink, content with the idea that he would most likely be drinking alone.

"Ok, slow down Ari. Who is here?" Bailon asked.

"You will see," she answered with sparkling eyes as he followed her into the dining area.

The man holding a glass of red wine spoke, "Captain Bailon, I am so glad you could join us. Your lovely fiancé has been telling me all about you," as he turned he recognized Therion.

Bailon looked at Ari's beaming face that the last ruling member of the Mage Council and the ruler of Courduff was at her father's inn, waiting to speak to her future husband. Bailon did his best to smile back, but the numbness of shock and dread were already creeping through his body. "Thank you sir," he saluted, stepping forward to meet his fate.

Chapter 24

"Five minutes sir," Harold's voice came over the intercom.

Camden and Suki stood next to the loading door of the cargo bay as the *Snow Break* prepared to drop them off. The plan was to retreat to a safer area before swinging back to pick them up once they had the rescued Amaya and Alyssa. The ride was a bumpy one as Harold quickly swung the ship low through the edges of Courduff, dodging the patrols tipped off to them by Bailon and Cid.

"This reminds me of five years ago," Camden remembered.

"What does?" Suki asked.

"Kail and I rushing to Courduff to rescue Angela."

Suki remembered part of that day. She had woken up at the Ebonmore Inn after being in a coma nearly dead for several days. Along with her half brother and the Mastersons, they had flown to Courduff to rescue the three of them from the top of Therion's tower.

"This time though it's different," he said.

"It's more important," Suki said softly.

Camden nodded his head in agreement. "I had given up."

"What?" Suki asked, not understanding where the comment had come from.

"When we rescued Angela. I had given up. Kail hadn't," he admitted.

"What do you mean?"

Camden looked at Suki before answering. "Everyone was dead. It was just the two of us there in the jungle. It was Kail and his magic that found Angela. He wasn't going to give up on her, or you, or me for that matter."

"He loves her," Suki pointed out.

"Yeah, but it was more than that. I think I know why he risked everything now."

"Why?" Suki asked.

"Is the world worth saving, if you can't save those closest to you?" he questioned.

Suki thought about his words for a moment before answering. "You don't have to save the world. If you try, you will forget to save those closest to you. Save them, and you will save the world in turn."

Camden nodded. The essence of what he tried to say was there. He had spent so many years trying to forget the death of his first crew that he had built a wall around himself shutting out everyone else. The more he thought about it, the more he realized that they all had. He started to see where they had treated people as resources and numbers. That same line of thinking lead to some of the bad decisions, like the failed attack on the gateway outpost where the *Wind*

Runner was lost along with her entire crew. Even getting the bindings from Cahir could have been handled much better. "You were right from the beginning. I just didn't see it until now."

"Don't let everything worth living for pass you by," Angela's words came to her. The wink that Camden had given her just before they attacked the gateway outpost flashed in her mind. She thought of him holding her when she broke down earlier, and him telling her that he would not tell anyone that she had been crying. *"Don't step quietly,"* she said quickly to herself.

"What--?" Camden's words were stopped by Suki's mouth crushing his. It took him a few seconds to realize what was happening. She had to stand on her toes to pull him down to kiss him, and he found himself kissing her back just as fiercely.

"Touch down in thirty," Harold's voice broke the moment.

Suki backed away to face the closed loading ramp while straightening herself after kissing Camden.

"Ready?" Camden asked, tasting his lips where she had kissed him.

Suki didn't say anything but nodded her head. Camden pulled down on the leaver. The loading ramp began to lower itself as the wind and noise kicked up around them. The *Snow Break* landed for less than ten seconds before it took to the sky again, leaving Camden and Suki a short distance away from where her brother had told them where Kail and Angela's daughters were being held. They watched in the fading daylight as the *Snow Break* flew out of sight.

"Let's go get them," Camden said.

"Let's save the world," Suki corrected.

Cid had just taken the first sip of his third drink when Captain Bailon returned to the lobby area. "I figured you had started the honeymoon early," he said, choking on the alcohol when he saw Therion step out of the dining area right behind him. Cid scrambled to compose himself and salute with as much dignity as he could wearing half a spilled drink.

Bailon closed his eyes to Cid's floundering and continued towards his lieutenant. Before he could say anything Therion spoke.

"I hope I have made everything clear Admiral," Therion said. "Do not keep me waiting," he finished.

"Yes sir," Bailon said, saluting again. Therion nodded as he continued to walk towards the front door of the inn, his body dissolving in a vortex of magic as he teleported away.

Cid gave him a confused look as Ari with a smile stepped to Bailon's side to take his arm.

"Prepare the horses. We are taking the *Lotus* to Courduff," Bailon said. "Now lieutenant," he snapped when Cid hesitated.

"Yes sir," Cid nodded and quickly left to do as ordered.

"I know this is big, but there is no need to be harsh," Ari said as she straightened his jacket and smoothed out a wrinkle.

"Unexpected is more accurate," he corrected. "It may be a while before I return."

"I know," she said, still smiling at him. "Don't worry. You need to focus and I understand that. Now, get going, as he said, you don't want to be late," she finished with a kiss.

Bailon nodded. "Ma'am I take my leave," he bowed and exited the inn.

Cid was waiting for him with both horses. "What just happened?" he wanted to know.

Bailon just shook his head. "I wish I knew."

"Admiral?" Cid asked.

Bailon gave Cid a sideways glance at the mention of admiral. "Apparently news of what happened in Cahir has already reached Therion, that along with our performance at the gateway outpost and the treating of the wounded. We, or more correctly I, have become some sort of poster child for the air force."

Cid's forehead burrowed as he factored Bailon's words in his mind. "And this is a bad thing?" he asked.

"Everything and I mean everything from now on will be looked at under a microscope. What we do, what we have done. He even wants Ari and me to get married in Courduff as some grand spectacle," Bailon said between gritted teeth.

Cid still wasn't quite sure why his captain, no admiral was in such a sour mood.

Bailon took a deep breath. "Therion is going to meet us on the *Lotus*. We are to escort him outside of Courduff."

Cid felt the same dread fill the pit of his stomach as he finally understood why Bailon was acting this way. "He's seen the same reports I have," Cid said. "He wants to see firsthand who has been using his access code."

Bailon's answer was to spur his horse in the direction of the Aldervale air field where the *Lotus* was stationed. He could only hope that his sister and the *Snow Break* were long gone before they arrived.

Camden and Suki had not seen anyone as they made their way from where the *Snow Break* had dropped them off near the building where Amaya and Alyssa were being held.

"Why are there no people?" Suki whispered as they watched the building from across the street under the cover of darkness.

"It's night and this area looks more like abandoned industry than downtown," Camden answered. "Also if I had to guess, the area is kept clear on purpose if this is supposed to be a secret jail of some kind."

A tiny flicker of light caught their attention as a hidden guard bored with the night had decided to light a cigarette. Camden looked back to give Suki an 'I told you so' look.

"Stay here," he whispered, stepping around the side of the building. Suki almost instantly lost sight of both Camden and the guard who had revealed himself. Her heart beat so loudly in her ears that she was sure everyone within a mile radius could hear her. Even her breathing sounded so loud that she had to cover her mouth and nose while she waited minute after minute for Camden to return.

She nearly fainted dead from a heart attack when he touched her shoulder. "Calm down and breath Suki," he said in reaction to her jump. "I took care of the guard, but I found two others on the way back."

Suki did as he recommended and took several deep breaths before nodding that she was ok.

"I think we're ok to move across the street, but we need to hurry. There is no telling what kind of system they have set up here. We might have an hour or maybe less than a minute before they realize something is up," he said.

"Let's make it a minute then," she said, not wanting to run the risk of being here any longer than absolutely necessary.

Camden nodded and pointed to a shadowy strip that ran across the street to the side of the secret complex. Leading the way and staying low, the two of them crossed the street. "This could be bad," Camden assessed.

"What?" Suki pried.

"There is only the one door so far," Camden said pointing to a well lit metal door. "If that is the only way in, it's going to be hard to open it unnoticed."

"Is there another way?"

"Don't have time to find one," Camden sighed. "I have an idea. When you see me signal, come as fast as you can."

"What?" she asked frustrated, but Camden was already walking towards the metal door.

Camden casually walked along the side of the building as if he belonged there. He kept his hand along the cement wall to use his magic to make the rest of his body just as hard. *No reason to get shot and killed*, he reasoned. When no one had tried to shoot him as he neared the door, he saw another problem. Instead of a normal door handle, there was a large lock. Taking one quick glance around, he placed his hand over the lock to fuse his hand to it. It only took a couple of seconds for his hand and arm to turn into the same steel as the door and lock. It didn't require much pressure for the entire front of the lock to break free still fused to his hand as the door opened an inch.

He signaled to Suki as he opened the door, quickly checking to see if there was anyone on the inside. The hallway was clear so he shut the door after Suki stepped inside. He almost set the piece of the lock on the ground when he thought better of it. Having a piece of steel to turn his body into might come in handy.

"This is defiantly a jail of some kind," Suki whispered, looking up and down the hallway. The walls were whitewashed as in a hospital, and there was one steel door after another spaced every twenty feet. "How are we going to find them in all this?"

"Same way we did when we found Angela," Camden said, rushing to the first door. "Look in every one," he finished. The steel door had a smaller door on the front of it for passing items or food into the room. The steel screeched as he slid the smaller door open to quickly glance into the room. He shook his head at Suki to let her know that it was empty as they moved to the next door. Each empty room made the seconds and minutes seem like hours and days as they rushed to find the twins.

Bailon was starting to get used to the uncomfortable presence of Therion on the bridge of the *Lotus*. The crew as well was putting on their best performance once they knew of his arrival on the ship. Once again he was amazed with Cid. Somewhere he had managed to find the time to replace his uniform after spilling a drink on it earlier that night. Both men kept a close eye on their commanding officer as the lights of Courduff were starting to be seen on the horizon.

Bailon had a dozen questions he would like to ask Therion, but kept them to himself. With the few encounters he had with Therion he knew that he was the type of man who came to you, not the other way around.

"Admiral," Therion said, standing at the front of the bridge viewport.

Bailon gave Cid a knowing look as he went to stand next to Therion. "Sir?" he asked.

"Once I am through with this curiosity in Courduff, we will be returning to Canyamar and The Eternal Gateway."

"Yes sir," Bailon acknowledged.

"In the coming days, I am going to need someone I can trust," Therion said. "Are you that man Admiral Bailon?"

"Yes sir," Bailon said without hesitation.

Camden held his hand over the guard's mouth to keep him from crying out as he felt the man go limp in his arms. He was the second guard that he and Suki had managed to get the drop on since entering the jail complex. Suki opened one of the empty jail cells as Camden dragged the dead man's body inside.

Both Camden and Suki were running on pure desperation at this point. Each empty cell slowly brought doubt. Was this the wrong building? Had the twins already been moved to a new location, or maybe something even worse, that they refused to put into words.

Another empty cell forced Suki to put voice to their concerns. "They are not here," she said.

"We still have many more to look through," a determined Camden said. "And there is another floor as well."

Suki nodded as the next two cells checked out empty.

"Do you smell that?" Camden asked after catching whiff of a sour smell.

Suki concentrated then nodded that she could smell something as well. Rushing they checked the next cell to find it empty as well. The following cell brought them up short as the smell was clearly coming from inside the room.

Camden covered his mouth and nose giving Suki a concerned look as he slid open the small center door to look inside. His heart skipped a beat and at the same time it felt like it had been cut from his chest as he saw the little dark haired girl curled up on the floor next to the far wall. "Stand back!" he growled at Suki.

The metal door was locked and reinforced within the cement walls. He didn't care if it was a mile of solid steel or granite separating them, it wouldn't be enough to stop him. Camden placed his hands on each side of the door and pushed his magic to its limits. Slowly his hands pushed into the steel and concrete. Fusing his hands to other objects was something he had done countless times, but he had never before tried pushing his hands inside of an object. He could feel and see his magic cause his hands to pass through the different materials.

Suki watched with baited breath as Camden tore at the door. The cement walls began to crack and chip around the door as the big man grunted.

Sand, Camden thought. Cement had sand inside of it and his magic obeyed his command as the reinforcing steel inside the wall turned to sand. He felt the door and its frame pull an inch towards him out of the wall. With a final groan, the cement edges around the door crumbled as the heavy steel door and its frame broke free. He didn't care about the loud noise it made as he tossed the metal door down the hallway with a crash.

Suki was inside the room in a flash. Alyssa had sat up cowering in the corner as Camden ripped the door from the wall. Her cell contained bits of spoiled food and fetid water. Clearly no one had bothered or cared enough to know how to take care of a little four year old girl. Alyssa's clothing as well as much of the floor were soiled.

Camden quickly followed Suki who was trying to get more than a flinch response from Alyssa. "So help me god, I will kill every single one of them," he promised.

Suki ran her hand to smoothed out Alyssa's hair. "It's going to be ok Alyssa. We're here, you're safe now," Suki soothed. Alyssa slowly began to recognize her and Camden. There were no tears as they had long ago run dry for the little girl as she began to open and close her mouth.

"Uncle Camden?" her tiny voice rasped.

Suki let loose a choked sob and hugged Alyssa. "Yes, yes, it's us. Everything is going to be ok," she cried.

"Take her and go now," Camden ordered. "I will find Amaya and meet you at the pickup spot," he said, rushing back into the hallway. Checking for locked doors was faster than peeking inside each one. The only locked door they had come across so far was the one containing Alyssa. Open, open, open the same result for each door as he ran down the hallway and around the corner to the next. It didn't make sense to him to have separated the twins by this much in a place this large.

"Damn it," he cursed, reaching the last of the empty cells. *Upstairs*, his mind yelled at him as he ran back to a stairwell, racing up the flight of stairs.

Suki held tightly onto Alyssa as she marched through the jail, going out the same door they had come in through. She knew that there might be guards or soldiers hiding in the darkness, but she didn't care. Her only thought was to get Alyssa away from here and to the safety of the *Snow Break*. She kept track of each sniffle and whimper Alyssa made. She would find a way to make whoever was responsible spend the rest of their life paying for each and every one of them.

No one had jumped out of the darkness at them when she reached the empty lot where the *Snow Break* had dropped them off. Setting Alyssa down she took off her pack to find a clean cloth to start cleaning the grime from Alyssa's face. "It's going to be alright," she said, tossing the dirty cloth away.   Pulling another clean cloth from her bag she continued. "It's going to be alright," she repeated.

"I know," Alyssa said.

"Camden will be here soon with Amaya, then we will all go home, where it's warm and safe," Suki continued.

"No," Alyssa said, shaking her head.

"Don't be silly," Suki choked, starting to work on her third cloth.

"She told me so," Alyssa countered.

"What are you talking about?" Suki asked still focusing on cleaning up Alyssa.

"The burned man took her."

Suki finally stopped to pay attention. "What?"

"Amaya said it was time, and he took her."

Suki gave the little girl a puzzled look. "She said what?"

"She is not coming. She has to go back and save Uncle Camden," Alyssa said.

"Amaya said this?" Suki said even more confused.

Alyssa nodded her head.

The second floor of the jail was different from the ground floor. Gone were the stark white walls with endless rows of empty cells. Here the jail reminded Camden of the mage tower where Angela had been held all those years ago. There were also additional guards and soldiers on this floor as well. The earlier rage he had felt was starting to fade. If he kept charging on like a bull, who knew what would happen. They had found Alyssa so making a stupid mistake now was unacceptable.

Camden knew time was starting to run short as he dragged a fourth guard's body into a small room. At some point he was going to have to decide to give up stealth in favor of speed. The *Snow Break* would be coming for them soon.

The familiar crack and sizzle of magic alerted Camden. Waiting behind the door of the room where he had just hidden the bodies of the guards he had killed, he listened as the footsteps approached and then passed by. A quick glance confirmed his worst fears as he caught a glimpse of Therion turning the corner at the end of the hallway. Time had run out. *That decided things*, Camden thought, pulling out one of his revolvers as he hurried down the hallway after Therion.

The next hallway ended at the entrance to a large room. Again Camden waited until Therion had moved out of sight before following. As he neared he could hear the voices of other people in the room. Keeping low, he took a quick glance into the room. Several people were gathered, most stood stiffly in the presence of Therion, but luck was on his side as the room was filled with desks and other office equipment, allowing him to slip into the room unnoticed.

"What do we have here?" he heard Therion ask.

"Falconcrest's kid," said an unfamiliar voice. "Two of them actually, but this one doesn't cry or cower like the other."

Camden found a small break between the desks and could see Therion kneel down next to Amaya.

"Filthy things, children," Therion stated.

"You should see the other one," the man said disgustedly. Camden didn't recognize the man as he came into view, but he knew the type, *bounty hunter*.

Therion stood. "It is the seed of Falconcrest. Where is the man who was with you? The one with access codes?"

Treylane shrugged. "Around. The man is a psycho, the less I see of him the better."

Camden swallowed hard as he slowly pulled the hammer back on his pistol. Keeping his eye on the men in front of him, he held his breath as the gun's faint click sounded like thunder to his ears as the hammer cocked for firing. Amaya slowly turned her head to stare right at him. Her small sapphire blue eyes blinked as she continued to look at him. Camden put his finger over his mouth in hopes that she did not give him away. She smiled as she turned back to Therion and Treylane.

"Kill it so we can leave this place," said a new voice that froze Camden.

Impossible, Camden's mind screamed, as Xavier Ross came into view. Xavier, the man who had killed his entire crew. One of the men that Mr. Eleazar had gathered years ago. The same man he himself had watched be torn apart one tiny bit at a time by the blue wisp that used to live inside the *Snow Break's* power core. Camden's body refused to obey his command as he stared at what was impossible.

Amaya looked at Xavier with fierce determination.

"I've seen that look before, that's why I did all this," Xavier told her. "You will thank me *Therion*," Xavier said with contempt. "Besides, they are already here. The other one is already gone."

"I can see no reason to disagree," Therion said. He seemed unconcerned by the news that Alyssa was missing. He had no intention of confronting whoever '*they*' were at this time. Holding his hand out towards Treylane, the bounty hunter handed him his serrated blade. "This will hurt them in a way from which they may never recover."

Camden froze and his mind screamed as Amaya's body fell to the floor. Her little face stared at him as the light faded from those blue eyes. Light that he failed to save. Like everyone else he had failed to save on the *Snow Break*. Even Xavier was alive, and here once more to torture him. "*I am going to let you in on a secret. She dies and there is nothing you can do to save her,*" Xavier's words from the past stabbed him again. "*I wish you could have been there.*" Camden was here, locked in a stare with Amaya, the daughter of his best friends who had on countless times entrusted him with their safety and love. A stare that ripped through his soul.

His ears filled with a high pitch ringing, and tears crept from his unblinking eyes to slowly fall onto the floor of his hiding place. Even after the flash and hiss of Therion teleporting himself and the other men away he could not flinch or move. There was only Amaya. He couldn't remember moving, but he had the little girl in his arms, holding tight, pleading for her to wake up. He would never say no to her again if she would only come back. He promised her to let her always win at any game she wanted to play.

"You can't be here for this," Mr. Eleazar's voice said softly.

Camden coughed as he wiped away tears with the back of his hand. "Be here for what? You're too late," he said. As his voice failed him he shook his head at the irony of Mr. Eleazar showing up here and now.

"I can't tell you."

"Answer me this then," Camden countered. Mr. Eleazar remained silent. "Was it worth it?"

"I don't know," Mr. Eleazar replied. "Right now, no. I don't think so. But tomorrow, maybe. Yesterday perhaps."

Camden wiped away a new set of tears as he held Amaya tighter and continued to shake his head at Mr. Eleazar's words.

"Suki is waiting for you."

"Damn it Camden where are you," Suki cursed in the darkness. The *Snow Break* should be on its way back to pick them up.

"He will be here soon," said a deep voice from the darkness.

Suki held Alyssa close to her as she held her gun in the direction of the voice. "Who's there?" she demanded.

Stepping from the darkness an older gentleman with more grey in his hair and beard than color held up his hands. "You won't be needing that," he gestured towards the gun.

"I'll be the judge of that," Suki answered by pulling the hammer back, stopping the man's approach. She turned her body to put more of herself between the stranger and Alyssa.

"It's ok," Alyssa said.

Suki looked at the man then back to Alyssa in confusion. "No, it's not ok."

The man lowered his hands as he held one out to Alyssa. "It's time dear," he said as tiny blue eyes peeked over the top of his shoulder.

Suki relaxed her grip at the sight of familiar being that she had not seen in several years.

Alyssa struggled out of Suki's grasp to run over to the man.

"Alyssa, step away from that man, now," Suki said.

Alyssa smiled at Suki. "Good bye Aunt Suki."

"Are you ready?" the stranger asked Alyssa.

"Yes Grandpa," Alyssa said, waving at her and grinning to the wisp.

Duke Falconcrest looked back at Suki with pity and sorrow. *I'm sorry*, he mouthed as the two of them disappeared.

"No!" Suki screamed, running towards where they had stood. She made it only a few steps before tripping over Camden who had suddenly appeared in front of her. "Cam, he took her," she cried, shaking the big man. "He took her!"

Camden looked at Suki like a zombie. "He killed her," he said flatly.

"No, he took her, just now," she pleaded trying to get Camden to his feet.

"Therion, Xavier, they killed her."

Suki understood now. Amaya was not with him. "No, no, no," she refused to believe him. Alyssa stolen right in front of her and now Camden telling her that Amaya was dead. "That's not possible. Xavier is dead."

"I watched her die," Camden whispered.

Suki slapped him hard. "No! They are not dead, that man took them."

"I held her in my arms!" Camden yelled. "I saw the life drain from her eyes," he screamed, getting to his feet.

"You're lying," Suki cried. Camden had never yelled at her before, but she could see it now. The pain in his eyes told her it was true. "No," she shook her head. "This can't be happening," she said backing away. The noise of the *Snow*

Break roaring overhead caused her to look up. Losing her balance she fell to the ground, unable to hold back her tears.

Admiral Bailon frowned when he saw that Xavier Ross stood on the bridge of the *Lotus*. He remembered the burned man from the Aldervale hospital where he had personally delivered his discharge papers. The other man he did not know, but held his tongue in Therion's presence.

"Admiral, there seems to be an issue in need of your attention," Therion said, pointing to the distance.

"Yes sir," Bailon acknowledged.

"Approaching ship identified as the *Snow Break* sir," an officer called through the bridge.

Cid gave him a sideways glance, but Bailon did not return the look. "Ready cannons, and bring us around for an attack vector," Bailon ordered.

"This is better than the first time," Xavier said, pulling out a cigarette from his pocket. He lit it and took a satisfying drag.

Bailon shot Cid a warning look when the Lieutenant was about to approach Xavier in regards to the lit cigarette on the bridge of their ship. Cid backed down when Bailon shook his head. Therion clearly held these men in favor. Starting something now was the last thing they needed, given the situation. "Fire when ready," he ordered.

"Aye sir," the officer said, relaying the order to the weapons deck.

Camden staggered over to where Suki lay crying on the cold ground. He was about to tell her that they would find Alyssa when the night sky lit up from explosions. Both of them stared in horror as shell after shell punched into the side of the *Snow Break* above them. "No," Camden whispered as the ship, which was his home, began to list as her pilot tried to move the ship away from them.

"No," he screamed again as terror filled him. Cannon fire exploded inside the noble vessel. The *Lotus* pursued never letting up the assault. As the *Snow Break* broke apart in the sky there was one final flash of blue energy from the heart of the ship. The magical energy core was breached.

He heard Suki scream '*why*', just as the escaping energy engulfed the *Snow Break* causing fire to rain down across the edge of the city.

Camden didn't think he could possibly feel any worse than he already did, but the death of the *Snow Break* tore away any life left in him. It was as if someone had extinguished all feeling from inside his body by tearing the last part of him away. First, Amaya dying in front of him while he did nothing, then Alyssa taken and finally, the betrayal by those they had foolishly trusted. Numbness set in. No feeling, no pain, no breath, no life.

"Why?" Suki screamed louder, now more animal than human, clutching her arms as she began to claw at her stomach continuing to scream.

Chapter 25

Suki sat alone in the passenger car of the train. The rhythmic clacking and vibrations did little to massage the numbness in her hollow heart. It had been over five days since they had tried to rescue the twins. Five days since her brother had betrayed them and destroyed the *Snow Break*. Five days since Camden had abandoned her. She yelled and screamed until her voice bled as he ran away into the darkness after a man she knew was dead. Five days since the world had ended.

Her only desire was that Kail and Angela would take pity on her and kill her. She would have done it herself, but she lacked the courage. The irony of it all was that everyone around her moved about like nothing had happened. A cruel new hell existed, and they were oblivious to it. The train started to slow down, and the screech of the metal breaks sounded like the devil's laugh as the train finally jerked to a stop. The conductor's disembodied voice filled the car telling the passengers that they had arrived in Silverton. Arrived for judgment.

"I don't care what the wire says," Kail argued. "I want confirmation," he finished angrily, dismissing Randal Wood and Duncan Deline from the room. The propaganda coming from Courduff claimed that the *Snow Break* had been shot down on the outskirts of the city. He knew it was a lie because there would be no reason for Camden or the *Snow Break* to fly to Courduff. Each passing day that they were overdue made him want to spare the time and manpower to go looking for them. The Mastersons had said the ship was in bad shape so that they most likely had landed somewhere for repairs and would be showing up any time now.

The alarm that went off sent adrenalin through his body. Confused he listened as the noise faded. It was unlike anything he had heard before. He was running out of the room before he even realized it.

"Angela!" he yelled, finally recognizing that it wasn't some new alarm but an anguished voice he heard. He knocked Duncan to the ground as he ran down the hall to where the noise had started again growing louder. As he raced into the room, he saw Randal looking confused and helpless as Angela struggled to get to her feet but fell towards the wall.

"Angela, what's wrong, what's going on?" Kail asked. He feared that maybe the magic from the rune staff had caused this. Even when she was dying, she was not in this much pain.

"Sir," Randal interrupted as he pointed to another person in the room.

Kail stood to see Suki sitting in a chair. She looked drained of life and slowly the rumors of the *Snow Break* being destroyed were starting to be a possibility. Before he could ask Suki what was going on, Angela screamed again and bolted for the door. "Find out what happened," he ordered Randal as he took off after his fleeing wife.

"Angela!" he cried out, running after her. "Angela stop!" he pleaded as she ran away from him stumbling and catching her shoulder on the wall as she almost fell again.

Growing scared the called again to Angela. He caught up to her just as she burst outside. He pulled her around to face him. "What is it?"

"They have killed our daughters," was all she said. Stunned he let go of her watching her shoot into the sky.

He ran back to the room where he had left Suki and Randal. Grabbing Suki by the shoulders he shook her to make her focus. "What is going on," he demanded.

"Sir," Randal said, pushing his way between them.

Kail knew it was true. He was intimately familiar with the look on Randal's face. He wore the same look every time he had to tell a mother or father that their child was dead and now, *here*, Randal looked at him with the same face. "No," he begged. "No."

The gentleness in Randal's voice robbed him of his anger as despair settled over him. He knew Randal was doing his best to comfort him by keeping him from doing something foolish. Angela had run, and he didn't blame her. With all of the magical power at his fingertips, he was useless, he would give it all away to change this. He would make a deal with the devil himself to trade places with them. He had promised Angela that he would tear the world apart to save them, but now, not even that would work. Death had robbed him of that option.

"Thank you Randal," Kail said emotionless. "I need to find Angela," he said without looking at Suki. Somewhere during it all Randal had told him that his aunt and uncle were dead. The Kelly farm burned and his twin daughters kidnapped. That explained why Suki and the others were in Courduff. He wanted to blame them with every fiber of his being, but he knew he would have made the same choice. Alyssa was alive, maybe, according to Suki, but Amaya was dead. He didn't care how long it would take him, but there were two men who had the answers: Mr. Eleazar, and his father, Duke Falconcrest.

Chapter 26

The following spring...

"It's time, are you ready my dear?" Ari heard her father ask. Glancing back one final time at the mirror she nodded. *Everything is in place, and whatever I missed, well, too late to worry about that now*, she thought.

"Just make sure I don't fall," she said, taking her father's arm.

"I'll do my best," he laughed, "but now that you brought it up, I hope I'm not the one who falls."

Ari smiled as she struggled to contain her laughter as well. "That would be quite the sight. Oh, I need to calm down," she said, waving her hands to get some air to her face. "Ok, let's go."

Together they left the dressing room. Felicia had been waiting for them and her excitement was on the verge of undoing her. "You are so beautiful," she squealed. Ari stopped her before she got her arms around her for a hug. "Sorry," she apologized when she realized she was about to crush the flowers Ari held.

"You're alright. Can you get the train?" Ari asked her bridesmaid.

"Oh, of course, I almost forgot," Felicia answered as she stepped around Ari and her father to pick up the hem of the white and ivory colored wedding dress that Ari wore.

Taking a deep breath Ari asked, "Are we ready?"

Felicia's reply made her smile, and her father patted her hand and nodded. The usher at the end of the hall nodded as well as he signaled into the next room. The soft beginnings of the bridal march reached their ears.

Wilhelm Bailon stood at the altar of the Grand Church of Courduff. He wore the formal white and gold dress uniform of his admiral's rank. Next to him was his best man, Cid Daltry in a polar opposite black and gold formal uniform.

"Breath sir," Cid whispered.

"I am breathing. Just make sure I don't fall," Bailon ordered through his nervousness. He knew this day was coming well in advance, but it didn't make anything easier. The church was filled with world leaders, ambassadors, diplomats, and everyone in between. He knew only a small handful of the people present. The worst was the press. They had been following Ari and him almost nonstop for months. After "saving" Cahir, Therion promoted him to admiral. That very night he had shot down the *Snow Break* in Courduff. Hero was the lowest praise he had received.

"I don't think you will have to worry about that, sir."

"Your confidence is all I need," he replied dryly as the music started, and everyone rose to their feet.

Turning, he saw Ari enter with her father. The crowd seemed to melt away into nothing when they locked eyes, and he saw her radiant smile. Cid's words also mumbled away as he watched his bride to be, slowly make her way down the aisle.

Therion stood in front of The Eternal Gateway. The outpost around him had been built up and reinforced to the point that outpost was no longer the correct word. All of the locks on The Gateway stood open except for one. The one lock that The Guardian had secured, the one lock that separated him from history, from destiny. He understood now the significance of the times stuck on the clock face of the final remaining lock. After recent events, one of those times was now missing. "Knowledge is power," he said to himself.

"You may kiss the bride," the priest announced.

Bailon lifted the thin lacy veil that separated him from his wife. Softly cupping the side of her face he drank in the sight of her. Ari smiled in return and bit her bottom lip in anticipation. When their lips met, the gathered guests stood to applaud. When the kiss continued cheers erupted before they finally broke the kiss. Together Mr. and Mrs.

Bailon shook hands and accepted congratulations from the crowd in the church.

"Are you ready for this?" he whispered to her, putting on his best face.

"Nope," she answered back.

The vaulting doors of the church were opened for them, and they stepped out together. The tens of thousands gathered outside the church erupted into cheers as Courduff's hero and his beautiful new bride appeared. The noise and power of the assembled crowd was almost overwhelming. Confetti began to rain down from above as they smiled and waved to the crowd. Chants for them to kiss began to dominate. Nodding to the will of the crowd, Bailon kissed Ari as the crowd redoubled its cheers.

High in the sky above them, the *Lotus*'s cannons were fired in salute. Fireworks filled sky, and countless flash bulbs went off capturing the moment.

Therion smiled as he reached up to the final lock and slowly dialed the time back. With satisfying click, the final lock rotated away. With a push, the doors of The Eternal Gateway swung open. Therion smiled as he looked upon the vastness of eternity. "And the last to rule shall lord over all," he quoted the prophecy.

Dust kicked up by gusts of wind from the train cars suspended on the monorail tracks swirled around her. The hooded cloak kept her skin from becoming burned in the desolate heat and shaded goggles protected her eyes from dust and sand filled air. She returned her pistol to its holster as she kicked the desert snake to make sure it was dead.

Tiny blue eyes peeked out from the protective cover of the hood as well. Together the pair walked the canyon floor. "It should be around here somewhere," she said.

The wisp played with the black and red strands of hair and agreed.

She concentrated while she mixed divination with chronomancy. The wisp tugged at her hair and whispered into her ear as it pointed to the distance. A soft glow of magic responded to her call, buried beneath the dirt.

Kneeling down she began to brush the dirt away. The wisp braving the sanctuary of her hood helped sweep away the dirt as much as its tiny hands could. Silvery runes of indestructibility appeared as they cleared away the sand that buried the Keratin war blade. The wisp clapped its hands as she held up the ancient blade. She slid the blade into the empty sheath, reuniting the blade with its twin after more than a decade of separation.

Turning to face the direction of The Eternal Gateway, she felt the time magic ripple over her as it opened for a new master. "It's time," she said with a smile. The wisp returned to the darkness of the hood. Looking at the passing train cars above her, she flew into the sky and out of the canyon. The Gateway called for its sentinel.